THE CHALICE WELL

Printed in Australia
Cover and internal design by Shawline Publishing Group Pty Ltd

First Printing: August 2023

Shawline Publishing Group Pty Ltd
www.shawlinepublishing.com.au

Paperback ISBN 978-1-9229-9364-9
eBook ISBN 978-1-9229-9376-2

Distributed by Shawline Distribution and Lightning Source Global

A catalogue record for this work is available from the National Library of Australia

More great Shawline titles can be found by scanning the QR code below.
New titles also available through Books@Home Pty Ltd.
Subscribe today at www.booksathome.com.au or scan the QR code below.

THE CHALICE WELL

S B POSTLEWHITE

Also by S B Postlewhite:

The Dumnonian Compass

Dros Andy.
Mae ein hanes yn bwysig. Gobeithio fod hyn
yn eich helpu i gofio eich un chi.
Fy nghariad i gyd.
Sharon x

I wait.
Through tilt and wheel, cycle, hour.
As eons roll their relentless passage on
I wait.

I watch.
Horse, then steam, oil, power.
The progress of century's achievement
I watch.

I know.
What was and what will be.
The promised once and future. He comes
I know.

CHAPTER ONE

FOSSICKING FOLLY

Simon had found nothing but empty dirt lately, and frankly, he was sick of it. He kicked at the soil and sighed.

'Nothing but natural.'

Archaeology was his first love; as a child he had watched Indiana Jones fight his way around the big screen and he had been hooked. Now he lived for the thrill of the chase for knowledge. Searching the past for answers, picking away at them like an itchy scab. But he was done. Weeks of scratching around in ground as hard as cement hadn't turned up anything significant. They had surveyed, dug test pits. Even the detectorists searching the spoil heaps had come back empty-handed. If it hadn't been for the sense of awe he had for this place, he would have packed it in already.

Glastonbury Tor rose behind him, a physical reminder of why he was here. He had worked with Pippa and Tom Bennet last summer at Tintagel while still a student. When he heard they were heading up the team at Glastonbury, it seemed a natural progression to work with them there. So after finishing his degree last year, he had applied and joined the team at The Well dig.

Glastonbury. The name itself conjured mystery. Its origins shrouded in the unproven suggestions and folklore that over the centuries, had become blended with its actual past. To work on a dig here was an archaeologist's dream. The chance to uncover something that proved one of the stories to be true was not to be missed. Besides this, he'd scored tickets to the festival.

Simon looked at his watch. 'Eleven thirty; lunch time.' He dusted off his trowel, wiping it back and forth across the leg of his army store fatigues before stuffing it, trowel end first, into his right back pocket. Picking up his bucket, he walked to the spoil heap and dumped its contents unceremoniously on top. The heavy chain inside his shirt irritated his chest hair, and he scratched at it absentmindedly.

'Hi Simon.'

He jumped, quickly securing the chain deep inside his shirt once more.

'Hi Darcy.' He grabbed her up in a big bear hug. Loving the clean, fresh smell of her hair as it tickled his nose. 'How ya been, lover?' He released her slowly.

'Yeah, good. You?'

'So, so.'

He shrugged. There was something in his eyes. It was far away at the back, but as fast as it was there, it was gone. He smiled down at her.

'Hey, I have something for you,' said Simon.

He reached into his pocket and pulled out a slip of card, passing it over to her. His smile changed into a grin, almost from one side of his face to the other.

'What's this?' Darcy took the card from him and turned it over in her hand.

2002 GLASTONBURY MUSIC FESTIVAL.

1 ADULT ADMISSION. ALL STAGE PASS.

'Will you go with me?'

'Go with you? This is amazing! Of course. But are you sure? Wouldn't you rather take someone else? One of your uni friends?'

'No. I can't think of anyone else I'd rather be there with.'

'Okay, well, that's it then. You've got yourself a date.'

Simon's grin widened.

*

Pippa looked into the rust-coloured water of the well, trying to focus her mind. She could not keep either it or her body still. She returned to pacing back and forth.

She's late. What's keeping her? Why doesn't she ring me?

Ever since Darcy's accident two years before, Pippa had smothered her daughter. Perhaps in an attempt to make up for any shortcomings Pippa imagined she must have as Darcy's mother.

Darcy had finished high school last year and had since been at a college in Exeter. She had sailed through her AS year. Tom and Pippa were thrilled by her straight A's in all subjects and a commendation in History.

Pippa stamped her foot, banging her clenched fists against her sides.

Where was she?

'Mum?'

Turning, Pippa looked up into the frowning face of her daughter.

She had got so tall.

'Oh! It's wonderful to have you home.'

Pippa's arms flew around Darcy's neck, and she held her tightly for a long moment before stepping back. Scrutinising Darcy for anything that might suggest she was in less than perfect health, Pippa's gaze was drawn to Darcy's bare midriff.

'You're so thin. Are you eating?'

Darcy rolled her eyes. 'Yes, Mum. Of course, I am. Right now, I could eat a mouldy donkey. Where's Dad? He does know we're supposed to be meeting for lunch?'

'Yes, he does. I reminded him about it only this morning. He's just gone to have a quick word with Simon.'

Darcy's frown deepened. 'Why? What's the matter with Simon?'

'We're not sure. He's distracted. Not himself.'

'I'll talk to him.'

'Why do you think you would have any more success than your dad?' Pippa smirked.

'Because Dad is clueless when it comes to anything other than archaeology. You know that.'

Pippa laughed.

'You know I'm right Mum.'

'Yes love, I do.'

Darcy and Pippa heard footsteps on the gravel behind them.

'Hello gorgeous. You look great.'

Tom Bennet smiled and hugged his daughter tightly.

'She looks thin,' said Pippa.

A frown, so much like her daughter's, appeared across her forehead.

'I'm hungry,' said Darcy. 'Feed me.'

She made a face and imitated an animal begging for food.

'Come on then,' said Tom. 'Let's get going or there'll be no lunch left.'

*

They walked along Chilkwell Street, chatting happily together until, turning into Bere Lane, they found the entrance to the Rural Life Museum and went on through into the Grain Store Cafe.

'So, what's up with Simon then?' said Darcy.

She had been studying the menu but lifted her eyes now, fixing both her parents opposite with a serious stare.

'No idea,' Tom said. Darcy's father shrugged and sipped his glass of water. 'His heart's just not in it anymore. I talked with him this morning, and all he could think about was the festival. It's like he's lost all interest in work.'

'It is next week Dad. That's pretty distracting for most people. You do know Bowie headlined last year? Thirty years since his first gig there. Tickets are like gold dust.'

'Maybe a week off is just what Simon needs, Honey,' said Pippa. 'He can get whatever this is out of his system.'

A waitress interrupted them, quipping about the state of the British summer before taking their order and moving off to another table.

'I expect he's just tired,' Pippa continued. 'I know I am. This summer has been one long fight with the dirt. I had to take a mattock to a trench yesterday. Hard as a concrete slab it was, I just couldn't shift even an inch of topsoil without nearly breaking my arms off.'

Darcy laughed. Her mother's face was screwed up in an affectation of agony as she rubbed at her shoulders.

'You're just getting old,' said Tom. 'Either that, or you need more practice.'

He poked a bony finger at his wife's shoulder and winked at Darcy. The waitress was back, this time with food and more chatty platitudes. Darcy accepted her plate gratefully, immediately tucking into the pile of pasta. Pippa glanced across the table and smiled as she watched her daughter eating.

'Stop it, Mum.'

'Okay, okay. I have nothing more to say on the subject.'

*

He was freezing. Early morning in the castle's courtyard was always icy, even in the height of summer. He swished water from the trough over his face. The cold and the water only combined to make his lack of sleep painful. The walls rising around him were even more prison-like this morning. They stole his breath, space, and any chance of peace of mind he clung to. He had to get out.

*

The sun was relentless. Pippa untied the sleeved shirt from around her waist and slipped it on over her red arms and shoulders. She was drawing and labelling the layers of stratigraphy in her trench. This was her thing, and she was great at it. Tom had to admit that his wife's sketches were intricately detailed and beautiful. Much better than his. He looked at her, tutting. She would be very sore later.

Tom bent low and scraped. Yes, it was there, the ever so slightly darker line in the dirt indicating something had rotted away hundreds of years before. He retrieved his water bottle and carefully poured it over the mark. The dark circle became clearer as the water seeped into the soil, just as it had with the others. Later he would try to locate the marks left by rain dripping from ancient eves hundreds of years before. That would add weight to his substantial Saxon building theory. Right now, though, he was off to look for Simon.

Where had he got to?

Quite frankly, Simon's attitude had been crappy lately. Tom was going to have it out with him once and for all. He'd tried yesterday, but it had been a waste of time. If Simon couldn't do his job, he would have to go. There was no room on this dig for passengers. Everyone must pull their weight.

'Simon! There you are.'

'I was just getting a cup of tea from the shed.'

'You've been gone an hour. It had better be a bloody good cup of tea.' Simon winced. 'What's going on with you. Are you sick?'

Simon shook his head. 'Come on, mate. I'm doing my best here, but you know I'm useless with this sort of thing. Do you need help? Anything?'

Simon just looked at the ground. 'Oh, for god's sake, just tell me.'

Simon started to unbutton the front of his shirt. Tom watched him, astonished. When Simon reached the button just above his waist, he pulled the shirt open, revealing his chest. It was swollen, and great red welts stood up from the skin as if he'd been punched.

Tom's breath drew in through his clenched teeth. 'Bloody hell. What have you done to yourself?'

'I don't know.'

'You need to see a doctor. Make an appointment and go today. And Simon, whatever this is, this thing that's going on with you. Fix it. Have your festival break next week and come back fixed. You understand what I'm saying?'

'Yeah, I hear you. Loud and clear.'

*

Simon walked back into the shed. He slammed his cup down on the sink drainer and took the weight of himself on two arms splayed on either side. His breath was coming fast and shallow. Closing his eyes, he gripped the freestanding drainer's edges, squeezing until his fingers were a bloodless white. His breath started to slow, and he opened his eyes again.

His bag lay in the corner where he had left it that morning. Reaching inside, he pulled out the chain. Even in the darkness, it glinted. The compass swung back and forth as he held it. He'd taken to keeping it in his bag soon after the welts appeared; how could he have known he would be allergic to whatever type of metal it was made from? Copper, but what else? He hadn't been able to find out yet.

When he'd found the compass two years before at Tintagel, he'd logged it with all the other finds, lovingly recorded it, and boxed it away ready for storage. But before the end of the dig, he had snuck into the finds room and taken it. Simon didn't know what impulse had driven him to take it, but he couldn't be parted from the compass. He just knew it was important. Nobody even missed it until months later, by which time there was no way of knowing what had happened to it. David, Tom, and Pippa had been devastated. They quizzed everyone, searched everywhere, but it had remained lost.

CHAPTER TWO

SUMMER LOVIN'

Simon pulled the camp trolly onto Pennard Hill Ground. The many domes of tents spread out before him, a patchwork of multicoloured bubbles straining against their peg anchors. He tugged at the handle of the trolly; the wheels stuck, sinking into the mud.

'Come on, pull!' shouted Darcy. She held the back end of the trolly and was pushing for all she was worth. 'If we don't hurry up, there'll be nowhere left to pitch this thing.' She kicked the left back wheel, and the trolly trundled forward again with a jerk, bouncing haphazardly along with its contents jumbling as it moved.

They headed for one of the last spots on the field that was tentless and staked their claim. Twenty minutes later, the tent was up. The kettle hovered precariously above the tiny camp stove, and Simon hoped it would stay put long enough to boil the water. Darcy was belting the tent pegs into the ground with such abandon that the little stove shook with every thwack.

'There, all done.' Darcy stretched her back and surveyed her hard work with hands on her hips.

'Here.' Simon passed her up a cup of tea. She looked at the dark brown liquid with bits of grass floating in it.

'Sorry, no milk.'

'Don't worry about that.' She sat down beside him and gave a reassuring smile. 'There's nothing to keep it cool in anyway. Let's get some beer later. You'll have to buy it, though. I've still got two months till I'm legal.'

'No need.' Simon reached into the camp trolly and pulled out a tiny box.

'I thought that was for tools or something.'

He opened the lid to reveal six perfectly packed green bottles. Condensation droplets beaded on their glassy surface. Darcy licked her lower lip.

'Later.' Simon shoved the lid back on and stowed the box in the tent. He handed her back the cup of tea. 'You can stick with that for a bit.'

'Okay, spoilsport. You're worse than my parents.'

'Don't remind me.' Simon was at the festival, with Darcy, alone. He didn't want to think about her parents at all. 'Come on,' Simon grabbed Darcy's hand and pulled her to her feet, 'let's go and check out The Pyramid.'

*

His horse felt solid beneath him. His fragility faded into the beast until they were strong together. The rhythm of pounding hooves gave a sensation of weightlessness as they covered the ground between the castle and forest. Almost there. A few more seconds, and he would be out of sight.

*

The sun was almost at the horizon as Darcy and Simon reached The Pyramid field. It was already buzzing. People were streaming in from everywhere. The stage, like a black hole, drawing everything towards it. Tonight, the whole world had shown up to hear The Manic Street Preachers.

The hairs on the back of Darcy's neck and arms prickled. She was here.

'I haven't felt like this since... since Dumnonia.'

'What was that?' Simon looked down at her.

'Oh! I didn't realise I said that out loud.'

'What about Dumnonia?'

'Nothing, I was just thinking how great it is to be here.'

'Why Dumnonia? It's not been called that for thousands of years.'

'Or three years...' Darcy muttered.

'You are a funny one, Darcy Bennet. The first thing you do when you arrive at one of the greatest music festivals in the world is start waxing lyrical about the land. Why don't you admit you're as hooked on history stuff as I am?'

Darcy smiled.

If only you knew...

*

The Preachers were amazing. Simon looked at the faces of other festival goers. Everyone was enjoying the moment, the connection. The feeling that they were part of something more than just themselves.

A dark figure moved at the corner of his vision. He blinked, turning to face it. A woman in black moved quickly amongst the crowd. As if feeling his eyes on her, she stopped, turned, and nodded.

'Teithiwr,' she mouthed toward him.

Darcy grabbed Simon's arm. 'It can't be.'

'It can't be who? Darcy? Wait, where are you going?'

Darcy was off into the crowd. Simon pushed his way through after her.

'Oi mate, watch it!' said a muscular man he'd accidentally bumped.

The guy pushed back at Simon.

'Sorry.'

Simon patted the guy's shoulder in apology. As soon as he looked away, he knew he'd made a mistake. Darcy was gone. He tried looking for the woman, but she'd disappeared too.

What now? Come on Simon, think.

He scanned the entrances, thinking that Darcy must be heading for one of them. He was right. There she was at the gate, but she wasn't alone.

What's she doing? Is she hugging her?

Given the density of people dancing around him, progress toward her was slow. Eventually Simon made it to the edge of the field. There was Darcy, but the woman had gone.

'Who was that?'

Darcy paled. 'You saw her?'

'Of course I saw her. What do you think this is, an episode of Dr. Who or something?'

'That was Jenna. She's an old friend.'

'She didn't hang around. What did she want?'

'Remember that compass you found at Tintagel? She's looking for it; it belongs to her.'

Simon's heart beat a bit harder, but there was no way Darcy could know he had the compass still.

'Yeah, right. I found it two feet down in the dirt. The only thing it belongs to is the past. Besides, nobody knows where it is. Did you tell her that?'

'Yes.'

'And?'

'She seems to think it's closer than we realise.'

Simon waggled his fingers in the air and made a ghost noise. Darcy punched him in the arm.

'Ouch! What was that for?'

'For being an idiot.'

Just through the gate was a burger van. A girl at the hatch was taking orders and shouting them over her shoulder to the cook in the back.

'Hungry?' said Simon.

'A bit.'

He grabbed her hand and led her to the van.

'My treat.'

He smiled. Darcy couldn't help but return it.

*

'Where are you going?'

He turned and was face to face with the wizard.

'I had hoped to escape without notice,' he said.

The wizard crossed his arms and shook his head.

'The son of a king does nothing without notice.'

The wizard indicated to the horse. Tut-tutting, he ran his hand down the beast's sweat-lined flank.

'You didn't think to spare him a little in this heat? He is one of our best and not your beast to flog in such a way.'

'Take him if he means so much to you. I have no more need of him. I will travel on foot from here.'

*

'That was amazing, thank you.'

Darcy leaned into Simon as they dawdled along in the direction of the tent, taking turns to swig gulps of beer from their shared bottle.

'It was, wasn't it? I haven't had a night as good in a long time.'

'You're kinda sad, aren't you?' Darcy laughed at him and reached up to ruffle his curly mop of hair. Simon leaned in and kissed her. It was clumsy and the minute it was over, he saw the stunned look on Darcy's face and regretted it.

'What on earth did you do that for?' Darcy's frown had caused deep furrows on her forehead. Simon remembered what his mother would say: *If the wind changes direction, you'll stay looking like that.*

'Simon.'

'It felt right.'

'Well, not to me. We're friends and I don't want to spoil it.'

'How would us being together spoil anything? I haven't made any secret about how much I like you.'

'I was hoping you would get over it.'

'Ah.' Simon removed his arm from her shoulders and walked ahead of her. Darcy let him put a few strides distance between them. All too soon, they reached the tent. Only an hour before, Darcy had been looking forward to sharing a night with a friend. They could have talked about everything and nothing,. Now it was awkward sharing such an intimate space.

'I'm going to wash,' said Darcy.

She grabbed her things and bungled off in the direction of the portaloos.

'I'm such an idiot,' muttered Simon, watching her hasty retreat. He scrambled into the tent, flinging his jeans off into the corner. Grabbing his sleeping bag, Simon hunkered down into it, fumbling with the zip until he was cocooned inside with only the top of his head visible. He caterpillar shuffled onto his side, facing the tent wall, and closed his eyes.

Not long afterward, Simon heard the tent zip open as Darcy returned. She didn't speak. The zip closed, she scrambled into her bag, and that was that.

*

He sat with his head in his hands, elbows resting on the scrubbed wood table. His head was heavy. The Wizard watched by the door of the shepherd's hut, alert to the slightest sound. He, on the other hand, was so tired. No amount of sleep would leave him rested.

A man entered the clearing by the hut. The Wizard held forward his hand.

'Who goes there?'

'Culhwch, the king's nephew. I have come for help.'

*

Darcy was awake. She rolled onto her back and immediately regretted it.

'God, it's hot in here,' she said. She turned to look at Simon but there was only an empty sleeping bag scrunched up in the corner where he should have been. 'Ugh!'

Darcy scrunched her eyes up tight. The sun's glare through the canvas was excruciating. She caterpillar rolled until she was able to sit up and extricate her legs out of the sleeping bag. Outside, the light breeze made the heat less intense. There was still no sign of Simon.

Sometimes you can be a complete idiot.

Back in the tent, Darcy dressed quickly. She dragged a brush through her hair. It caught in the knotted ends; she had to work it loose with her fingers.

'Ouch!'

She threw the brush into the corner. Grabbing hair and pulling it back into a Scrunchie, Darcy crawled outside and zipped up the tent.

Right. Where have you gone?

Darcy wandered in the direction of the music stages. There were a few stragglers who hadn't made it back to the camp grounds the night before. Ambling along, they were singing to each other, reminiscing.

Oh Simon, where are you?

Darcy stood with her hands on her hips, turning in circles. She bit her lower lip until it lost its usual pink colour and turned white.

'Does that hurt?'

'Simon.' She hugged him then quickly drew back. 'I was worried.'

'Why? Did you think I was stolen away in the night?'

Darcy smiled.

'That's more like it. You look so much better when you're not trying to disfigure yourself.'

'Ha, ha. You're hilarious.'

'Yeah, your hilarious mate Si. Good ole dependable, salt of the earth Si. Always there when you need him.'

'Simon.' Darcy touched his arm. It was a feather-light touch. 'I do love you,' she said, 'you're my best friend. But I don't LOVE you.'

'Yeah, I know.'

'Yeah, I thought you did too. So, I don't understand why you kissed me and why you were so upset?'

'I'm sorry about that. I was a bit drunk.'

'What, on one shared bottle of beer?'

'Okay. Not drunk then, but I got carried away.'

'All I wanted was a few days with you at this amazing place. But now I feel like I want to go home. It's too much. Too difficult.'

'Hey.' Simon took hold of Darcy's hand and held it between them. 'I'm sorry I spoiled it. I'm an idiot. Can we just pretend I didn't kiss you last night? Please stay. I'm bloody useless on my own.'

She sighed. 'I'll stay on one condition. No more stupid moves. Deal?'

'Deal.'

'Now, you owe me a cup of that awful, stewed stuff you call tea. And don't forget the bits of grass either. I want the works.'

'Your wish is my command, oh fair one.'

They walked back to the tent together.

CHAPTER THREE

PARTIAL REALITY

'I need to get away from here for a bit,' said Darcy.

'What's up?'

Simon finished tidying the tent. It had been another great night. They had both crawled exhausted into sleeping bags at two am. Now it was mid-morning.

'I feel penned in. There're too many people; I just need some space.'

'Okay. Where do you want to go?'

'I was thinking maybe Bude.'

'That's miles away. Besides, it will be just as busy. Is it because of that woman?'

'Jenna? Partly, and because I haven't been there in ages. Seeing her the other night made me miss the place.'

'I'm surprised you want to go back. It wasn't exactly your best summer.'

'No. But it did have some compensations.' Darcy smiled.

'Don't do that. It teaches me to hope, and I need to stop, or I'll never get laid.'

Darcy's laughed.

'Okay,' said Simon. 'Bude, it is.'

*

They finished packing up the tent and trundled back to the car. Although they hadn't intended to leave the festival early, it felt right. As if going now, before the festival was over, meant it wouldn't end.

They decided to take the Taunton/Barnstable route to keep them away from the M5, which was always a nightmare. Two and a half hours later, they searched for a parking space in Bude town centre.

'It hasn't changed a bit,' said Darcy

'It's only been a year or so since you were here. Did you think that the wheels of commerce and industry would turn the place into another major city in your absence? This is Cornwall. The passage of time has no effect.'

'I know what you mean.'

'Where do you want to go?'

'Just down the high street. I want to check something.'

They wandered amiably under the hanging baskets, dodging other people doing the same. Halfway down the street, Darcy stopped. Simon walked a few more steps before realising she wasn't beside him.

'What's up?'

'I'm going in here.'

Simon looked up at the faded signage.

'What is this place?'

'Tredinnick's Emporium.' Darcy went inside.

'Okay, I guess. Wait for me.' Simon stepped through the doorway. 'My god.' He spun in all directions. Shelves filled with quirky and strange objects stretched out in rows before him. The smell of a mixture of herbs, tainted by the stench of dead things, assaulted his nose. 'Where are we?'

'Shush! Don't you dare embarrass me,' said Darcy. 'Just keep quiet. I don't expect you to understand but try not to make a fuss.'

A woman appeared next to Simon.

'Ello me dearee,' she said.

The plump, jolly-faced woman only came up level with Simon's elbow.

'Jenna, have you got shorter?' said Darcy. The light in the already dim shop suddenly vanished.

'Woah!' Simon steadied himself against the nearest thing he could find. 'Yuck! What is this?' Gunk ran slowly through his fingers. He could hear it plopping onto his boots. A mist swirled around him. As it started to clear it became light enough to see again. Simon looked down at his hands. 'Oh my god.'

The dark, red, gloopy substance continued to drip down the front of his t-shirt. It was unmistakable. He could smell the metallic tang of it. He wiped his hands down his jeans.

'Simon, what have you done to yourself?' said Darcy.

'He's fine,' said Jenna. 'It's just a broken bottle of 'Abhorrence'; it turns into whatever we fear the most.'

'I didn't know you were afraid of blood,' said Darcy.

'I'm not afraid,' said Simon. 'It makes me a bit queasy; it's the smell.'

It took him a few moments before he could look around again.

'Wait. You're the... you're Darcy's Jenna. But where's the other one? She was just here. The little one with the funny hairdo?'

Jenna and Darcy both laughed.

'She is also me,' said Jenna. 'We are one and the same.'

'I don't understand.'

Simon felt the burning rise in his throat. He gagged and vomited on the floor.

'Okay,' said Jenna, 'let's get you cleaned up. Darcy, please take your friend out the back. I will be there after I have sorted this mess.'

Darcy led Simon away. Over his shoulder, Simon saw Jenna wave her hand over the vomit, blood, and broken glass on the floor. It rose in a whirling mess before evaporating into putrid black smoke that drifted out the door. 'That's better,' she said.

Jenna scooted after them to the back of the shop, popped under the counter and through a door in the back wall.

Simon changed into a clean pair of jeans and a t-shirt that had, peculiarly, been waiting for him in the room out back and were identical to the ones he had been wearing. His face was still a murky grey colour, but he had stopped vomiting at least.

'I have so many questions,' he said as Jenna entered. Simon pulled out a chair from under the table that filled the centre of the room and sat down. 'I don't know what to ask first.'

'Well, why don't you let me ask you a question,' said Jenna. 'What have you done with my compass?'

Blood flowed back into Simon's face. His cheeks burned with it. He couldn't find anywhere comfortable to set his eyes, so he just looked at the floor.

'What's she talking about Simon?' Darcy's tone made Simon shiver. He could feel the vomit rising in his chest again. He reached into his rucksack.

'She's talking about this.' Simon held up the compass. It twisted clockwise on its chain until it could go no further and started to unravel the other way.

'I don't believe it,' said Darcy. She ran out the room, slamming the door behind her. Simon got up to follow, but Jenna's hand was on his shoulder.

'No, you don't. I'll speak to her.'

Simon slumped down in the chair.

She'll never trust me again.

*

'Try not to be too upset. It's not entirely his fault,' said Jenna.

Darcy started.

'Oh! I didn't hear you creep up on me... What do you mean?'

'He did steal it, we can't avoid that corker, but he was pushed into it.'

Darcy shook her head. 'I don't get it. How was he made to take it? My parents were so upset when it went missing. I was upset too. How could he do it to us? After I lost it coming back from Dumnonia, I never thought I'd see the compass again. Then it turned up at the dig site, and I had a small hope that one day... maybe... it might be possible to go back. I was holding onto that, and then it was gone again, and all that hope went with it.'

Darcy's eyes filled. Jenna offered her a perfectly laundered handkerchief, so white it glowed in the dark hallway.

'All I have to say is this. Have you considered there might be other things at work here? Simon took the compass, we know that. And yes, it was hurtful that he lied to you. But he doesn't know why he took it. Did you see his face? He is drawn to it...'

Jenna wiped Darcy's eyes with the handkerchief.

'...I think he was forced to take it by something that he has no power to resist.'

'What's that?'

'Fate, Darcy. His and yours. I've always felt you would return. But this time, you won't go alone.'

'You think that I can go back?'

'Yes.'

'How? When?'

'Ah. Now, those are the questions I don't have answers for. I was always good at the prediction stuff, not so good with the logistics.'

'I can't forgive him.'

'Right now, I'm not asking you to. But leave a little room for sympathy. As your friend, he deserves that at least.'

*

'Let me get this straight,' he said. 'You have set yourself against the giant Ysbaddaden Bencawr to marry his daughter and, in so doing, bring about his demise.'

Culhwch looked straight at him, unblinking.

'I do not wish his death, but if I cannot have one without the other, then so be it. That curse was not of my making. I will marry Olwen; her father must do what he will.'

*

Simon sat with his head in his hands. He looked up as Darcy, then Jenna, returned.

'Darcy, I'm so sorry,' he said.

'Save it. Right now, I can't even look at you.'

'I never wanted to hurt you.'

'Well, you have, and it makes what I want to say next extremely hard. You have questions about Jenna, and we'll get to those. You're not going to believe what I say at first. It took me a while to understand. You'll think you're going mad; that everything you hear is a trick or a dream. But then, you don't wake up.'

'Darcy, you're talking in riddles,' said Simon. He scratched at his itchy chest. The marks left by the compass suddenly irritating again.

'We're going away, you and me.'

'Away where?' said Simon, taking the tub of ointment Jenna held out to him and sniffing it.

'Here.'

'Now I'm confused.' Simon rubbed the ointment into the skin under his t-shirt.

'What if I was to tell you that it's possible to leave and still be here at the same time?'

'I would say you're bonkers and suggest you see a doctor.'

'Well, even so, it is possible. There's a place I want to return to. Dumnonia.'

'You're obsessed. This is Dumnonia. We're in it.'

'No, this is Cornwall. I'm talking about returning to when it was Dumnonia; only this Dumnonia is not like any place you may have heard of. My Dumnonia is full of people and beings that only exist in stories or the imagination. In my Dumnonia, there are witches, wizards, and faeries. Pixies make mischief and get people lost. But most important of all, in my Dumnonia are my friends, and I want to see them again.'

'Have you been drinking?' Simon's eyes narrowed.

'No! You know I haven't.'

The room darkened as Jenna stretched out her arms. Slowly she changed. Shrinking a good foot in height right before Simon's eyes. Her waist gradually expanded along with her chest until she was round in shape. The colour of her hair changed to a mousy grey and swept itself into a bun that teetered precariously on the side of her head. She was wearing a scruffy worn dress made of green garden twine. Lastly, her face settled into the shape of the old woman who had welcomed them earlier. Her transformation had taken only a moment, but she was completely changed.

'Well, dearee,' said Jenna. 'What do 'ee think of me now?'

'How...?'

Simon shook his head.

'How is not important,' said Jenna. 'Remember that this is real. It can and does happen. People like me do exist. Everything Darcy told you is true. Dumnonia is here, but not now. It's not in the past either; it's very much alive. The rumblings are in the air. I have felt it and so have you. That's why you took the compass. Dumnonia is calling to you.'

'Calling me? What for?'

'I don't know. I can feel the turbulence brewing. The how and the why of it, though escape me.'

'Okay. Say I believe you and agree to go. How do we get there?'

'That question is for Darcy.'

Darcy frowned.

'Give me the compass,' said Jenna.

Simon passed it over. Jenna unravelled the chain and carefully lifted the compass. The hands whirled round the dial. She popped the chain over Darcy's head. The second it touched her skin, the hands stopped.

'Hmmm. Northeast,' said Jenna.

'What does that mean?' said Simon.

'It means there is a way into Dumnonia somewhere northeast of here,' said Jenna.

'That's not Tintagel,' said Darcy. 'That's completely the opposite direction from here.'

'The gate at Tintagel is still well and truly shut,' said Jenna. 'No one will be going through that way. No, this is a new gate, or a long forgotten one. It's up to us to find it.'

Simon got up and swung the rucksack onto his back.

'Right. When do we start?' he said.

Jenna smiled and squeezed Darcy's hand.

'Now.'

CHAPTER FOUR

A WILL AND A WAY

Darcy and Simon sprinted back to the car.

'What about Jenna?' said Simon.

'It's okay, she'll find her own way.'

'But you've got the compass, how will she know?'

'Jenna is Jenna. Need I say more? Now. Come on, let's get going.'
In the car, Darcy rechecked the compass. 'Still northeast. That's back
the way we came, towards Glastonbury.'

'Well, that's as good a starting point as any. We'll head back. You
just keep an eye on that thing and tell me if it changes.' Darcy held
the compass cradled in her hand. A sacred thing. It felt familiar and
strange at the same time. The old fear sat like a ball of fire in her
stomach. She pushed it down hard. 'Keep a lid on it, Darcy.'

'What's that?'

'I was talking to myself.'

'Been doing that a lot lately?'

Darcy laughed. 'I'm not going mad if that's what you're thinking.'

'Hmmm. You do need to start talking, though.'

'Do I?'

'Yes. You must tell me everything. If you're expecting me to go
along with it, then you'd better start talking.'

'I don't know where to start.'

'The beginning's a good place. Take your time, and don't miss anything out.'

Simon drove and listened. He didn't interrupt; he just let it all flow out of her. She cried in parts, laughed in others. He realised why Darcy had been the way she was after her so-called accident. So interested in the Tintagel dig after the compass was found, and then not wanting to be anywhere near it. She had been afraid, and it was no wonder.

*

He watched as Culhwch slapped the horses on the rump and sent them racing back the way they had come. Culhwch hadn't wanted to let them go, but horses are never good travellers in the close confines of a forest.

'We must go on,' said the wizard.

Even now, after days of hiding out, he still felt eyes on him everywhere. Escape seemed impossible. They skirted the forest's eastern edge to use the light while maintaining their cover. Hours later, he stood by the rust-coloured water and looked into the depths.

*

When it was over, Darcy slumped in her seat.

'How on earth did you manage to keep that all in for so long?' said Simon.

'I didn't. I had Jenna. When everyone else was fussing around me, she made sense of it all.'

'I feel terrible. I was no help to you.'

'You hardly knew me back then. The truth is, you've been more help to me than you could have ever realised.'

Over the last two years, for a reason she could never quite put her finger on, Simon had reminded her of Kea. There were similarities in how they looked, especially the wavy, out-of-control hair. But that was where it ended. Simon was quick witted, as sharp as a tac. Kea had been strong and dependable, but never very fast on the uptake. Their personalities were as different as could be, but after her return from Dumnonia three years ago, Darcy had been drawn to Simon. He had eased her sense of loss. Her time there seemed more real when she was close to him. Simon was the big, dependable friend she had lost when Kea was killed, and he talked about the past like it was a place. He could bring Dumnonia back to her in the way he explained history with such passion it would cause her to drift off into remembrances. Before she knew it, Darcy was back in the Willow's cottage, or Morwenna's home, drinking tea with her friends. And her heart was full.

'I've never told you before... well... I couldn't tell you, but you remind me so much of Kea. He was the most loyal and brave person I have ever known. I miss him. You look so much like him; it helped being around you, it still does.'

'Well, I suppose I'm good for something then.'

'Oh, Simon.' Darcy looked down at the compass. 'Still the same.'

'We'll be back in Glastonbury soon. Any suggestions what we should head for?'

'The last gate was at an ancient monument. Maybe we should be looking for the same.'

'The Tor. You can't get much more ancient than that.'

'You're right. It's got to be.'

'The turning is just here.'

Simon pulled the car around into the lane. The tyres screeched, and the chassis moaned. Darcy held onto the passenger side handle above her head.

'Take it easy.'

'Sorry.'

'We can park at The Well and walk from there.'

'Your parents might see the car. I won't risk that. We should pull over here. The Tor is just at the end of this lane; it's only a couple of miles to walk.'

Simon pulled the car into a lay-by.

'What do you think we will need?' he said.

'The trouble is, we won't know until we get there. Let's just take a change of clothes each and your toolbox. Anything else will just weigh us down.'

'Do you think it's alright to leave the car?' said Simon.

'I don't believe you. We're about to head off to the other side of goodness knows where, and you're worried about the car.'

'I've got priorities.'

'Ha!'

'If you two are ready,' said Jenna, leaning in through the passenger side window. 'Shall we go?'

'Where did you come from?' said Simon.

Jenna tapped the side of her nose.

'Mind your own,' she said, laughing.

They walked the rest of the lane and up onto the path that meandered its way up to the ruined church.

'How will we know if this is the right place?' asked Simon.

'Believe me,' said Darcy. 'We'll know.' They ran up the path. Darcy fought back the dead weight in her legs as the muscles protested.

'Can we please slow down a bit?' Jenna had stopped and was holding her side, breathing hard. 'I'm way too old to be running around the countryside like this.'

'Don't be ridiculous,' said Darcy. 'You're not much older than me.'

'Not in this body. I'm old enough to be your grandmother and some.'

They stood, taking in the sunshine and the view.

'Come on old lady; we need to get going,' said Darcy.

They carried on up the path, slower this time. As they neared the top, Darcy stopped. Her eyes fixed on the door at the side of the ruined church.

'Look at that.'

Simon turned. 'That's just the church door.'

'No, Simon,' said Jenna. 'Really look.'

In the gap between the stone surround, something was happening. The space was undulating as if a light breeze were wafting a piece of fabric or you were looking up at the surface of water from underneath.

'It's like water,' said Simon.

'A bit,' said Darcy. 'But it's more like walking through a cobweb. It kind of sticks to you, then it pulls you through. There's a second when both sides want to hold on, then it's gone, and you're on the other side.'

'And what's on the other side?' said Simon.

'Magic,' said Jenna.

*

As he stared into the water, something drew him in. The Wizard's hand was on his shoulder just in time.

'Careful. Some have lost themselves in this place. The water speaks, though few know what to listen for.'

Ripples rolled outwards from the centre, forming larger rings on the pool's surface until they threw themselves against the lip at the edge and vanished. The tip of something glinted and rose out of the water. Heavy hammered steal, cut upwards to free itself from the murky deep. A hand wrapped around the hilt held the sword high above the water's surface.

'The lady has a gift for you,' said the Wizard. 'It is Caliburnus.

Your birthright. You must claim it before the witch returns it from whence it came.'

'Whomever that is in there, I do not think they will give up that prize easily,' he said.

Mawgan sighed. 'There is only one way to find out.'

*

Simon and Darcy approached the ruins.

'Be careful, it might pull you in,' said Darcy

'Isn't that the point?'

'Not yet. I have to say goodbye first.'

'I don't understand.'

Jenna was behind them.

'Be careful, stay safe and don't forget to come home,' she said.

'What? You're not coming with us?' said Simon.

'No, I am needed here. When Pippa comes looking for Darcy because she hasn't returned her calls, someone needs to give her the cover story. She'll take some convincing.'

'What will you say?' said Darcy.

'I will tell her what I always tell her. You will be back when you're hungry or need clean laundry. That always works; I have no idea why. Some people are easily persuaded. When you're on the other side, head for Mawgan's cave. Even if he isn't there, you'll be safe, and the cave has everything you could need. Wait for him; he will come to you.

It's a long walk from The Tor to the cave, and risky, so be careful not to draw attention to yourselves. Dumnonia is a much more peaceful place than it was, but there are still dangers, and your arrival may upset some.

Hold to each other. Don't lose sight of friendship. It will be tested, but it will not break. Trust each other.'

Darcy grabbed Jenna and hugged her. 'We'll be fine.'

'Yes, but will Dumnonia?' said Jenna.

Simon held out his hand. 'Well, you're the strangest person I've ever met, and I'm an archaeologist.'

'Reserve your judgment on that one until you come back through that gate. We'll see if you still feel the same then.'

Simon lowered his head and kissed Jenna on the cheek. 'Thank you. I still have questions, but I'm guessing that the answers are through there.'

'Yes, you're probably right. But answers often raise even more questions. Good luck, and safe travels.' Jenna walked a few steps back down the Tor. Before she had gone any further, a puce-coloured oval door appeared ahead of her. It hung suspended in the air. She took hold of the large handle, opened it and stepped through into whatever lay beyond. The door closed swiftly behind her. In a blink, she was gone.

'Shall we?' Simon took hold of Darcy's hand.

'Are you sure you want to do this? We have no clue what might be waiting on the other side.'

'You know what's there; that's enough for starters. Besides, there is no way I'm letting you go on your own.'

'Come on then.'

The rippling was faster now. It blurred everything on the other side. Darcy felt the familiar tug. Like her bones were about to be pulled through her skin.

'This is it. Just go with it; we'll be on the other side in a second.'

Simon squeezed her hand, but he didn't say anything. Darcy closed her eyes, took a deep breath, and stepped forward.

For the smallest part of a second, there was nothing. They felt the sticky sensation of being held suspended somewhere, not moving forward, not able to go back., but it was over in an instant. With their next breath, they were through. They hadn't stepped into a building as they would have done if they had stayed in Somerset. Instead, they were standing on the top of the Tor, in the open air.

'It's the same,' said Simon.

'Yes. But it's different. You can feel it.'

Darcy turned and looked back through the doorway. She could see the Tor on the Somerset side through the ruined church entrance.

'If you're not sure about this,' she said, 'go back while you still can. You may not get another chance. The doors move, and there's no guarantee this one will still be here when we want to return.'

'No way, you're not getting rid of me. Besides, Jenna told us to stay together, and that's what we're going to do.'

'The only way is down from here. Let's get going before something spots us; we kind of stick out dressed like this.'

'Why? What should we be wearing?'

'Something older in style. Denim doesn't exist here, and these T-shirts are far too underdressed. Don't worry, we'll find what we need in the cave. We have to get to it, and the sooner, the better.'

They ran down the path. In Somerset, the outskirts of Glastonbury town run up to meet the Tor, but here it was different. A thick forest lay stretched out before them, and they ran into its cover like diving under a blanket.

'I don't know this place,' said Darcy. 'Or what might be in here.'

'It's just a forest.'

'We'll see.'

They ran in a southwest direction towards the cave.

'Stop,' said Darcy. 'It hurts to breathe. The air's stuffy, I feel sick.'

'We've only gone about half a mile.'

'We'll never make it like this. We're noisy and not being careful enough.'

Darcy scanned the green dark under the trees. She shivered. Tiny goosebumps rose on her arms. She spun around at a rustle in the darkness behind.

'What was that?' said Simon.

The rustling sound started again. It had a slow rhythm. Thud. thud.

'That's footsteps,' said Darcy.

'It's a big bloody noise for footsteps.'

'That's because it's made by something very big.'

First, the beady black eyes caught a speck of light as they blinked. The thud, thud was getting faster. A closely feathered and crested head quickly followed by a hooked beak. The green darkness gave up its secret bit by bit, and the creature came into full view.

Darcy and Simon froze. Darcy brought her mouth slowly up to Simon's ear.

'Run.'

CHAPTER FIVE

FOOLS AND THEIR MONEY

The Wizard and Culhwch watched as he entered the water. Tentative at first, his feet searched for a solid purchase on the bottom. He waded slowly to the centre. The red water was now waist deep.

The hand still held the sword aloft. He took it, grasping the blade; instantly regretting it as he felt steel bite into his fingers. Blood ran down his arm and dripped into the water; the shades of red swirled. He adjusted his hand to the swords hilt, realising as he did so he was now the only one holding it. The disembodied hand had gone. He was alone in the water.

*

Darcy had forgotten how difficult it was running in thick woodland. She felt a jabbing pain shimmy up her leg as her boot hit something hard. She stumbled. Simon's hand was quickly on her elbow. Steady again, they ran on.

The creature was still behind them, but its sound was fading; Darcy and Simon were smaller and faster. Its clumsy pursuit was far away now. Darcy slowed her pace and Simon followed. They heard the creature squawk in frustration before its sounds trailed off. It had given up the chase and turned away.

'What was that?' said Simon.

Darcy bent over, hands on knees, breathing fast and shallow.

'A buzzard.'

'It was huge.'

'Actually, it wasn't a big one, probably only a youngster. There may be others. We need to go on.'

They walked quickly, making as little noise as possible, which was difficult given the amount of dried leaves and other matter on the ground.

'Is it just me? Or is it getting lighter?' said Simon.

'Yes, but I don't know why. We're nowhere near the edge of the forest. You're right though, it's definitely less dark.'

'What's that?'

Darcy followed Simon's finger to where it pointed at a speck of green light. A flicker of recognition crossed her face.

'I know what that is. Come on.' She ran toward the light. 'Hurry!'

When Darcy caught up with the light, it erupted into a thousand sparks, so bright, Simon stopped and rubbed his eyes. When at last he could see again, Darcy was standing hugging someone and jumping up and down in excitement. None of that seemed particularly strange except that this other person had wings.

Darcy had explained the types of creatures he was likely to meet in Dumnonia, but nothing had prepared him for his first encounter with a pixie.

Nix was tall. She had the lightest coloured wavy hair that fell to her knees in soft curls. Her face was plump and round like a young girl's and she had the sweetest smile. But her eyes... they held such age; she could describe the passing of centuries.

A soft green tunic fell past her waist. Her legs encased in breeches of the same material. She had boots on her feet, and a ring of daisies haloed her head. She was an amalgam of every fantasy character he could remember from the stories his father had read to him as a child, with one notable difference... she was real.

'It's so good to see 'ee again Darcy.'

Nix slowly stepped back, cupping Darcy's tear-stained face in her small, neat hands.

'This is not the girl I knew. 'Ee is a woman now. I knew one day 'ee would return to us. I always knew it, although Mawgan doubted you would come back. But here 'ee is, and with a stray in tow too.' Nix turned to Simon. 'Who might 'ee be?'

'Simon.' Simon shoved his hand out in front of Nix. She looked at it, grasped it tightly, and smiled.

'Hmmm. Interestin',' she said. ''Ee have an over-exaggerated loyalty complex. It's goin' to get 'ee into trouble.'

'I think it already has,' said Simon.

'We were on our way to the cave,' said Darcy. 'But we ran into a buzzard, and now I'm not sure of the direction anymore.'

'Hmmm. The buzzards are roamin' free now. They were trouble enough when Narcasta had 'em, but they've been worse since he went back to the Fae. Well, there's nothin' for it. I'll have to go with 'ee. There's no sense in lettin' ye get 'eeself lost. Come on.'

Nix pointed. 'It's that-a-way.'

Getting themselves lost had taken most of that day. They were tired, hungry, and becoming grumpier by the minute. It was getting dark, and they still had a long way to go.

'Piddleton Village is just down this lane,' said Nix. ''Ee can rest there.'

'Piddleton Village. That's where Morwenna is.'

'Not anymore.'

Darcy looked at Nix. Her face was fixed, but she had caught the edge in her voice.

'Still smarting, are we?'

'I don't want to talk about it.'

'Okay. So, if we're not going to Morwenna's, where are we going?'

'The pub. They have rooms.'

'Sounds good to me,' said Simon. He strode off down the lane with a newfound spring in his step.

Piddleton Village was as Darcy remembered it. The clock tower stood in the central square with tiny homes arranged around its perimeter from the church to the pub at the end of the lane.

'I'm off for now,' said Nix.

They stood outside the pub. The windows were cheerful, lit by the glow of candles and fires. Voices, merry with drink and chit-chat, floated out to meet them.

'I can't go in. They're not keen on the likes of me. But you'll be fine from 'ere. I'll see you first thing down the lane there, just before you get into Willow Wood.'

Before either could answer her, Nix was gone. Her body evaporated, leaving behind the small spec of green light that buzzed off into the darkness.

Simon walked up to the door and pushed. It creaked loudly as it swung inwards. Everyone inside turned to look at the strangers as they entered, but soon returned to their drinks and conversations.

The bar was at the far end of the room. A plump, red-faced publican stood polishing an ale glass with a towel. He smiled, showing brown tobacco-stained teeth.

'What can I get ya?' he asked.

'What do you recommend?' said Simon.

'The mead is good this year, 'n goes well with the meat 'n potatoes from the kitchen. Want some?'

'Sounds great, make it for two.'

'Comin' right up.'

'We're looking for somewhere to stay.'

'We have rooms upstairs, two shillings a night each.'

'Two shillings. Hmm. I suppose that's okay. Thanks, we'll take them.'

Simon joined Darcy by one of the fires.

'We have a problem,' he said.

'What's up?'

'We don't have money.'

'What are you talking about. I have my purse, and I saw you put your wallet in your rucksack.'

'Unless you have old currency, shillings to be specific, we don't have money. I've just ordered dinner and somewhere to sleep, but we can't pay.'

The Publican brought over their food and drink. They thanked him, and he left.

'What are we going to do?' said Darcy.

Simon looked around the lounge. In a corner by another fire, were a couple of locals playing a card game on the small table between them. Simon squinted to see.

'Eat up,' he said.

'I'm not sure I feel like it now.'

'See those two guys over in the corner.'

Darcy looked across to where the men were sitting.

'Yes. Actually, now I think about it. They look familiar.'

'They're playing Noddy.'

'Ha! Really?'

'It's like Cribbage but without the crib, and you happen to be looking at a pro.'

'What do you mean?'

'I learned to play at uni. We didn't do much else actually for the whole of the first year. Do you see... they're playing for money.'

Darcy looked across again and saw the small piles of coin.

'I'm going to win us our dinner.'

They ate, gulping down mouthfuls of their drinks in between bites.

'This is so good,' said Darcy.

'It's mead, honey wine.'

'I feel a bit light-headed.'

'And your cheeks are flushed.'

Darcy's colour heightened even more.

*

He swung the sword in a backward arc, feeling the weight, the balance of the blade and hilt. The runes and scrollwork that set Caliburnus apart from other swords caught the light. He glimpsed his history there in the steel. Wondering what the smiths would carve in years to come in remembrance of his deeds. Would there be anything?

Culhwch approached him.

'The Wizard is impatient to leave, so am I. We must go; the wheel of the year is turning fast. Time is getting away.'

*

Simon approached the card table.

'Can I get you a drink?'

A weathered man looked up from the cards. Cocking his head to one side. 'Who's askin'?'

'The name's Simon.'

'Mine's Bill. What do ya want Simon?'

Bill's eyes narrowed as he looked Simon up and down.

'I was hoping to join your game.'

'Play a bit of Noddy, do ya?' He didn't wait for a reply. 'If you're wantin' to join, you'll 'ave to do more than stand a couple of pints. We're playin' for coin; one shillin' a hand. Can you stand that?'

Simon reached into his back pocket and took out a set of keys. He took off the key ring and threw it onto the table. There was a silver shilling attached.

'Fancy. What does ya reckon Harry? Shall we let the lad join?'

The other player, Harry, shuffled his feet under the table and hid his mouth behind his hand. 'We don't know 'im Bill; he might be sharp.'

'Doesn't look that sharp to me, looks a bit wet behind the ears. Pull ya self up a chair whateva ya name is. You're in.'

Simon pulled his chair up to the table. He beckoned to Darcy, who joined them. On a closer inspection of Bill and Harry, she remembered where she had seen them before. The night they had come searching for Morwenna, Kea had collided with a drunken Bill by the clock tower.

'What ya starin' at?' said Harry. ''Ere. You look familiar.'

He squinted at Darcy, drumming his fingers on his chin.'

'Na, I can't place ya. Must just be me old mind playin' tricks.'

Darcy kept silent as she saw Simon's raised eyebrows; she lightly shook her head.

'I'm real thirsty,' said Harry.

'I'll get them in,' said Simon. 'Same again?'

Harry passed across his tankard.

'That'll be grand. And Bill'll have the same.'

After they finished their drinks, they played cards. Simon won the first hand, and so he now possessed three shillings. He deliberately lost the second hand but won the third and fourth, earning him six shillings.

'This is thirsty work,' said Harry.

Simon took the hint and put another round of drinks on his tab.

'Let's play,' he said.

He won the fifth hand. Deliberately lost the next two hands and went on to win the hand after that, putting eight shillings in his pocket.

He put his keys back onto the ring.

'One more hand fellas? A chance to even the score?'

'If you're buyin' 'ow can we refuse.'

Harry was slurring now. His eyes were glassy, and the smile on his face, empty. Simon got Harry and Bill another drink before dealing the cards once more.

'Last hand Darcy, promise,' said Simon. He smiled at her and leaned forward, addressing the men. 'The words 'candy' and 'baby' mean anything to you?'

Darcy stifled a laugh, covering it with a cough.

The final hand went quickly. Bill and Harry were too drunk to notice that Simon had won again, and he let the last three shillings plop into his pocket to join the other seven.

'Thanks for a good night's play fellas. Let me get you one for the road.'

'Don't mind if we do,' said Harry.

After they had finished their drinks, Harry and Bill left. They leaned on each other, reaching the door with a great deal of effort before stumbling out into the dark singing.

'Both times I've seen those two, they've been drunk,' said Darcy.

'Just as well. I don't think I would have gotten away with it otherwise. Ten shiny shillings.'

Simon was grinning like a Cheshire cat as he jingled the change in his pocket. 'Enough to pay for the meals, drinks, and the rooms. My uni days weren't wasted.'

*

'Is that really you Darcy?'

She started. Her mind raced and her heart beat its way up into her throat. Darcy had known it would happen. Had deluded herself that she wasn't longing for it. But she had wanted to meet him on her terms, when she was ready and not before. She wasn't ready.

'Glewas. How are you?'

It was as cool as she could make it.

'Surprised to see you. How are you here?'

'We found another gate.'

Darcy gestured towards Simon.

'Aren't you going to introduce us,' said Simon.

He smiled, but there was a strangeness in his eyes—a flicker of something.

'Simon, this is Glewas.' He shoved his hand out. Glewas took it for a second then let go just as quickly.

'Hello,' said Glewas before turning back to Darcy, his dark, heavy-lidded eyes fixing on hers.

'Have I got dirt on my face or something?' she said.

Glewas shook his head.

'You're staring at me,' said Darcy.

'Am I? Sorry. I am staggered you are here. I thought we said goodbye for good. When Nix said you were at the pub, you could have knocked me down with a feather. I had to see you for myself. You do look well.'

'So do you.'

'Is anyone tired?' said Simon. He yawned into to back of his hand. 'It's late.' He handed Darcy a key. 'I'll see you in the morning; breakfast is at six, apparently.' He went upstairs.

'We're going to the cave,' said Darcy. 'Come with us?'

Glewas took her hand, feeling its small, soft warmness in his own. He smiled. 'Of course.'

*

He looked down the deserted street. The clock tower chimed the eleventh hour.

'It's late,' said Culhwch. 'Where are we?'

'Piddleton,' said the Wizard.

42

Two men stumbled out of the public house. They sang as they held each other up in a precarious arm sling wobbling their way across the square.

'Not again,' said the Wizard.

His hand was on the other man's arm, whose in turn had found the hilt of the sword.

'That won't be necessary,' said the Wizard. 'There is no harm in these two, just too much liquor. Come, there is nowhere for us to rest here. A quiet, unobserved night in the wood is the best we can hope for.'

They skirted the village unnoticed and lost themselves in the darkness.

CHAPTER SIX

THE CAVE

Simon was whistling to himself as he walked out the door of the pub. Thoughts of the night before filled his head. He had played the game of his life, filled his belly with the best meat and potatoes he'd ever tasted, and the mead had run down his throat like rich honey, leaving behind a warm tingle that had lasted pretty much the whole night.

Darcy caught up with him.

'You're happy this morning.'

'What's not to be happy about? Did you taste those kippers at breakfast? Amazing.'

'Do you think of anything other than food?'

'Not much.'

Darcy laughed. 'You're getting more like Kea by the hour. It must be this place.

'Or maybe I'm just being myself. Come on, it's down here.'

They walked to the end of the lane, past the last home, stopping at the signpost marking the edge of the village. The first trees of Willow Wood sprinkled the trackway with their leaf litter, the forerunners to the dark green mass ahead. Darcy shivered.

'What's up?'

Simon stopped, his hand on her arm.

'Nothing. I was just thinking about the last time I came through here. It was the first time I saw Imps.'

'There's no Imps here now, are there?'

'No, it's just the memory of them, it got to me for a minute.'

'Ahem.' Glewas was smoking a long, thin stemmed pipe, leaning against the trunk of a tree. He blew out a series of decreasing smoke rings that rose between them in the clean air. Nix stood next to him, hopping from one foot to the other.

'If 'ee are ready, can we please get goin'?'

Simon bent over Darcy. 'You didn't tell me he was coming.'

'No. Is that a problem?'

'No.'

'Good, because there is absolutely no reason for you to be jealous.'

'Jealous! Really?'

Simon's eyebrow raised. Darcy punched him on the arm.

'Ouch.'

'Come on, we're getting left behind.'

Nix and Glewas were already at the edge of the wood.

'I forgot to tell you. Wizards and pixies; they're fast.'

The darkness caught Darcy by surprise. It felt like an elephant had stepped on her chest. Sweat prickled the white skin on her face and arms as she clutched at the front of her T-shirt.

'I... I... can't catch my breath.'

Just as her legs buckled, Simon grabbed her up in his arms.

'You're having a panic attack. Breathe... slowly... in... out...'

'What's wrong?' said Glewas.

By the look of him, Simon thought he might collapse too.

'She'll be fine in a minute.'

Darcy's shaking hands stilled and her breathing became more regular.

'What happened?' said Glewas.

'I don't know. I couldn't breathe.'

'It's this place,' said Glewas. 'The last time you were here, we were being chased by the krone and the Imps. Those kinds of memories leave marks, they surprise us when we are least prepared.'

'You sound like Mawgan.'

As Darcy, Nix, Glewas, and Simon headed further towards the cave, they crossed a cobbled pathway.

'I know this,' said Darcy. 'It's the path to the dell.'

'Yes,' said Glewas.

He looked away. Darcy rested her hand on his arm.

'How are they. Gwen and Peter? Have you seen them?'

'I visit when I can. Peter is Peter, he does not show much, but Gwen; the life has all but gone out of her.'

'I should go see them.'

'No. I don't think that is a good idea.'

'Why? Maybe I could help or at least tell them how sorry I am.'

'There is nothing you could help with. Time is what they need now. Besides, l do not believe you would be welcome.'

'But I love the Willows. They were like another set of parents that summer.'

'Darcy, I am sure you have nothing but good memories of the time you spent with them, but they lost their son while he was away from home, looking after you. Can you not see? Please do not go. I do not want them upset any more than they already are.'

Darcy's stared at her feet. Tears pressed against her eyes, and her cheeks felt hot. She opened her mouth, but she couldn't find the right words. In the end, she walked away and caught up with the others, Glewas slowly bringing up the rear.

*

He woke to a cold stiffness in his joints. His head ached from sleeping on a stone all night. It had not made as comfortable a pillow as he had hoped. The Wizard was watching him from under an oak, smoking as he contemplated things, blowing the smoke rings so favoured by the Mages.

'Very pretty.'

'Thank you.'

'Where are we going? I think it is time you told me.'

'Somewhere we can think about what is to be done.'

'I thought that question was already answered. We will do what we can to help Culhwch. I am unsure we will be of any assistance in his fool's errand. But he is my cousin, my blood, and in that, the choice is made.'

*

Darcy walked in silence. Glewas' news had shaken her.

'You haven't said anything for ages,' said Simon. 'What's up? Lover boy put his foot in it, has he?'

Darcy kept walking.

'What? It's not like you to have nothing to say.'

'Well, as you seem to know so much about it, there is no need for me to comment, is there?'

'Ha. I knew it wouldn't last. What did he tell you anyway? Got a little wife or girlfriend stashed away, has he?'

'No, nothing like that. It wouldn't matter if he had anyway; we're not together.'

'So, why the big sulk then?'

'Oh, Simon.' Tears rolled down Darcy's face again. 'You remember I told you about Kea?'

'Yes. He's the big oaf I'm supposed to remind you of.'

'Not nice, but yes. I told you he died. The Imps attacked him, he was killed trying to protect me. Well, back there, the cobbled path we crossed, his parent's home is at the end of it. I wanted to stop and see them, but Glewas didn't think it was such a good idea.'

'Ah, let me guess. He told you they wouldn't be happy to see you?'

'How did you know that?'

'Darcy you can be so naive. Not everyone will think good thoughts about you all the time. These people are hurting, it makes it easier sometimes to have something or someone to blame. If you hadn't come here two years ago, Kea might still be alive. You can't fix this.'

Simons words slid beneath her skin and felt like chips of ice. 'Glewas said the same thing.'

'Did he? Well, that's something we can agree on at least.'

'Why don't you like him? You've made your mind up about him without even giving him a chance.'

'It's more that I don't want to like him.'

'Why?'

'It's easier if I keep my distance. If I get to know him, I may have to agree with you that he's a genuine, all-round, good guy. I've seen the way he looks at you. I'm not ready to do that.'

'You are an idiot.' Darcy laughed. 'Just promise me one thing. You won't write him off because of me.'

Simon nodded. 'I'll do my best, but I'm not promising anything.' Darcy punched him on the arm and Simon rubbed at the spot. 'Hey. This is getting to be a habit. I have bruises, you know.'

'Baby.'

At midday, Darcy noticed a familiar copse of closely grouped trees. The branches were woven together so closely there wasn't a centimetre of light between them. She smiled.

'We're here.'

Darcy and Simon watched as Nix, then Glewas, vanished into the thicket.

'Come on. It's easy,' said Darcy. She stepped forward. There was a second where she hesitated and then smiling again, she stepped through and was gone.

Simon looked into the mesh of branches. Narrowing his eyes, then widening them, hoping it would reveal some hidden entrance. Nothing.

Darcy's disembodied voice filtered through from inside.

'Stop thinking. Close your eyes and step through. Trust me.'

Simon filled his lungs with a deep breath; it was cool and clean, and ever so slightly earthy. He closed his eyes and lifted his face.

A hand, followed by its arm, grabbed the front of his hoodie. He felt the sharp twigs touch his face and then melt away as the arm tugged him forward off his feet and through the thicket. Simon landed hard on the stone floor. Glewas' hand, still gripped the front of his hoodie, he stood above Simon, smirking down at him.

'What did you do that for?' said Simon.

'You seemed to be having some difficulty,' said Glewas. 'Stop whinging; you got through did you not?'

Simon got to his feet, rubbing his knees as he did. It was only as the throbbing eased that he noticed a different hand thrust towards his. He grasped it firmly with his own and shook it. 'Thanks; I think I'm okay now.'

'Good,' said the owner of the hand. 'That was a bit of a tumble.'

The hand's owner sniggered and slapped Glewas on the back. Both erupting into laughter.

'Great,' said Simon. 'Now I'm the village idiot.'

'Please don't upset yourself. We needed a little light relief; I am glad you were here to supply it. If we had to rely on Culhwch there, 'he pointed towards another man at the far end of the room, in conversation with Nix, 'we would be starved of comedy. His mind is only on his love these days. He has no time for merrymaking.'

'You did look funny falling through there,' said Darcy. She leaned in and whispered, 'You'll never believe who this guy is?' Simon looked the man over. 'Stop staring at him. It won't help you.'

'Okay, well tell me then.'

The man finished speaking with Glewas and turned back to Simon and Darcy. He smiled and stuck out his hand once more. 'Arthur Pendragon. Pleased to make your acquaintance.'

CHAPTER SEVEN

PEARLS BEFORE SWINE

Darcy held on to Mawgan as if her life depended on it.

'My dear girl. I never thought to see you again,' he said. He stepped back and held her away from him. 'You are taller.'

'I was still a girl the last time I was here. I've done a bit of growing since then.'

'Hmm. How are you here?'

'Another gateway. We found it at the Tor this time, near the well. The compass brought us right to it. Jenna believes we were drawn back here for some reason, but she was pretty vague on what that might be.'

'Hmm. Jenna feels the vibration of things, but she has much to learn in the art of divination. She is young; but she is correct in this observation. It is timely that you have come back to us. Much has happened. The removal of Narcasta was for the good of all things, but his departure has created a vacuum, and many now vie for position.'

Mawgan looked across at Arthur talking to Simon. 'The young Pendragon,' he nodded in Arthur's direction, 'carries the hope of us all.'

'Mawgan, it's more than that.'

'How so?'

'In my time, there is a story of a king who united Britain. He was more than just another king. He embodied the heart of the people. He's known as the 'once and future king.' People actually believe that he will come back and be king again. And his name...' Darcy leaned in closer to Mawgan. '...is Arthur Pendragon.'

Mawgan hummed thoughtfully. 'Our stories are starting to converge.'

'Doesn't it strike you as odd?'

'What?'

'That there are two Arthurs, yours and ours. One that lived thousands of years ago in my time and this one, here right now?'

'Odd? No. Interesting? Absolutely.'

'Mawgan!'

'Ahh Darcy, you have so little imagination. The idea is interesting, but why would you think it odd there would need to be two Arthurs? You are looking at this from the perspective that we are somehow a past to your present. This is not the case. We don't exist in your past; we live parallel to you. But the most interesting thing with space and time is that it undulates. Like stream water meeting a riverbank, never the same water hits the same part of the bank twice. Darcy, this Arthur maybe both yours and ours. That at some point in his future, he finds himself in your past.'

*

'Oh yeah,' said Simon. 'The space–time thing. There's no proof that any of it is real. There may never be any, but it's damn interesting all the same...'

Simon and Darcy looked through the bookshelves at the masses of large volumes stashed there alongside other curiosities. Darcy pretended to listen as Simon prattled on next to her, but she was thinking about something else.

'...Darcy, did you hear me?' Simon rapped his knuckles gently on the top of her head. She brushed his hand away.

'Look. It doesn't matter what we can prove at this point. He's here. We are standing in the same room as the Arthur of *The Sword in the Stone*. The Arthur of *The Knights and the Round Table*. Excalibur and ladies in lakes. He's here, and we're here. I want to pinch myself.'

'Shh. Keep your voice down. He'll hear you, and whatever happens, he can never know.'

'Why not?'

'Because maybe it'll change everything. You remember that old movie your parents made us watch. What was it? *Back to the Future*? Now I'm not for one minute saying that it was true, but what if there is something to the principle of the thing? We should be careful of messing with time. Darcy, you must promise me you won't tell him anything. Whatever we say could potentially change the future for him and us. He has to find his own way. No help from us.'

'And you don't think the space-time thing is real?' Darcy smothered a smirk with her hand.

Simon rolled his eyes. 'Yeah, well. Let's just do the right thing and see what happens.'

*

The cave was much as Darcy remembered it. The smooth granite walls rose so high that the lamps scattered about here and there could not completely penetrate the blackness overhead. Overstuffed chairs and floor cushions were arranged around fireplaces carved out of the solid rock. Darcy rested her head on the smooth scrubbed pine table that stood between the bed recesses and the massive bookshelves and closed her eyes. The table felt cool under her cheek.

'Do you remember the last time we were here?' said Glewas. He gently ran a finger over the top of Darcy's head and smoothed a wisp of red hair from her cheek.

She sat upright as Glewas took the chair next to hers. 'Yes. Like it was yesterday. I remember being so tired that first night, crawling into that bed over there and sleeping in till late the next day.'

'It was a difficult thing, almost losing Morwenna like that. You were such a strange and uptight little thing. Worried about getting home. Well, worried about everything actually.'

'I had travelled through a gateway that was only visible during an eclipse to find myself stuck on the wrong side of it with a group of strangers that knew no more about getting me home than I did. There was a lot to be worried about. Besides, I felt responsible for Morwenna. She would never have been injured if I hadn't lost my nerve in those woods out there.'

'You take too much on yourself. There is no way of knowing if your actions that day could have changed any outcome for Morwenna. Anyway, she survived.'

'Kea didn't.'

'No.'

Glewas sighed. 'Kea wasn't your fault either. We all knew what we were doing.'

'We were just kids.'

'We were old enough to know that there was a price attached to the adventure and that any one of us could have paid it. We went along anyway.'

The rest of the group had crawled into the bed recesses and were already asleep. Darcy covered a yawn with her hand. Glewas brushed the back of his fingers along her cheek, leaving a trail of goosebumps on her skin. Darcy reached up a hand to cover his.

'Time to sleep. We can talk more tomorrow.' He kissed her lightly on the lips before turning away, and walking to his bed recess and lying down. Darcy sat at the table, hiding the way her legs felt suddenly wobbly. She traced a finger over her bottom lip where Glewas's mouth had touched hers, the sensation fading. Only then did she walk to her bed recess and crawl under the thick coverlet. She closed her eyes as sleep crept up and carried her away.

*

Darcy woke early. She knew it was early because the tiny amount of light that found its way in through the thick mesh of branches disguising the entrance was not yet covering the floor. She sat up and allowed her warm feet to find the stone beneath them.

'Ooh.'

She rubbed each hand quickly up and down the opposite arm. She found her shoes, slipped them on, then grabbed the coverlet off her bed and wrapped it around herself.

'It's chilly this mornin'; autumn's in the air. We'll be pickin' apples and lightin' candles for Mabon before 'ee knows it.'

Nix sat at the table sipping from a mug. She smiled across at Darcy as she sat down beside her.

'Can I have one of those please?'

'Of course, darlin' girl.' Nix waved a hand over the table's surface in front of Darcy. A cup of steaming hot chocolate appeared. Darcy gathered it up in her hands, hugging it to herself.

'I love how you do that.' She smiled and sipped her drink.

Nix raised an eyebrow. 'It can be useful.'

'How do you know if you can do magic?'

'Fer the likes of me n' Hicca, it was in us and around us from the minute 'ee was born.'

'What about humans? How do they know?'

'Oh sweetie, every human can do it. It's just that most are afraid, they don't understand it, or think they're superior and don't need it. Those who see the old religion as somat' to be feared or something evil have all but driven it out, and those that practice it often have to keep it secret. People should know better. 'Ee all have somat' to bring, 'ee all need each other.'

'Could I learn it?'

Nix giggled. 'Darlin' girl. 'Ee has been practicin' yer own brand of magic for some time now.'

'That's not what I mean.'

'I know.' Nix looked across to where Simon and Glewas were still sleeping. 'Yer gonna 'ave to put one of 'em out of their misery soon yer knows.'

'I know. I've already told Simon that I don't think about him that way.'

'I don't think he's gotten the message yet, but he will soon if Glewas has anythin' to do with it.'

'I don't know how I feel about Glewas either. Why does everything have to be so complicated? I just want everyone to be friends.'

''Ee is not taking their feelin's into account, Darcy. Choose one, or choose neither, but if 'ee wants to stay friends with 'em, 'ee'll do it quickly. That's my advice.'

'What's all this?'

Mawgan had reached the table before Darcy and Nix realised he was behind them.

'Nix, I left you on watch.'

'My watch is over Mawgan. The sun's been up a good hour or so. You overslept.'

'Hmm.' Mawgan sat at the table and waved the palm of his hand just above its surface. 'Ætywan.' There appeared another steaming hot mug of chocolate.

*

Culhwch sat staring at the mug of hot chocolate Mawgan had conjured for him a moment before.

'Come on man,' said Arthur. He slapped Culhwch on the back. 'What is wrong with you this morning? This melancholic behaviour is not your nature.'

'I dreamt all night of a sweet girl with creamy skin and flaxen hair, and as she walked, white flowers grew where her feet had stepped. It was the most beautiful dream. I was not ready to leave it when the day arrived.'

'You truly have gone mad, my friend. This is not like you Culhwch. You have had many women; none have ever had this effect. This girl has bewitched you. That is the only answer.'

'If I am bewitched, then I hope I never recover.'

'You have never even met her.'

'I know I must find her and ask her to marry me. I need to find her Arthur. We must leave now while the day is still young and there are many hours of light left.'

'Not until you have broken the fast and bathed. You smell like the pig pens you were raised in. Besides, there are more of us now to consider. The girl, have you noticed she looks at me strangely. As though she is waiting for something to happen.'

'You are imagining this, Arthur. Though they are strangely dressed, I give you that. Mawgan explained they are from a great city, very distant from these parts. Perhaps the girl stares because she considers us strange.'

'No, it is something else. I mean to discover what.'

Culhwch stuck his nose in his arm pit and screwed up his face. 'You are right my friend; I smell like a pig.' He went off to bathe, leaving Arthur alone at the table.

Arthur reached down and unsheathed the sword from the hilt around his waist. The symbols exquisitely etched along its broad side glinted in the light. A dragon, claws bared, its arrow tipped tongue pointing outwards through a mouth of razor teeth. It was the symbol of the Pendragon house, and it stared back at him accusingly. Further down the blade were the three swirls of a triskelion, inextricably joined at the centre—the symbol of his sister. Arthur frowned.

The less said about Morgawse, the better.

His eyes moved along to a swan, so finely etched it appeared to move as the light caught it. His mother, Igraine, had worn a pendant of the same that she had treasured until the day she died. He reached up and touched the front of his loose shirt. He could feel the pendant through the thin fabric. The swan was for her. Arthur's eyes travelled almost to the hilt now. There were no more symbols, just bare steel. He was nowhere to be seen on the sword's surface. As if he didn't exist.

Arthur shoved the sword down on the table; it sounded a twang as it hit the wood. The light caught something he had missed right at the tip.

Se Cyning nu and æfre, se ānes and æfre.

'What does it mean?' Arthur muttered under his breath.

'It is in the old tongue,' said Mawgan. He now stood beside Arthur. 'It means: *The King of now and ever, the once and always.* A prophecy. It speaks of someone to come greater than any king before him or after.'

'Who?'

'That is still to be seen. There is a blank space on the sword for you Arthur, not because you are unworthy of note but because your time is not yet written. We shall see what we shall see.'

Simon, who had been reading by the bookshelves, rushed to the table. 'Is that what I think it is?' Mawgan shook his head at the ground, and Simon realised his error. 'I-er, I haven't seen a long sword this close up before.'

'You have led a very sheltered life,' said Arthur. He held the sword out to Simon. Mawgan's hand reached for Arthur's wrist and gripped it hard. 'No, Arthur, only you can take up this sword. No one else must touch it; make sure of that.'

Arthur sheathed the sword once more. 'I will guard it with my life and, in turn, hope that it does the same.'

Culhwch rejoined them at the table. 'Not so pig-like now?' He slapped Arthur on the back.

Arthur leaned towards him and sniffed. 'You will do.'

Nix and Darcy joined them.

'Now everyone is present,' said Mawgan, 'let me tell you a story... Beyond the sunken forest of Lyonnesse lies the realm of the giants. Their leader, a particularly gruesome individual named Ysbaddaden Bencawr, is fortunate to have a daughter whose loveliness is known throughout the four kingdoms. She has skin the colour of milk and hair as fair as a wheat field. So lovely is Olwen that white flowers bloom in her footprints as she walks. Many have tried for her, but her father will not consent to a marriage. It is said that when Olwen of the giants leaves the islands to marry her love, Ysbaddaden Bencawr will be no more.'

Culhwch paced the floor.

'Mawgan, if she will not leave her father, what am I to do?'

'Now, now, Culhwch. That is enough of that. There is no point in worrying about something we cannot know at this stage in the proceedings. I am sure the solution will come to me at the appropriate time. Let us concern ourselves now with what we can do. Pack up that stuff on the table there. Fill up those bags with provisions. We are going to hunt a giant.'

CHAPTER EIGHT

A LITTLE HELP FROM FRIENDS

They were outside the cave an hour later. It was late summer; the leaves were already falling. Looking up, Darcy could see a dull, grey sky which only a few weeks before would have been completely obscured by the green canopy.

'It's going to rain,' said Darcy.

Simon smiled. 'It's Cornwall; I don't suppose it's any different here than back home.'

No sooner said, the weather broke, and the first spits drummed down on their heads.

'This ain't no fun anymore,' said Nix. She transformed and buzzed off ahead of them.

'I love it when she does that,' said Darcy.

'I suppose it's one way to avoid the rain,' said Simon. He pulled his hood over his head and hunched into it. 'Is there anything about magic you don't love?' he asked.

'I'm not sure how I feel about the Fae; they're weird.'

'Ha, Fairies. Oh yes, all that sparkly magic dust and tiny glittering wings all sounds very scary.'

'You don't know what you're talking about. The Fae aren't tiny, exactly the opposite. There's no magic dust and no wings. They don't fly, well, at least, I don't think they do. Not with wings anyway.'

'Okay. So when do I get to see them?'

'I'm not sure that's in the plan. I get the distinct impression everyone's avoiding talking about them.'

'Why do you say that?'

'Morwenna, Jenna's sister; she's with a Fae man. But every time I talk about her, the subject gets changed. Something has happened, and no one will tell me what.'

'You might be imagining it. Why don't you ask them straight out?'

'I guess I'm afraid of what they might say.'

'Yes, well... that's the risk, but at least you'd know.'

They walked on in silence. The rain subsided a little, and the day settled into a subdued greyness. Their spirits were as damp as their clothes. The only person unaffected was Culhwch.

'You are happy, my friend?' asked Arthur as he walked beside him.

'Happy that we are on the move. It makes me happy that I shall soon see Olwen at last.'

'You don't even know what she is like. Sure, she might have a beautiful face, but what about the rest of her? Suppose you don't like each other.'

'What is not to like about me?'

Culhwch winked at his friend who smiled.

'Yes, yes. Well, we shall see. Do not blame me if she has a heart as cold as her father's and a voice that could grind steel. A pretty face will not be enough to sustain a long and happy life. In time even beauty fades.'

'You will not make me think less of her, Arthur. We are destined for each other. All will be well.'

As they reached the edge of Willow Wood, it started raining again. This time with bigger drops. It took less than a couple of minutes to soak clothes to skin. The sky grumbled and promised far worse.

'If I didn't know better,' said Mawgan. 'I would conclude there are other forces at work in that sky.' He looked up into the swirling clouds. A massive drop splotched onto his eye, the remainder running down his cheek like a giant tear. Nix buzzed around their heads doing an impression of an angry green bee. Simon forgot himself as he went to swat her. Darcy grabbed his hand just before it made contact.

'What is wrong with her?' said Simon. 'She's gone nuts.'

'Look up,' said Darcy. 'Something's happening.' The clouds were rotating, whirling round like a washing machine cycle, drawing all into the centre.

'That's not right,' said Simon. 'I've never seen anything like that before.'

'That is because it is conjured,' said Mawgan. 'And we appear to be at the centre of it.'

The swirling clouds were descending. Second, by second, they drew closer. Darcy swallowed hard a couple of times, and fake yawned as her ears popped with the pressure.

'I've got a feeling of déjà vu,' she said.

'What do you mean?' said Simon.

'She means, this is not the first time we have been subjected to adverse weather conditions,' said Mawgan. 'You are recalling an afternoon spent in the home of the Lord of the Fae?'

'Exactly.'

The clouds were just above head height now. Making them all scrunch down.

'What is this Mawgan?' said Culhwch.

'I think we are about to find out,' said Arthur.

Two boot-clad feet appeared at the centre of the clouds, followed by legs, torso, and arms. As the feet touched the ground, the clouds reversed. Swirling in the opposite direction, they lifted. Long, dark hair fell onto large shoulders. Upwards went the clouds until, at last, the head was clear. The darkness lifted, and the rain ceased.

'Hello Cadan,' said Mawgan.

'I thought you said fairies don't fly,' said Simon.

'I said I don't *think* they fly,' said Darcy. 'That's not the same thing.'

Nix was battering the new arrival about the head with such abandon it was hard to hear anything above the buzzing.

'What on earth is wrong with you, Nix?' said Cadan.

He waved his arms, fending off the angry pixie. He caught her with a swipe, and she landed hard on the grass with a fizzle, full sized.

Nix sat on the grass, rubbing her head. 'Where's my Hicca yer beast? 'Ee is keepin' him locked up somewhere. I just knows it.'

'That's why you were in the forest the day we arrived,' said Darcy. 'You were looking for Hicca. Why didn't you tell me?'

Nix wiped away her tears and blew her nose loudly into a white handkerchief before getting to her feet.

'Nix, I can assure you,' said Cadan. 'Hicca was safe and whole the day he left to return to you.'

'Then where is he? He was comin' home two weeks ago, n' no one's seen 'im since.'

'We are just as concerned about his disappearance as you, Nix. Morwenna is beside herself with worry. She insisted on coming with me, but I persuaded her against it given her condition.'

'Wait. What condition?' said Darcy. 'What's wrong with her?'

'Nothin's wrong with 'er,' said Nix. 'She's 'avin' 'is baby is all. She's fine. But my Hicca isn't. If he ain't with 'ee, where is he?' Nix cried into her handkerchief again. Darcy put her arm around her shoulders. It did not help, Nix only cried harder.

'Darcy,' Cadan said, 'you have come back to us. I have often considered the possibility that one day you would do so. I said as much to Morwenna, and here you are. Who is this?' Cadan poked a long finger into Simon's chest with enough force that Simon took a step backward.

'This is Simon.'

Cadan looked him up and down a few times. It made Simon uncomfortable.

'Hmm. So, you have come then,' said Cadan.

'I'm sorry,' said Simon. 'What do you mean?'

But Cadan had turned aside to where Mawgan, Culhwch, and Arthur talked.

'He's a pain in the neck. But what am I supposed to do? My Morwenna loves 'im.'

Nix brushed herself down.

'Why didn't you tell me about Hicca, Nix? We could have helped you look for him.'

Darcy put a hand on the pixie's shoulder.

'I feel so embarrassed now, fussing about getting to the cave when all the time Hicca's been missing.'

'Oh, darlin' girl. It's not your worry. I will find 'im, 'n when I do, I'll ring 'is bloody neck fer puttin' me through all this, the silly idiot. There's nothin' fer it. I'll 'ave to go and search fer 'im.'

Simon looked at Darcy. Her face was implacable, her jaw set. 'Uh oh.' He knew that look.

'Nix, we're going to come with you,' said Darcy. 'They don't need our help with this giant thing anyway. We want to help you find Hicca.'

'That will not be necessary,' said Mawgan, his booming voice grabbing everyone's attention.

'I don't think that's your decision,' said Simon. He placed a hand on Darcy's shoulder, turning on Mawgan, glaring.

'Forgive me,' said Mawgan. 'I didn't mean to upset you. Darcy. What I meant to say is that I do not believe Hicca needs your help. I am the reason he has not returned home yet. I needed a spy, someone trustworthy who would not be suspected of any wrongdoing if caught. Hicca was perfect for the task. He is small, fast, and frankly, can charm the bees out of the hive. He has not returned to you Nix, because I needed him elsewhere.'

'Why on earth did you keep such knowledge to yourself Mawgan,' said Cadan. 'I have had my people searching the length and breadth of the kingdom for him, Morwenna insisted on it.'

'Because if he had,' said Arthur, 'Hicca would not be a successful spy for very long, would he?'

'As it happens,' said Mawgan, 'Hicca has been very successful.'

Darcy spun round on him. Her face was strawberry, and her eyes looked as if they might pop out of their sockets. 'Don't you have any feelings at all Mawgan? You should have at least told Nix. All this time, you let her think Hicca was lost. It's a horrible thing you've done. Horrible.' Darcy picked up her bag, slung it over her shoulder, and stormed off to where a stile was on the fence line bordering a field. She climbed it and disappeared into the barley rows.

'Like she said,' said Simon, following after her. Nix buzzed away in the same direction.

*

'I do not think they are impressed with you Mawgan,' said Culhwch. 'Why did you keep Hicca's whereabouts a secret? I agree with Darcy. You should not have done that.'

'I sent Hicca to spy on the giants; he has been sending me valuable information for weeks,' said Mawgan. 'If there was a chance of that information falling into the wrong hands, then my actions were warranted. I will not apologise for that, though I am sorry for Nix. Shall we go?'

Glewas, Arthur, Cadan, and Culhwch followed Mawgan over the stile.

'What information did Hicca give you Mawgan?'

Glewas spoke so softly, only Mawgan heard.

'The giant is aware of our plans. He is expecting us and will not make things easy. This may be the hardest thing we have done yet. You and I will need all the resources at our disposal.'

'I understand.'

Glewas' hand folded around the wand securely stowed in his pocket.

'I will be ready.'

*

Darcy stopped at the edge of the barley field. She sniffed the air, raising her face as she did.

'Mmm. Bacon and eggs, and I think I smell toast too.'

'I smell it,' said Simon. 'Where's it coming from?'

'From a little farmhouse just over that ridge of trees. Come on; there's a couple of people I want you to meet.'

CHAPTER NINE

THE CAER

Mawgan pushed his chair back from the kitchen table. It scraped across the flagstone floor. He leaned back, rubbing his very rounded belly.

'Another good meal Mrs. Tussock. You spoil us as usual.'

'Aww, Mr. Mawgan, ye is always so kind.'

'So, ye 'ave eaten of our provisions, Mawgan, what brings ye an' this motley crew to our door. Hidin' again are ye?'

Mr. Tussock narrowed his eyes as he looked in turn at each of the occupants of his kitchen table. Finally, his gaze rested on his wife; he smiled and winked at her.

'Tussock, you are shroud,' said Mawgan, 'but alas, I am unable to enlighten you further.'

'Oh, don't be daft man,' said Mr. Tussock. 'Yer pesky pixie friend 'as already been 'ere tryin' ta get information out of us, and I'll tell ye the same as I told 'im. I don't know nothin' about no giants. We keeps ourselves ta ourselves 'ere.'

'It's alright Tussock, I wouldn't want to put either of you in any danger,' said Mawgan.

He leaned forward, his forehead lined with crisscrossing furrows, they resembled the craters on the moon.

'I know you know more than you have let on. The halls of the giants being less than a day's walk from this place, you could not avoid them, or they, you. Tell me, how do we gain an audience with Ysbaddeden Bencawr?'

Mr Tussock leaned back, releasing a long, loud belly laugh.

'Are ye soft in the 'ed?' he said. 'No one sees Ysbaddeden; at least, no one comes back. Ye knows he likes the taste of human flesh. Is this somat ta do with them again?'

Mr Tussock pointed an arthritic finger at Cadan.

'No, not this time,' said Mawgan.

'Just as well, they've done enough damage.'

Everyone was looking at Cadan now, but he seemed unaffected as he fiddled with the toggles on his coat.

'Well, this will never do.'

*

Mawgan looked at the group sometime later, shaking his head.

'I had thought we would arrive at the giants' halls with some idea of the lay of the land. I had asked Hicca to prime Tussock so I could question him, as I am sure he knows more than he has let on. Alas, Hicca was not successful.'

'Tussock's just scared Mawgan,' said Simon.

They stood in the yard, ready to set off again.

'I don't know him at all, but I do know Darcy, and she trusts him. So, I would say that if he chooses to keep quiet, it may be nothing more than a man protecting his family and property. If it were me, I'd do the same.'

'Yes, I agree,' said Glewas. 'But it does not help us much.'

'No shit, Sherlock,' said Simon.

'I don't understand,' said Glewas.

Darcy laughed and patted Glewas on the back. 'Don't worry about it Glewas; he's just messing with you.'

*

'That was very brave of you just now,' said Darcy. She and Simon walked with Glewas apart from the rest of the group to the end of the yard and headed out into the fields once more.

'What are you talking about?' said Simon.

'The way you spoke to Mawgan back there. Very brave.'

'Well, the guy needs to lighten up on everyone a bit. He thinks he's in charge, obviously, and that he knows everything. I was just reminding him that it's not a given.'

'What is not "a given"?' said Glewas.

'That Mawgan makes the decisions for everyone all the time. He certainly doesn't for me, and he shouldn't for you either. Anyway, what's the worst he could do?'

'He could turn you into a toad,' said Glewas.

'Ha, not likely,' said Simon. 'I have a funny feeling. Something Cadan let slip earlier. I think there is something I have to do.'

'Hmm,' said Glewas, 'What do you think?'

'I've no idea,' said Simon. 'I'll find out at some time or other. I don't suppose there's much point trying to wheedle it out of him.'

Glewas shook his head. 'No. Teeth would be more easily extracted.' His eyes raked over Simon's face. 'You don't seem to have a very high opinion of Mawgan.'

He maintained a leisurely pace between Darcy and Simon.

'I don't dislike him,' said Simon. 'I just object to his high-handed attitude and the way you all follow his orders without question.'

'We have the advantage over you Simon...' Glewas casually slipped his hand into Darcy's as he strolled beside her. She was momentarily startled but didn't draw away, though she felt a twinge of discomfort as she saw Simon wince.

'...We have known Mawgan much longer than you. As time progresses, you will come to understand the Mage's judgment can be relied on.'

*

They stood at the edge of a vast, broad plain. It stretched in front of them as far as the eye could see and was equally as wide. On the horizon was a blob, but it was so far away it resembled a pimple in the distance.

'What is this place?' said Darcy.

Nix had joined them on their stroll through the fields, taking it upon herself to buzz Cadan's head when he least expected it. Full-sized now, she stepped up to the edge of the plain and squinted at the blob on the horizon.

'This is the Great Plain,' she said. 'And that spot on the line of the horizon there is The Caer. It belongs to the shepherd Custennin.'

'That it does, Nix,' said Mawgan. 'And it is where we must go.'

'What about his hound?' said Arthur. 'I have heard that it is such a beast in size and ferocious with it.'

'We are a long way off yet,' said Mawgan. 'I have an idea to fix the dog when the time comes, but for now, we must walk. We need to get a move on too, no more of this dilly-dallying nonsense, the day is drawing on.'

'What's a 'Caer' Mawgan?' said Darcy, as they walked on.

'It is a fortified place. It could be a camp or a piece of land. In the case of this Caer, it is Custennin's home. It is fortified because it is on the other side that the giants live, and because of this, it is the greatest Caer that has or will ever exist. It is not only that it keeps the giants in, it keeps the people out.'

'So, this isn't going to be easy then?'

'No Darcy, this will be the opposite of easy.'

*

The plain itself was a deserted place. Nothing grew apart from stubbly grass, bleached brown by the sun. They would pass the stump of a tree or a frizzled-up bush every so often. Each stood as sombre markers on the landscape, blackened and dead.

'What happened here?' said Simon.

He touched what was once a hawthorn bush. The black leaves fell off in his hand. He scrunched them between his fingers, and the breeze took the dust away.

'That's the work of Custennin's dog,' said Arthur.

'His dog?' said Culhwch.

'The hound can kill anything living with its very breath,' said Arthur. This plain has become a desolate place because of it.'

'I've heard of dogs having bad breath,' said Simon. 'But that's ridiculous.'

'Hmm,' said Mawgan.

I agree,' said Cadan. 'If he can do that to a bush, what might he do to you?'

They walked on. The ground was soft, but not the springy softness of grass. It was a sinking softness; a bog. They had to lift their knees to waist height with each step, and they were getting tired. The sun was level with the blob on the horizon.

'I have to stop,' said Darcy. 'Just for a minute.'

She raised her hand over her eyes.

'Is it just me, or does that Caer thing look as far away as it ever did?'

'It is not you,' said Glewas. 'I was thinking the very same. Morgan, we've been walking for hours. We are no nearer the Caer than when we entered this place. What is going on?'

Glewas tuned to look back the way they had come. He lost his balance as his feet sank and failed to turn with him.

'Steady there, mate,' said Simon, helping him upright again.

'What the...'

'What indeed,' said Mawgan.

They were all looking back the way they had come. If they were to take only a few steps in that direction they, would be right back where they started.

'We have not made any progress,' said Cadan. 'What sort of magic is this?'

'Ancient,' said Mawgan. 'We will camp here tonight. Do not worry; things are not always as they first seem.'

*

Darcy wrestled in her sleep.

'No. Stop it. Get off me you rotten thing. Get off.' She lashed out at her invisible assailant, hitting Glewas across the face as he slept beside her. He sat upright, catching her hands in his own before she could hit him again.

'Darcy, wake up. Come on; nothing is attacking you. I am here. You are safe.' She woke with a start. 'Shhh,' said Glewas, 'it is all right.' He held her.

Surprised at how peaceful it felt leaning into him, she couldn't pull herself away.

'I love you,' Glewas whispered into her hair. Darcy looked up at his face, just visible in the light from the campfire. She didn't know what she was feeling; she had never felt like this before.

'I... er... I don't know what to say,' she said.

'It is alright Darcy. I do not expect anything. Sleep now. Tomorrow will have its own set of problems for us; we do not need to make our own tonight.'

She lay in Glewas' arms until morning.

*

It was cold. The first frosts lightly blanketed the dead grass, making it sparkle. The fire had long since fizzled out. Cadan waved a hand above its charcoal remains, and it crackled back to life.

'That's a good fire,' said Simon. Cadan smiled, and Simon happily sat defrosting his fingers and toes. One by one, the others joined them. The fire was hypnotic. Flames leaped in an exotic dance. Simon was sure there were things alive in the glow.

Mawgan stood a little way apart, straining his eyes, searching the horizon.

'It is no closer this morning, my friend,' said Cadan. 'What will we do?'

'We will walk,' said Mawgan. 'And we will walk again tomorrow and the next day. We will walk every day it is necessary until we reach the Caer. This magic is made to defeat those not of a stout mind. It is only by determination that it will be overcome. Persistence pays.'

So, they walked the second day, and the third. On the fourth day they noticed that the Caer was growing bigger on the horizon. As they walked into the evening, an enormous flock of sheep scattered around them. It was so large, all they could see was sheep for miles.

'What will we do now, Mawgan?' asked Arthur.

'We will go through it,' said Mawgan.

They walked into the flock, shooing the sheep one way then another, causing a ripple as the sheep scattered before them. Arthur took Caliburnus from its hilt. He grabbed a lamb by the scruff of its neck and sliced its throat cleanly. Then slung it over his shoulder.

'We need to eat tonight,' he said.

The metallic tang of the fresh blood stung at Simon's nostrils. His stomach lurched uncomfortably, and his hand shot up to cover his yawing mouth. Nobody took any notice. They were listening to the howl on the wind.

'What was that?' said Darcy.

'Custennin's dog,' said Arthur. 'He is coming. All of you, get behind me.'

Arthur dropped the lamb; Caliburnus in his hand ready.

CHAPTER TEN

CUSTENNIN

A sleek black shape lolloped across the Great Plain. It was the size of a dray horse, but this was no horse. Massive paws splayed wide as its feet took the weight of its body. For all that, it padded over the soft ground soundlessly, like a wading bird through a marsh. Sweat lathered its coat, and drool oozed from its mouth, spraying the ground with large white globules as it passed by. The wide jaws hung open, showing two rows of pristine teeth, each the size of an adult human finger.

Mawgan placed a firm hand on Arthur's arm.

'This is no job for you, my son. More than hard steel and courage will be needed to stop this beast.'

He stepped in front of Arthur, Cadan stepped up beside him.

'We will do this together Mawgan,' said Cadan. 'It will take both of us.'

The footfalls were getting louder, but Darcy still couldn't see what was making the sound.

'Where is it? I can't see a thing,' she said.

Simon grasped her hand and squeezed it. 'It's okay. Don't be scared.' His hand was shaking.

'I'm not scared,' said Darcy. 'Are you okay?' Darcy smiled, and Simon's hand stopped shaking.

'I've never done anything like this,' said Simon. 'I've never been in danger really, ever.'

'It's okay,' said Darcy. 'This is where you just have to trust us. Mawgan knows what he's doing.'

Mawgan and Cadan both looked toward the horizon.

'I can hear it, Mawgan, but I cannot see the thing.'

The sky was prematurely dark and threatening. As the first drops of rain splattered the ground, they had their first sighting of Custennin's hound. The sheep herd parted down the centre. The terrified animals scattering left and right.

'I see it,' said Mawgan.

Nix, who had been buzzing above Mawgan and Cadan like a demented bumblebee, now shot off in the direction of the dog.

'Nix!' yelled Cadan.

But it was no good. She hovered now above the dog's massive head before dive-bombing the tip of its nose. The dog yelped and raised a giant paw over the place Nix had struck. With a speed quicker than anything of its size should move, the dog swung round. Nix was now just out of reach above its head. The dog lunged upwards, its jaws wide. In one fluid action, the jaws closed around the pixie, the dog swallowed hard, and she was gone.

'Nooo!' The sound Darcy made was more scream than word.

Cadan lunged towards the dog; arms outstretched. A darkness seeping from his hands. The dog twisted around itself as the dark engulfed it, blinded. Mawgan raised his wand.

'*Acennan Adl.*'

The dog stopped its twisting, its front legs splayed as its stomach heaved. The corners of its top lip turned up as its jaw clenched. Another heave, then another. Its stomach lurched with every effort until, with one enormous heave, the dog's mouth opened wide and out poured a thick, yellow liquid. There, in the centre of the yellow mess, lay Nix; still, her hair matted and thick with spit and bile.

The dog collapsed. All attention now was on Nix.

'She's not breathing,' said Arthur. 'What do we do?'

'Move out of the way,' said Simon. 'Please. Just move aside.' He rolled Nix onto her back, tilted her chin upwards, wiped the gooey mess away from her mouth and nose, took a deep breath himself, covered her mouth with his own, and blew.

'Excuse me,' said Culhwch. 'Is this appropriate?'

Simon ignored him. He placed one hand and then the other over Nix's breastbone and pushed down hard once, then again as he started to sing, 'Nelly the elephant packed her trunk and said goodbye to the circus...' He came to the end of the first stanza and breathed into Nix's mouth again. Her chest inflated then fell back. Simon returned to the chest compressions and another couple of lines.

'This is ridiculous,' said Culhwch. 'You can't sing her back to life.' He moved to intervene, but Mawgan's hand was on his shoulder.

Darcy knelt beside Simon, one hand on Nix's head. 'It's not working,' she said. 'We have to try something else.'

Simon didn't respond; his whole focus was Nix. Breathe, compressions, breathe again. Darcy sat beside him, stroking Nix's yellow hair. Glewas knelt and wrapped his arms around her, resting his head on hers. Everyone watched as Simon worked. The Great Plain, the Caer, everything melted away. There was no sound, no air, just Nix, and no one watched the dog.

*

The hound raised its enormous head and blinked. The stuffy darkness had gone; he could move again. He watched the group on the ground. His nostrils flared with the smell of sweat and vomit. His mouth dripped saliva; he licked his lips. It was a good smell. The hound flexed the muscles in his legs and wobbled to his feet.

Towering now above the group, he could see them crouched around the annoying, stingy thing. He had stopped it and now, it could not sting him again. The dog leant closer. He had wanted to make the stingy thing stop, but he could now see that he had hurt it. He hadn't wanted that.

The one with the sword stood watching the stingy thing. That made him angry. The one with the sword had cut one of the lambs. He could still smell the blood hidden amongst the other smells. He moved forward. The hairs on the back of his neck bristled. One gigantic paw soundlessly following the other. Crouch, creep, then crouch again, the silent rhythm of the hunt. He would get him; he would not fail.

Nix coughed.

'She's breathing,' said Darcy, shrugging herself free of Glewas. 'You did it.'

Simon slumped back onto the grass. His arms and shoulders throbbed. The palms of his hands were numb. He laid down on his back and closed his eyes.

Nix spluttered through a few raspy breaths then threw up. Her blueish pallor slowly changing back to pink. Darcy held back the mass of yellow curls from Nix's face as she vomited for a second time.

'Breathe, Nix,' she said. 'Just breathe.'

Glewas was once again at Darcy's side. 'Can I help?' he said.

'No. Please just check on Simon.'

Culhwch, Arthur, Cadan, and Mawgan hovered over Darcy and Nix. Glewas turned to look at Simon behind him. He froze.

A large drop of white slime splattered the top of Arthur's head. He reached up to touch it.

'Uh, yuck.' He examined his hand. 'What is this?'

Culhwch leaned over. 'I do not know.'

Arthur looked up. Above him, loomed the massive jaws of the

hound. Another large globule of drool hit him in the face. The dog's mouth clenched; lips turned out. A rumbling growl filled the air.

'Watch out!' said Culhwch. He pushed Arthur out of the away as the dog snapped down on them. It was quick, but Culhwch and Arthur were faster. The hound bounced around the field, snapping at anyone and anything. Darcy hunched down low over Nix. They lay still in the bleached grass. It worked; the dog ignored them; all his attention on Culhwch and Arthur.

Simon, seeing the danger, jumped up and ran. Mawgan followed him.

'We must stay out of this trifle,' said Mawgan. 'Wait, this is far enough.' He pulled on Simon's arm. They stopped running. They had put a fair distance between the fight and them. 'You are untrained in combat of this nature, I think.' Simon nodded at the ground. 'Do not be ashamed boy. There is no shame in knowing one's limitations. What is not known can be taught, if you have a mind to learn. Someone who believes mistakenly that they already know everything makes for a very dumb expert.'

Simon searched. 'I can't see Darcy. My god, I left her behind. What was I thinking? Where is she?'

'She is there,' said Mawgan, pointing to the far left of the group, 'She is caring for Nix. She is safe.'

'I should never have left her.'

'You would only have drawn attention to them by staying and put them in more danger. Your gut instinct to get out of the way was the right one. We must choose which battles we stay and fight. Sometimes withdrawal is the more strategic option.'

Mawgan looked at Simon. He had the oddest expression on his face; Simon could not place it. The next moment it was gone; he only winked and smiled.

Glewas, Culhwch, Arthur, and Cadan engaged the dog in an elaborate game of tag. It was only a matter of time though before those huge teeth would manage to find an arm or a leg. Arthur kept trying to release his sword from the sheath around his waist, but the dog would not leave him alone for a moment. It pursued him with such venom in its belly that Arthur felt the fear return. He had not felt it for a long time.

*

Away at the distant Caer, a door opened. A large man and a small light burst out onto the plain. The man ran towards the mix of dog and people, closely followed by the light. They pushed their way through the flock of sheep, scattering them further. Once on the other side, they launched into the mess of flailing arms and legs.

'STOP!'

The dog froze at the sound of its master's voice, his jaws hanging wide around Arthur's dark-haired head, poised to eat him at any moment. 'COME.' The dog dropped Arthur unceremoniously on his backside and moved away to the right. 'THAT'LL DO.'

The dog sat in the grass, licking itself.

Custennin's rage burned in his face, making his alcohol reddened nose the same colour as the rest of his skin. He breathed heavily, clenching his fists and closing his eyes, mouth moving as he breathed. 'Six... seven... eight... nine...' he said.

'Who is he?' said Nix

'I don't know,' said Darcy.

'...ten,' said Custennin. He breathed deeply once more, and the beetroot colour faded. His complexion returning to its usual sallow tones.

A sound resembling a fan started. It was soft at first, but as it gradually grew louder, one by one, their attention was drawn to it.

'What is *that*?' said Arthur. I cannot hear my own thoughts anymore.'

'It's coming from that green light,' said Simon. He and Mawgan had re-joined the others.

The light continued to whirl above their heads, settling at last over Nix and Darcy. It bust apart, scattering little shards of light in every direction. Darcy rubbed at her eyes. When eventually she could see again, she let out a little whoop.

'Ello me lovely.'

Hicca grasped her hand in both of his, smiling. Then he was by Nix. 'Oh, me darlin' are 'ee well? I mean, do 'ee 'ave any bits missing?' Without waiting for an answer, Hicca turned on Custennin. ''Ee an' that blooming' dog of yours. It would be shot or worse if I had me way.'

A quiet, musical voice reached his ears. 'Where 'ave 'ee been Hicca?' said Nix. 'I thought I'd lost you.'

Hicca turned and took Nix's hand in his. 'My darlin',' he smiled and stroked Nix's cheek with a long slender finger, 'You could never lose me. I'll always turn up eventually.'

Custennin let out a deep chortle. 'He's been fretting over being away for so long,' said Custennin. 'It's pitiful if you ask me.' The giant man grabbed his dog by the scruff of its neck and led him away. 'Come on then, will you,' said Custennin. Looking at the group; he frowned. 'What a rabble you are. You had better come with me.'

They were walking across the plain once again. This time the Caer grew steadily larger.

CHAPTER ELEVEN

MY SISTER'S SON

They reached the Caer just as evening was sinking into night. Its outer wall stretched as far as could be seen in either direction, so high an average person would need a long ladder to reach the top.

'What could need a wall like this?' said Simon.

As Darcy looked back across the Great Plain, she could see the last rosy glows of sunlight melt into the earth.

'Hey,' said Simon, 'you okay?'

Darcy frowned. 'I don't know why we're here. I guess I thought we'd step through, and after I'd found them all again, there'd be time to enjoy Dumnonia. I want to see the places I experienced last time and take it all in.'

'Like a holiday?' said Simon.

'The last time I was here, there was always something to do, somewhere we had to get to. This time I was hoping it would be different. It's not what I thought it would be. They don't need us here; we're just extra baggage. Maybe we should go back.'

'Or, maybe this time, it's not all about you, Darcy,' said Simon.

Darcy's eyes darkened.

'Come on, don't be like that,' he said. 'I know things so far haven't been what you thought they would be. It's three years on. Things never stay the same. You've got older, and they've moved on. I do know though, we are here for something. I've felt it from the moment we arrived. I've seen it in Mawgan's face. What I mean is; maybe this time it's not you. Maybe this time it's me.'

Darcy looked at Simon. He was so precious, a loved older brother. Solid and dependable, he was safe. She thought about Kea. She'd had the same feelings about him, and he was dead. Kea was born and raised in Dumnonia, but it had still found a way to kill him. What if the same thing happened to Simon? His knowledge of Dumnonia was even less than her own, what chance did he have?

'Come on,' said Darcy, quickly changing the subject, 'They're leaving us behind.'

Custennin flicked the latch on a gate in the wall and pushed the heavy door. It creaked as it slowly swung inwards. The dog trotted on through into a yard beyond, his tail held high.

'Wife.' Custennin's voice echoed off the walls, the sound jarred in Darcy's ears.

He stood in the centre of the yard, looking towards a door in the wall of a round hut. An earthy smell clung to the insides of their nostrils and hung in the air like a fog. It seeped out of the hut's thatched roof, and rose from other places around the yard.

A large woman appeared through the door; her rough hands spread across voluminous hips. Sunken eyes as grey as the frazzled hair around her face gazed at them, unfeeling.

'Who's this then?' she asked, looking at them each in turn. Her eyes narrowed, and her thin mouth drew back in a tight smile as her gaze rested on Culhwch. 'My sister's boy,' she said. 'Oh my, how long has it been? I don't think I've set eyes on ya since you were a lil' man.'

She opened her arms wide and ran towards him. When Culhwch was just out of her reach, Cadan stepped between them. The woman's arms wrapped around Cadan in the hug meant for Culhwch, the smelly fog rose from their bodies and hung in the air.

'That's weird,' said Darcy. She watched as the fog continued to drift upwards.

'Woman. Stop!' shouted Mawgan.

Simon's hand rested on Darcy's arm. Something was happening to Cadan.

The Fae's body was shrinking. He shrivelled before their eyes, the skin over his face tight across the bones of his skull and like paper, it broke apart. Darcy thought there would be blood, but there wasn't. The very life was being squeezed out of Cadan, and there was nothing that could be done to stop it.

The whole thing was over in a moment. As the last spark of life left Cadan's body, his withered remains dropped to the ground in a pile. Darcy was in a dream. Simon, horrified, was rooted to the spot; his hand still resting on Darcy's arm.

'My god,' said Arthur. 'What have you done?' He drew Caliburnus, pointing it at the woman. Expecting her to launch herself at Culhwch again and ready to stop her with any force necessary.

The woman stumbled backward, tripping on a stone she fell, crying.

'YOU KNEW THIS WOULD HAPPEN!' Mawgan shouted.

'You killed a lamb,' said Custennin. 'You took what was not yours, and you expect that I would allow that to go unpunished? The sheep are the property of Ysbaddaden Bencawr. What do you think he will do when he hears one has been lost?'

'He'll want to know what's been done about it,' said Simon.

'Yes,' said Custennin. 'And now I can tell him how a life was given for the life that was lost, and he will be satisfied.'

'It should have been my life,' said Arthur.

'Yes, it should have been,' said Custennin. 'But no matter. It is done.'

Custennin bent low and rifled through Cadan's remains.

'Don't you dare touch him.' Hicca spat the words. 'He's my son. My daughter's lover.'

'Then I am sorry for you, and her,' said Custennin. Custennin picked his wife off the ground. She stumbled to her feet, leaning on him, and they went inside the hut, closely followed by the hound.

Hicca produced a box from his pocket and stared at it. The box grew until it was the size of a packing trunk. He carefully placed Custennin's bones inside. Once the lid closed, the box shrunk again, and Hicca put it back in his pocket.

'We need to leave you now, Mawgan,' he said. 'We 'ave to take 'im home to Morwenna. She will need us both.'

Mawgan nodded. 'Please tell Morwenna how sorry we are,' he said.

'I doubt it'll 'elp much,' said Nix, 'but we will.'

'I understand,' said Mawgan. He looked at the ground and shook his head.

'Bye, pumpkin,' said Nix. She stroked Darcy's hair, and it was only then that Darcy snapped out of her frozen state.

'You're going?' she said.

'Yes,' said Hicca. 'We must. Don't be scared.'

Glewas came to stand by Darcy's side. 'I'll look after her,' he said.

'So will I,' said Simon. He looked sideways at Glewas as he said it. Glewas ignored him.

Mawgan, Arthur, and Culhwch were already inside the hut, but Darcy did not follow them. She clung to Nix's hand. Nix gently extricated herself, kissed Darcy on the cheek, and she and Hicca's lights sped off into the night. They were gone.

'Okay. Let's go in,' said Glewas.

CHAPTER TWELVE

AN EVIL LOVE

Mawgan, Culhwch, and Arthur sat at a table inside the hut. A small fire puffed in a central pit, the smoke twirling up into the roof space to find its way outside, but not before depositing its stinky reek on everyone and everything.

The walls were leached black by greasy soot that ran in tiny rivers onto the floor, pooling and hardening. Over the fire hung a pot of oily water and bones. It bubbled gently, emitting a foul stench. Darcy felt bile rise in her throat at the first whiff of it. She sat down at the table.

'I hope we're not expected to eat that,' she said. 'I don't think I could.'

'I doubt we are invited to dinner,' said Arthur softly. 'Not after... well... you know.'

'Why are we even in here?' said Glewas. He sat down. 'I thought, given the circumstances, we would be on our way as soon as possible.'

'And how do you suppose we do that,' said Mawgan. 'Custennin holds the keys to the other gate. We will need to persuade him to open it.'

They sat looking at each other.

'I think I could take him with your help, Arthur,' said Culhwch.

'Yeah, of course you could,' said Simon. He rolled his eyes and slumped back in his chair; arms folded. 'I'd like to see that.'

'I do not see you with a better suggestion,' said Arthur.

'We could do the obvious,' said Simon. He rocked back and forth on the back legs of his chair.

'What's that then?' said Darcy.

'We could ask him,' said Simon.

'I would like to see that,' said Culhwch.

Custennin and his wife entered the room from the far side of the hut. 'You are all still here then?' he said. He did not smile.

'We have no choice,' said Mawgan.

'Oh, I think not Wizard,' said Custennin. 'I rescued you from the jaws of my hound and the wrath of Ysbeddaden Bencawr. Nothing is keeping you here now; move on and be done with it.'

Simon got up from the table.

'See,' said Custennin. 'The boy has sense.'

'I'm not leaving,' said Simon. 'We will go when you open the other gate for us.'

'Ha!' said Custennin. 'You are funny. Puny, but funny nonetheless.'

Glewas opened his mouth to speak, but Mawgan laid his hand carefully on the table and shook his head.

'I'm not built for fighting, that's true,' said Simon. 'But I have a good brain, that's where my talents lie.'

Darcy covered her mouth with a hand.

'Is that so,' said Custennin.' 'We shall see.'

He reached into his pocket and pulled out a pack of cards. Darcy recognised them as the set from the pub in Piddleton Village.

'Do you play?' asked Custennin.

'If you know the owners of those cards, then you already know the answer,' replied Simon.

'Mmm,' said Custennin. He fumbled the cards slowly in large, crusty hands, feeling each in turn before laying them down on the table.

'Pull up a chair, boy,' he said. 'If you want that gate opened, you must earn it. There are no gifts to be had here.'

Simon thought for a moment. 'One hand. Winner takes all,' he said.

Custennin smiled. 'You think yourself a player, boy? We shall see what we shall see.'

Custennin cut the deck of cards. He took the top card from one pile; the King of Hearts and laid it on the table. Simon lifted the top card from the other pile, Ace of Spades.

'My deal,' said Simon. He shuffled the deck and dealt three cards to Custennin and three to himself. When he was done, Simon laid the rest of the deck down on the table, taking the top card and turning it over for Custennin to see. Seven of Hearts.

'Call,' said Simon.

Custennin blew out through pursed lips. 'Fifteen, peg two and a run of four to peg six,' he said.

Simon looked at his cards. 'Fifteen is two, another fifteen is four, twenty-five is seven, and a pair comes to nine,' said Simon.

'Humph,' said Custennin.

'Come now, Custennin,' said Mawgan. 'Don't be sore.'

'It is not over yet Mawgan,' said Custennin.

'Let's play our hands,' said Simon.

Custennin laid down the Four of Clubs, making four. Simon laid his Nine of Diamonds on top of it, making thirteen.

Glewas squeezed Darcy's hand. 'Breathe,' he whispered. 'You are turning blue.'

Custennin laid the Six of Diamonds on the Nine, making nineteen. Simon smiled.

'What?' said Custennin.

Simon didn't reply. He picked up his Six of Spades and placed it on the other cards.

'Twenty-five,' he said. 'That's another six pegs for me.'

Custennin frowned, his eyes disappearing into the deep folds of his skin.

He laid down the Five of Hearts, making thirty.

'Go,' said Simon.

'I'm out too boy,' said Custennin, Pegging one more for laying the last card.

'Yes!' Arthur jumped up, slapping Simon on the back. 'You are very useful indeed.'

'Is that it?' said Darcy. 'I still don't get it. Who won?'

'We did,' said Glewas. He didn't look pleased about it, but maybe Darcy imagined it.

'The shepherd pegged seven to Simon's fifteen,' said Glewas. 'We won.'

'Best of three?' said Custennin.

'Absolutely not,' said Mawgan. 'The rules were very clear; you played, you lost. Now please, unlock the gate.'

'Not before you promise me something,' said Custennin.

'There were no conditions,' said Mawgan.

'Mawgan.' Darcy touched his hand. 'Let's just see.'

Custennin dragged a box out from the shadows. It was large, like the boxes people keep at the ends of beds for extra blankets and such. The wood was ornately carved and blackened by age. Custennin undid the latch and lifted the lid. Out jumped a young boy. He could only be ten or eleven years old. His clothes were virtually rags and hung from his skinny body; they had been made for someone much larger.

'This is my son,' said Custennin. 'My youngest boy and the only one left.' He looked across at his wife. She scowled and sunk back into the shadows. 'The giant curses my house,' said Custennin. 'I had twenty-three sons; all are gone. Gorau is all I have left, and he will be gone too if I don't get him away from here, away from her. She loved them all, but as you have seen for yourselves, her love destroys all.'

'You can't keep him in a box,' said Darcy. 'It's cruel.'

'Not as cruel as being dead,' said Culhwch

Darcy shook her head. 'Mawgan, we have to take him with us. You heard Custennin; if he stays, she will kill him, even though I don't believe she wants to.' Darcy glanced at the woman weeping silently in the shadows. 'I feel sorry for her,' said Darcy.

'What can we do?' said Mawgan.

Custennin had been sitting with his head in his hands. He looked up now; his eyes pleading with them. 'If you want to marry that girl,' he pointed a finger at Culhwch, 'you will have to kill her father. That is the deal. If you kill him, my wife will be free, and so will we all be. Take Gorau with you. He is a good boy and deserves a better end than this. He will be useful.'

'That's debatable,' said Arthur. 'But I will not leave him here.'

'No,' said Culhwch. 'We will not leave him, whether he proves helpful or not. And if I must kill the giant to marry my Olwen, that is precisely what I will do. Just as soon as you unlock the gate to whatever lies beyond these walls.

'My boys, they are all gone now,' the woman sobbed from the shadows. She was sitting on a three-legged milking stool, shelling peas. They plopped into the boiling pot.

'They are gone because you couldn't keep your hands off 'em,' Custennin growled back at her.

'Do you have any clothes for him?' said Darcy. 'I mean, anything other than what he's wearing? Does he have any shoes at least, or a coat?'

'What does he need that he doesn't already have?' said Custennin. 'It's time you were all gone; you have troubled us long enough.' Custennin gathered up a large set of keys from the table and walked outside.

The sun was gone, replaced by the moon whose watery light was no substitute. Custennin unlocked the other gate. Once on the other side, the gate slammed shut and the key turned. There was no going back; the only way forward was to go on.

CHAPTER THIRTEEN

THE FOREST OF LYONESSE

What lay on the other side of the wall surprised them all. A line of shingle as far as the eye could see ran in either direction. Lapping against it, the sea, as flat as a black mirror stretching out in the moonlight.

'It's the ocean,' said Darcy. 'I had no idea it was this close. That's it; what do we do now?'

'There is no boat,' said Arthur. 'How do you suppose we cross it?'

'How do you think?' said Mawgan. He sat down on the shingle, resting his chin on his knees, and stared out at the water.

The moon was above them now. A perfect silver disc reflected in the black water. As they looked on, a black hole grew in the centre of the reflection. A point rose out of the water, shattering the image into thousands of glistening fragments. Many more points rose slowly with it.

'What is that?' said Simon. The points continued to rise, spreading large arms out as they went.

'They're trees,' said Darcy. Climbing now above their heads, the water all but disappearing; in its place was a boggy stretch of forested land.

'This is the sunken forest of Lyonesse,' said Mawgan. 'You asked how we will cross the ocean, Arthur, well here you have it, we will walk.'

'Walk, yes, but where to?' said Culhwch.

'Siluræ Insulæ,' said Arthur. 'I have heard of a place that lies in the sea. Islands that are reached through an ancient, buried forest.'

'Yes,' said Simon. 'I've heard this legend too. It's a children's bedtime story about the Scilly Islands. Siluræ Insulæ is the Roman name; the Greeks called them Hesperides and Cassiterides.'

'You are clever, my friend,' said Arthur. 'Did those stories ever tell you what the Islands are famous for?'

Simon and Arthur looked at each other.

'Giants,' they said together.

*

Considering the ground had been the seafloor just a few hours before, it was surprisingly easy to walk on. They made good progress, but it wasn't fast enough for Mawgan; he fussed at the rear of the party, chivvying them along, jumping up and down, poking culprits in the back and by physical coercion when they slowed too much for his liking.

'We must hurry,' he warned them. 'Come morning; the sea will return. I do not plan to be in this forest when it does.'

So, they walked. Darcy considered herself a professional at this now. Mawgan walked beside her; he was staring at Simon's back as he in turn walked beside Arthur.

'They seem to be getting along,' said Darcy.

'Hmm,' said Mawgan.

'What's wrong?' said Darcy.

'Nothing is wrong, my dear,' said Mawgan. 'Exactly the opposite, actually.'

'What do you mean?' said Darcy.

'No matter,' said Mawgan. 'Things are as they should be.'

Darcy's eyebrows drew closer together.

'You always talk in riddles, Mawgan. It'd be nice occasionally if you'd give a straightforward answer to a question.'

'Answers are not always straightforward, my dear. They can be complicated, and it is often better to say nothing at all when they are such. At least, until one is sure. Come along; we must hurry.'

The forest was thick now, making it impossible to see the sky through the many jagged branches above their heads.

'Is it me, or is the ground soggy?' said Culhwch. His feet squelched as he lifted one, then the other.

'The tide is coming,' said Mawgan. Sure enough, with the next breath of wind, a rush of water ran across their path.

'We'll be cut off,' said Glewas. 'Mawgan, is there nothing we can do?'

'Powerful, I may be,' said Mawgan, 'but not even I can hold back the tide. There is only one course of action I would suggest: run.'

The water lapped their ankles now. As they ran, it showered them in droplets until they were wet through. Darcy's lungs burned with every breath. She felt dizzy; spots dancing around in front of her, tiny specks in her eyes.

Arthur stopped.

'Look,' he said and pointed through the trees.

Darcy squinted. It wasn't spots in her eyes. It was lights along a shoreline. They twinkled prettily in the distance, a string of jewels in the night. The water was at their knees now. They ran on as best they could but they were slowing. After a few minutes, the water was at Darcy's waist, then her elbows. She was no longer running but wading; it was difficult to stay upright. The water pushed her sideways. Simon was suddenly at her side.

'Swim,' he said. 'Or we'll never make it.' They swam together and caught up to the others.

Darcy had swum regularly as a child. She remembered the lessons and her parents' insistence that she persevere until she mastered the fifty meters, then the hundred. They were so proud of the little embroidered badges sewn onto her costume when she achieved another proficiency level. Now Darcy's confident strokes powered her forward until she was ahead of the group.

Her hand brushed the sand as she took a stoke. Stopping, she pushed her feet down; they found the sandy bottom. As she stood, the water was at waist level. She walked forward and was standing on the shore in the first sprinklings of morning sunlight. The others were quickly with her. Darcy looked behind into the blackness. The forest was all but gone under the waves once more. She lay on the sand and let the exhaustion take her, closing her eyes to blot out the sun. Tiny red veins crisscrossed her eyelids, like red spaghetti lying across a translucent bowl. A breeze gently wafted across her body, warm, but she shivered anyway. Her mum would say it was someone walking over her grave. She wasn't superstitious; just tired. She felt the familiar slipping sensation that comes just before sleep, and then, nothing.

*

Darcy lay on the beach. Glewas was on one side, Simon on the other. The rest of the group were scattered here and there. No one stood watch this time; the soporific breeze wafted over them and they were helpless to resist it. Darcy yawned. Stretching her back on the hard sand, she ached all over.

'This feels like the worst hangover ever,' said Arthur, 'and I have had a few. I do not remember drinking anything.'

'We did not,' said Mawgan.

'Then why do I feel so bad?' said Arthur.

'It is in the air. The sea, the sweet smell of apples growing in the fields over there, it is intoxicating,' said Mawgan. 'It would floor a giant, and that is exactly what it is meant to do. If any giants were to reach this place, they would not get further, even if that was their intention.'

Culhwch sat up rubbing his eyes. 'What in the name of all that is holy are *they*?' He pointed toward the buildings that had housed the lights they'd seen in the distance the night before. Walking down the beach towards them were nine huge men. Each had a tethered mastiff. The nine dogs snarled and snapped, their rolled-up lips drooling. Their muscular bodies reminded Darcy of lions.

'Those are the Porters,' said Mawgan. 'Nine there are, and if you thought Custennin was difficult, these men will make him look all sweetness.'

'Oh great,' said Simon. 'That's all we need. Will I be expected to beat them all at cards?'

'I have a feeling,' said Mawgan, 'that this will be more a battle of brawn than of wits. Glewas, Arthur, Culhwch; it is down to you.'

Arthur drew his sword. It sang like a tuning fork as he pulled it from the sheath, glittering. The runes glowed, fracturing the light across the blade. The sword was the most automatic and natural thing to him. Holding it was like an extension of his arm, his heart. In his hand, it came to life, and he revelled in the glory of it.

CHAPTER FOURTEEN

THE NINE PORTERS

Culhwch drew back his bow. He felt the yew yield as he pulled until his index and middle fingers rested against the right side of his face.

'I have the man on the right,' he said. 'Just say the word.'

'Not yet,' said Arthur. 'Let them come.'

Glewas raised his wand. 'I am ready.'

'Keep that down,' said Arthur.

Glewas stuffed the wand back in his pocket.

'We will need it, but it would be better if it came with the element of surprise.'

The Porters continued down the beach towards them.

Simon grabbed Darcy's hand and dragged her further down the beach to a group of large boulders. Mawgan followed close behind.

'Stay here,' said Simon.

'What will you do?' said Darcy.

'Whatever I can.'

'I'm coming with you.'

'Don't be ridiculous.'

'And what help do you think you'll be exactly?'

'That's enough, both of you,' said Mawgan. 'I need you to do something.'

'What?' said Darcy.

'Well, seeing that you are both so accomplished at arguing, I need you to put on a little performance. Can you do it?'

Darcy got to her feet. 'Just watch,' she said. Darcy pushed Simon from behind. He stumbled forward, temporarily thrown off balance. 'You're bloody useless!' she yelled at him. She pushed him again. This time, he turned on her.

'What on earth is wrong with you? I did what you told me to do; why are you so upset?'

It was working. The nine men turned to look at the squabble; it was all that was needed.

Arthur swung Caliburnus high in a sweeping arc that took the first man's head, then swung back to do the same with his dog. Glewas pointed his wand, and a stream shot from the tip, frazzling another Porter until the blackened form dissolved into a pile of ashes. His dog whimpered before running back up the beach the way it had come.

Culhwch's bow twanged as an arrow left it and found its mark in the chest of a third man. This man's dog launched itself down the beach towards Culhwch. The dog covered the ground quickly. Culhwch fumbled at his back, pulling another arrow from his quiver and pulling back on the bow once more. The dog was only a few meters away when Culhwch fired the arrow. It sliced through the dog's neck, making the head jerk backward, spraying blood in all directions before it collapsed. Culhwch wiped his face just to see Mawgan and Arthur dispatch another two men. He quickly reloaded his bow and took out their dogs.

Glewas' wand once again shot a stream of light, but it missed its intended target. The man ran at him, pulling a knife from the short scabbard strapped to the top of his leg. When Glewas was an arms-length away, the man lunged. Landing on top of him, Glewas was flattened to the ground. The man stabbed, but Glewas gripped the man's wrist with both hands, struggling to keep the knife off his face. His attacker was large and strong. His body was squashing the breath out of Glewas, and he crept towards unconsciousness with every second.

Darcy was yelling but the words were meaningless. She ran towards Glewas lying under the Porter. She jumped on the man's back. Wrapping her arms around his neck, she squeezed as hard as she could. The man wriggled, trying to free himself. Darcy held on for dear life, digging her knees into his sides and tightening her grip around his neck. It could only have been a minute at most before the man fell sideways and slumped unconscious into the sand.

Darcy hovered over Glewas, he was barely breathing, but he was alive. She slapped the side of his face and Glewas took a deep breath. 'Oh, thank god,' said Darcy.

Glewas coughed and spluttered through a few deep breaths. He began to resemble his more usual colour as the blueness left his lips. Darcy touched Glewas's face. She leaned in and kissed him. They had kissed before, but it felt different this time. This time she had kissed him.

'I thought you were dead,' she whispered.

Glewas coughed. 'Not likely.' His dark eyes looking up into hers, unblinking. 'I will always be with you.'

'How?' said Darcy. 'I wish I felt sure. Everything feels strange to me; nothing is certain.'

'None of that matters,' said Glewas. 'You must trust this, trust me.' Darcy thought of Morwenna. Love hadn't helped her or Cadan. He was gone, and now she would face her future alone.

'Do not worry,' said Glewas. But his words had little effect.

'Come on,' said Simon. 'It's over.' Darcy looked behind her. The remains of eight Porters lay where they had fallen; the ninth still unconscious beside Glewas.

Mawgan appeared. 'Come, we must get moving. There will be others coming.'

Darcy pulled Glewas to his feet. 'Alright?' she asked.

Glewas nodded.

Darcy stepped over the man lying on the ground. As she walked away, a hand grabbed her ankle knocking her over. She landed heavily, her left wrist buckled and cracked sideways. She cried out. The man grabbed her injured arm, pulling her towards himself. Darcy screamed.

Glewas pressed his wand to the man's temple. 'Let go of her.'

The man smiled through bloody teeth.

'Make me,' he said.

'Very well,' said Glewas. He closed his eyes and breathed in long and slow; it was like a meditation. Spell work required immense concentration and strength of will. He breathed out; his eyes still closed. The tip of his wand made contact with the man's ear.

'*Ā-cwacian berstan*,' Glewas said. The Porter's head shook from side to side. At first, it was a tiny movement hardly noticeable until he cried out and grabbed his head in pain. The shaking grew. The man's hands dropped away, and his eyes rolled backward. His lower jaw hung loose, tongue lolling. The shaking increased again; now, his whole body jerked with the movement. It was a vile thing to watch. Darcy turned away. The Porter made the most bizarre chirping noise as the jowls waggled back and forth. There was a point when the vibrations reached their peak. It was a second of silence, a pause, just long enough for Darcy to turn and look before the man's head exploded in front of them.

*

Darcy could not remember if she had ever fainted before. As a child she had been sick with fever, broken from a fall down a cliff, so ill with the flu that her mum had once driven her to hospital in a panic. But never before had she fainted, until now.

Simon knelt beside her. 'Come on, Darcy, wake up.' She opened her eyes. 'There you go. Sit up slowly, that's it. Just take it easy.'

Darcy rubbed her head. There was a loud buzzing in her ears, and everything was spinning. The sensation slowed as the seconds passed, and the buzzing faded until she could stand again.

Glewas reached out to take her hand. 'Better?' he asked.

'Is that all you can say?' said Darcy. 'You butcher a man right in front of me, and now you want to know if I feel okay. No! No, I don't.'

Mawgan was already making his way up the beach again.

'Come on, Simon.' Darcy grabbed Simon's hand and followed after Mawgan. When they were a little further away, Simon spoke.

'I don't know why you're so angry with him. Glewas saved your life.' Darcy said nothing. 'What did you think? That the guy would just give up, surrender, and let you go?'

Her face hardened. 'I guess I just didn't think of him as a killer. I'm not sure I'm comfortable with that.'

'You're placing your values on a time that isn't ready for them. That guy would have killed you in a second. You know that, right? You've seen how these people behave; it's medieval. Glewas is the same. It's not his fault. But you... you can't protect yourself here, yet you seem to resent everyone's attempts to keep you alive.'

'I don't need mollycoddling all the damn time.'

'Then stop being so precious about it all.' As much as Darcy hated to admit it, Simon was right. She had been acting like a spoilt child. The truth was when she decided to come back into Dumnonia, she had imagined it would be an idyllic reunion. She hadn't thought about the risks, only concentrating on the enjoyment. The truth was something else. Dumnonia had changed; it was not the place she had left three years before. The fact was, she was disappointed. This journey so far had not been the one she had hoped for, and now she was being stroppy. Simon knew it; the others did too.

'I've been an idiot,' said Darcy.

'I suppose that makes a change; I'm usually the idiot,' said Simon.

'Nah, you're *always* the idiot.' Darcy laughed at Simon's expression. *He has kind eyes.*

Many times, she had considered if their friendship could be something more. When he had kissed her at Glastonbury, she had been in shock at first, but once that subsided, she'd imagined it comparable to kissing your brother, if she'd had ever had a brother. Simon was family, she loved him, but her feelings toward him were not romantic.

Darcy sat by a wall in the morning sunshine holding her wrist. It throbbed horribly and looked purple. Simon had seen this type of injury before. It was common among diggers. Your automatic reaction is to stick your arm out to try and save yourself from the worst of the impact. The trouble is wrists are weak points and easily broken.

'I'll have to try and set it,' he told her. 'It's going to hurt.' He looked at Mawgan. 'I need to strap it somehow and stop it moving. Any suggestions?'

Mawgan reached into the copious pockets of his cloak, pulling out a strip of cloth and something resembling the stick from an ice lolly. 'Will these do?' he said.

'They're perfect actually,' said Simon. 'Okay Darcy, you ready?' Darcy held out her arm. It was agony just lifting it. She turned away, screwing up her face. Simon took her hand gently, Darcy flinched. He was about to pull on it, but Mawgan stopped him. Holding his wand over the broken joint, Mawgan closed his eyes and drew in a long breath.

'*Rihtan Swipian,*' he whispered over the hand.

Darcy felt his breath on her limp hand. Cool and soothing, she was soon pain-free. She screwed up her eyes again, expecting any second to feel the pain return, but it never came. Opening her eyes, Darcy looked down at her hand in time to see Simon wrap the last of the cloth around it and the sticks and tie them in place.

'I don't know what you did Mawgan,' he said. 'But that was bloody amazing.' Darcy looked at Mawgan, then at Simon. 'Thank you.'

CHAPTER FIFTEEN

THE HALL OF GIANTS

The group of seven crept up the beach following the line of the wall, keeping themselves low, crouch-walking, single file, their backs pressed in hard to the stone. Darcy banged the elbow of her injured arm; it jarred painfully. She winced, grabbing her wrist and immediately regretting it as this only caused more sharp pulses to shoot along her fingers. The wrappings of the bandage were tightening, and where her hand peeped out, she could see purple bruising. It didn't look right, but there was no time to fix it now.

The wall ended just before the beach disappeared into the sea. In the gap, stone steps lead up to what Darcy imagined was where the Porters had been housed. She slumped down on the gravelly sand, her head resting against the wall; she was in agony.

Simon had been peering over the wall; he squatted down beside her, putting his hand on her head.

'You okay?' he asked. Darcy curled herself around her arm. 'Let me see,' said Simon.

'It's fine,' said Darcy.

Holding the arm away from him. Simon didn't take no for an answer and lifted the arm to see better. 'These bandages are far too tight. They're cutting off your circulation.' Simon undid the tie at Darcy's wrist. She immediately felt relief as the blood rushed back into her arm and fingers. He tied a much looser knot. 'There. Better?'

Darcy smiled. 'Much. Thank you.'

'What is the matter?' Mawgan was now peering down at them. 'Shall we carry on?' he asked. 'If you are finished, that is?'

'Yes, we're done,' said Simon.

'Good. Come on then.' They moved along the wall to join up with the others. Watching for any signs of movement from among the buildings above.

'It's not right,' said Simon. 'Nowhere should be this quiet at this time in the morning. The place is a ghost town.'

Arthur nodded. 'Yes. This is a fishing village. So why are the boats all pulled up over there? I would expect them to be at sea on a morning like this.' At the top of the steps, a cobbled path meandered its way up through the main square and towards the top of town. At the very edge of their view stood a massive building.

Simon stood in the main square contemplating it. 'It's how I imagined a Saxon or Viking hall,' he said.

'Yeah,' said Darcy. 'If Vikings and Saxons were twenty feet tall. It looms in a kind of depressing way. It's sad.'

'Sad?' Simon's face screwed up, and the lines on his forehead made little tributaries across his skin. 'How can a building be sad?'

'It just is,' said Darcy. 'I feel it.'

Gorau stood next to Darcy. He slipped his skinny little hand into hers. 'I hate this place,' he said. 'My father brought me here once. It gave me nightmares.'

Darcy knelt and looked directly into the boy's face. 'Whatever is waiting up there for us. I won't let anyone hurt you. I promise.' She squeezed his hand and stood. They made their way up towards the hall.

It took longer to walk the distance between the shore and the hall than expected. The street was steep and cobbled. They stumbled on the uneven surface, a little too much. Simon looked back down the hill only to be disappointed.

'Not this again,' he said.

'What is the matter?' asked Arthur.

'It's the same magic as the Caer. The harder we try to climb this hill, the further away from that hall we get.'

'Hmm,' said Mawgan. 'Never the less, we succeeded at the Caer; we will do so now again. It is purely a matter of will. We must think ourselves to the top.'

As Simon looked back down the street again, he was sure he caught movement in the buildings below. 'We're not alone,' he said.

'No,' said Culhwch. 'They are watching us.'

'Why are they hiding?'

'I do not believe they would be scared of you or me,' said Arthur. 'It is far more likely that they are concerned with what might come down on them from that hall and beyond. And by the look on the face of this young boy.'

He patted Gorau on the head.

'I would say their fear is not without cause.'

They continued up the hill. It took another two hours before they finally reached the entrance to the hall.

'Nothing this time is easy,' said Darcy. She stood, hands on knees breathing through the effort of the climb. Mawgan looked at her; his head cocked to one side.

'Why did you come back Darcy?'

She thought for a moment. 'I don't think I knew until now,' she said. 'It has something to do with Simon rather than me. I think I'm here for him.' Darcy looked straight into Mawgan's eyes. 'And something else,' she said. 'It has something to do with Morwenna too. I don't know how I know that; it's a feeling. It's strong, and it won't go away.'

Mawgan straightened his head and nodded. 'Your power is coming to you.'

'My power?' said Darcy.

'You have abilities outside of what most would consider usual. I have always known this. It is why you were chosen. It is why you are here now.' With that, Mawgan turned and walked into the great hall.

*

The wall and roof of the hall were constructed from whole tree trunks. They soared up and over their heads; giant redwoods brought here from another place. The floor was polished and slippery underfoot, their boots clip-clopped, echoing back at them and cutting into the silence. Mawgan cringed with every footfall.

'Stop it, Mawgan,' said Arthur. 'They knew we were here on the beach this morning. If they wanted to stop us, they would have done so already.'

'You forget, they already tried. This quiet makes me nervous. What will they try next?'

Darcy walked between Simon and Gorau. The boy still held her hand, his grip tightening as they went further in. At the far end of the hall was a platform. On it stood an enormous wooden chair; it was high-backed like a throne. Seated on the chair was Ysbaddaden Bencawr.

They approached him cautiously. The giant snorted.

'He's asleep,' Darcy whispered to Simon beside her.

'Don't be fooled,' said Culhwch. As he spoke, a huge eyelid flickered open slightly, then slumped closed again. The giant straightened his back and bellowed.

'Bring me my forks.' There was a flurry of movement to the side of the massive chair, and a burly servant appeared with two forks, which, given their size, would have been more suitable for gardening. She handed them to Ysbaddaden. The giant propped open his eyelids, one at a time with a fork. Darcy stifled a snigger. It was ridiculous; nonetheless, she didn't want to chance Ysbaddaden's displeasure.

'Careful now,' whispered Mawgan, his hand on Darcy's shoulder.

Arthur moved closer to the throne and cleared his throat. Ysbaddaden leaned forward to see him better.

'Who are you Englishman? I smell your stench from here.' Yasbaddaden's bulbous nose wrinkled.

'I am Arthur Pendragon. Whom do I address?'

'I am Ysbaddaden Bencawr, Chief of Giants. What business does a Pendragon have with me?'

Arthur paused for a second and looked around at Culhwch. 'I accompany my cousin Culhwch; he seeks your daughter's hand in marriage.'

Ysbaddaden screwed up his nose again and sniffed.

'That is Welsh blood I smell now. A better prospect. He will cook up nicely.' The giant licked his enormous bottom lip. 'Fa fe fi fo fum,' said Ysbaddaden.

'Not on your life mate,' said Simon.

'What?' Darcy turned to Simon. 'What did he say?'

'It's old English. It means, "Behold food, good to eat, sufficient for my hunger!" He thinks we're his next meal.'

'We're not here for dinner,' said Mawgan. 'We have come for Olwen and nothing more.'

'Where are my lazy servants?' yelled Ysbaddaden. 'Lift the forks. Let me get a better look at this son-in-law.' The burly woman was back, fussing. Ysbaddaden moved further forward on the chair as the woman raised the forks even higher until the giant's eyelids pushed up past his eyebrows. He concentrated on Culhwch. 'Humph. Come back tomorrow,' said Ysbaddaden. 'I will give you an answer then.'

Mawgan shrugged and turned to the others. 'We will do as he says. Come, let us return to the town. We will come back in the morning.'

As they turned to leave, there was a kerfuffle behind them. Arthur swung back around in time to see Ysbaddaden snatch up a spear. He poured a drop of liquid over the point and hurled it at them. Culhwch, lightning-fast, caught the spear mid-air. He turned it back and threw it with all his strength behind it. The spear hit the giant in the knee.

'Cursed son-in-law,' shouted Ysbaddaden. 'It will be so much worse now when I try to walk up a hill. Cursed are the smith and the anvil; it stings like a Gadfly bite, so painful. Everything is worse now.' He lifted his head to hurl more abuse at them, but they were gone.

*

On the beach where they'd spent the night, the day dawned cold and drizzly. Darcy ran her fingers through her hair.

'You look like you've lost a fight with a crimping iron,' said Simon.

'I don't have a brush and this,' Darcy held up an almost toothless tortoiseshell comb, 'well, it's seen better days.'

She dragged the hair on top of her head backward and pinned it at the crown with the almost useless comb. Gorau was curled up asleep next to her. He had been there all night. She ran a hand over his head.

'He likes you,' said Simon

'He's scared. To be honest, so am I.' Darcy cradled her broken arm.

'Is that still bothering you?' Simon asked.

'It's not so bad. What will happen to him?' Darcy continued to stroke Gorau's head.

Simon shrugged. 'If we can fix this thing, he can go home.'

'And if not?'

'We'll figure it out.'

Mawgan appeared. 'Come on,' he said, 'we are going back up.'

They walked into the hall as they had done the day before.

Ysbaddaden was asleep in his chair again. His enormous belly wobbled with every intake of breath, and as he exhaled, his rumbling snore shook the walls around them. The moustache that grew low, covering his mouth, fluttered with each breath.

Their footsteps echoed on the floor as they approached him. Ysbaddaden Bencawr stirred and shifted in the chair.

'Fa fe fi fo fum,' he said. 'You do smell good this morning.'

'We have returned for your daughter, Olwen,' said Culhwch. 'Bring her here.'

Ysbaddaden sat up in the chair. 'Where are my lazy servants?!' he bellowed. 'Good-fer-nothing, no-hopers.'

There was a scurrying from behind the chair. Out popped the burly woman, forks in hand. She shoved the prongs under Ysbaddaden's eyelids and pushed upwards until his pupils were once again visible. 'I have a big family,' said Ysbaddaden. 'Olwen has four great grandmothers, and each has a husband; all are still alive.'

Mawgan frowned. 'What has that to do with anything?' he asked.

'The elders must be consulted,' said Ysbaddaden. 'That is only proper. Come back tomorrow. I will give you their decision then.'

'Oh, for goodness' sake,' said Simon. 'This is ridiculous.'

'But necessary,' said Mawgan, scratching his head.

They went to leave, a repeat of the previous meeting. They were almost out of the door when a whistling came from behind. Arthur spun around just in time to catch the spear before it hit Gorau in the back. Darcy, who was on Gorau's other side, grabbed him into her arms to shield him. Arthur turned the spear and hurled it back at the giant. It hit Ysbaddaden in the chest.

'Cursed friend of this savage son-in-law! That stings like the bite of a big-headed leach. Cursed is the forge in which it was smelted! There will be a tightness in my chest, stomach ache, and frequent sickness when I go uphill now. Curses upon you all.'

They left.

CHAPTER SIXTEEN

THE ELDERS

Ysbaddaden harrumphed and cursed his way back and forth across the hall, limping and rubbing his chest. For hours he went on in this way. Evening fell. His servants brought food and drink to appease his mood, but Ysbaddaden would have none of it.

At midnight he yelled, 'Bring me my boots, sword and shield! I must go to the elders and seek their council.' Servants rushed here and there. Before long, there appeared a pair of boots. The servant flung them in Ysbaddaden's direction before hurrying off. The giant sat in his chair, pulling the boots over his feet and cursing the servant's day of birth. As he tied the last lace, he yelled again.

'Where is my sword?' After much kerfuffle, the servant reappeared, flinging the sword at Ysbaddaden, narrowly missing his head. The giant deftly caught the hilt in his left hand and sheathed the sword at his belt. 'My shield. Bring it to me. Useless waste of good air.' The servant approached the giant, bent double under the shield's weight on his back. He awkwardly crossed the hall to the chair where Ysbaddaden sat, red-faced, anger burning in his barely open eyes.

'Hurry.'

The servant tried to go faster but crumpled to the floor, crushed under the weight of his burden. Ysbaddaden rose off the great seat and walked the few paces to where the servant lay. Picking up the shield, he swung it up onto his back with no great effort. Relieved of the weight, the servant got up, only to be knocked down again by Ysbaddaden's boot in the middle of his back. 'Useless waste of air.' The giant kicked him before limping out of the hall into the night.

The air was fresh even for late summer. Ysbaddaden's laboured breathing threw clouds of vapour into the night that wafted away so slowly they appeared as solid shapes for minutes afterward. He lumbered further up the hill from the hall and the town below. He had been right. The spear to his knee and then his chest had left troublesome spasms of pain that slowed him down. His anger grew as he remembered the authors of his trouble and why he was now forced to stomp his way up the cursed hill to see the crones and wait on their advice.

He lengthened his stride, attempting to cover more ground with less effort, but it was no use. The long stepping motion stretched the muscle from his kneecap to his thigh. He blinked the wetness from his eyes, shaking his head, clenched fists banging against his sides.

In the distance, he saw winking lights and knew he was almost there. The glow filling the window spaces was a welcome sight. Ysbaddaden, tired now, trundled the last few paces up to the door and banged out the coded rhythm that would have him admitted as soon as it was heard.

The door crept open, and Ysbaddaden pushed inside.

Four crones sat around the fire grate, warming their feet in the ashes. Their heads rested back as they snoozed. The air was stifling and thick with smoke and the smell of sweaty feet. Ysbaddaden's bulbous nose wrinkled; he covered it with his hand. But it had no effect.

'Ahem.' Ysbaddaden broke the sleepy silence. The crones creaked into action, moving in the chairs to better look at their rude awakener. 'Mothers,' he said. 'I need your wise advice.'

His mother smiled a toothless encouragement; she was ancient now. At least four hundred years old. He had lived for three hundred of those years himself. His wife's mother sat to her left. She was only seventy years old. A mere child in his eyes. His wife was not from giant stock, and her parents were as human and fragile as she had been, dying giving birth to his beautiful Olwen.

How could he possibly give her up after that?

The other two women were his maternal and paternal grandmothers. Their age was as unfathomable as the deepest ocean. He would guess, but his understanding of numbers didn't reach that far.

'Someone has come for Olwen?' said his mother.

'How did you know?'

'The look on your face, my son. It is the same look you always have when you bring us this news.'

'It is different this time.'

The four crones looked at each other. His wife's mother leaned forward in her seat. 'This one is a possibility then? That is not all bad news.' She smiled at him.

'He is the Pendragon's cousin and my brother's, wife's, sister's son.'

'Custennin?' said his mother. Her face softened. 'Has he come home?'

'Mother, you know Custennin would never come here.'

'Why ever not?'

'Because I would kill him first.' Ysbaddaden's fist thumped down on a table. A shower of splinters flew around the room like tiny darts, embedding themselves in whatever they found.

'Stop this!' his wife's mother shouted.

'You have murdered almost every member of your family in one way or another.' Her face was bloodless. He could see her thoughts, and he was ashamed. 'Our darling Olwen has a chance to be happy.

To live a life outside of this prison you have built around us all, and you would deny her even that.'

'You know what will happen to me if I allow her to go,' he said.

'Maybe it is time.' His mother lifted her hand to his face. He was a monster, but he was also her son.

'Whatever you decide,' said his father's mother. 'You must not allow her to go easily. The son-in-law must prove his worth.'

'How?' He looked at each woman in turn. They responded in unison.

'Set him the tasks and let us see what will be.'

*

Ysbadadden trundled out into the early morning air. His tiredness was overwhelming. If he allowed his mind to wander just a little, he would sleep where he fell. He focussed his attention on the hall further down the hill and his feet, moved by sheer will, carried Ysbaddaden towards it.

The hall was silent. Everyone still sleeping, curled up in corners or strewn across random furniture. No one heard him return. Ysbaddaden slumped down on his great chair and instantly fell asleep himself.

CHAPTER SEVENTEEN

A GIANT'S EYES

It was the third time they had climbed the hill, and it was getting tiresome.

'Keep your minds on the destination,' said Mawgan. 'If we wander, we will not reach it.'

They struggled the last few steps to the enormous doorway and stepped on through.

Loud snores escaped from every corner. The halls occupants were all still asleep.

'It must have been a big night,' said Simon.

'I have a feeling this is how things always are in this place,' said Arthur. 'There is nothing to do here. It is as if there is no point to existence, nothing to live for.'

'That is exactly the point,' said Mawgan. 'Exactly.'

They crept over to the great chair. Its occupant snorted loudly, his moustache fluttering as he breathed. His enormous belly rising then falling back still showed the bloodstain where the spear had plunged through his shirt the day before.

'He looks pretty harmless today,' said Darcy. 'Sad even.'

'You are extraordinary Darcy Bennet,' said Culhwch. 'You see things differently.'

'I just think maybe there is more to why he doesn't want to

let his daughter go.'

'That maybe so, but do not be fooled. The monster asleep in that chair thinks nothing of destroying an entire village to have his way. He is no gentle giant.' Culhwch slipped the bow off his shoulder and nocked an arrow in readiness. Darcy saw Glewas take the wand from his pocket and hide it up his sleeve. She looked across at Arthur; he had his hand on Caliburnus' hilt. Mawgan and Simon moved in closer until they stood in front of Ysbaddaden. As Darcy joined Simon, he slipped his hand over hers.

'Be ready to run,' he whispered in her ear.

Ysbaddaden stirred. Snorting, he spat on the floor. 'Bring me food and wine.' He scratched at his belly with one hand and rubbed his eyes with the other.

'You may wish to delay that order,' said Mawgan.

Ysbaddaden jumped onto his feet, then fell back into the chair. 'Bring me my forks,' he yelled. 'I cannot see a bloody thing.' The servants scuttled from their corners. A very puny man with not one ounce of fat on his body scurried from a dark recess, forks in hand. He unceremoniously shoved them up under Ysbaddaden's eyelids. The giant grabbed the fork handles and leaned forward in his chair to look at his visitors.

'Huh! You again. I thought you had left.'

'We did,' said Arthur. 'With the promise to return and hear what the elders had to say about your predicament.'

'Perhaps they had nothing to tell me.' The giant let go of one of the forks to scratch at his head. It clanged onto the floor. 'Servants!' The puny servant rushed back from the shadows. He picked up the dropped fork and shoved it under Ysbaddaden's eyelid. The giant took the handle and leaned forward again. 'Fa fe fi fo fum. You all smell so good this morning, and I am ravenous. I will tell the servants that I only need wine; there is enough food arrived here for everyone.'

'If this is an attempt to scare us,' said Mawgan. 'It will not succeed.'

'I did meet with the elders last night,' said Ysbaddaden. 'It was a long, arduous journey, and I am tired. Come back tomorrow, and I will tell you their advice.'

'No. You will not do this again,' said Culhwch. 'We were promised an answer, enough of this. Tell me how I can win your daughter's hand.'

'There is no winning.' Ysbaddaden's voice was a growl. His enormous body lunged at Culhwch; he missed.

'You are old giant, and slow. Too slow.'

Ysbaddaden's face burned; he grabbed a spear and hurled it at Culhwch. The giant's aim was wide, and Culhwch caught the spear in one easy movement. He turned it back on Ysbaddaden in an instant. The spear pierced the giant through his left eye. 'Aaaaah!' Ysbaddaden screamed and pulled the spear out, throwing it across the floor. The puny servant ran and picked it up, carrying it off into the shadows.

'Cursed, savage son-in-law! As long as I live, for however long that may be, the sight of my left eye is now completely gone. When I go into the wind, it will water. I will get a headache, and I will be giddy every new moon because of it. I curse the forge in which the spear was smelted! It bites like a mad dog!'

'You should have thought about that giant before you tried to kill me again,' said Culhwch. 'Enough of this. Bring Olwen here so that I can propose to her, and we can be gone from this place.'

'Not so fast Welshman,' said Ysbaddaden. 'I told you that I would seek the counsel of the elders in this matter.' Ysbaddaden held his hand over his weeping eye. The tears flowed down his face, mixing with blood.

'What did they say?' Mawgan asked.

'They were concerned that my daughter should not go easily.

There are some things the young suitor must do before Olwen can be his.' Ysbaddaden leaned forward in his seat. 'Approach me.'

Arthur put a hand on Culhwch's arm. 'I will come with you,' he said. 'This giant cannot be trusted.'

Arthur and Culhwch came up level with Ysbaddaden; he was much bigger even seated. The giant fumbled in his trouser pocket and produced a roll of parchment. He unravelled it. Pulling a very large pair of spectacles from the pocket in his shirt, he perched them on the end of his nose.

'What is this?' asked Culhwch.

'The giant looked at him over the rim of his spectacles.

'These are your tasks. Complete them all, and provide me with the bride price, and my Olwen is yours. Fail, and you and your friends here...' He scanned the group in the hall. '...are mine.' He licked his lips. Darcy shivered.

CHAPTER EIGHTEEN

THE WHITE TRACK

She moves soundlessly along the track. Bare feet touching the cool, wet grass. Tiny flowers, as white as a snowflake, opening as she passes, their little heads lifting to the sun. Yellow centres shining a reply.

The red velvet dress brushes her feet as she steps, contrasting the milky skin. Its gilt collar sparkles with tiny pearls and gemstones sewn delicately in flowing patterns along the edge. The gold glows against her neck and face. Fair hair swaying in the breeze like ripe wheat. She has eyes of the lightest grey and cheeks as dewy pink as rose petals in the morning. Tall as a young willow and slight as a falling feather. She shines wherever she goes. She is Olwen, daughter of giants.

*

Olwen stepped from the shadows.

'Wow,' said Simon. Darcy thumped him on the arm. He frowned. 'What? She's very... tall.'

Culhwch moved forward. His hand rested on the tip of his bow as it hung over his shoulder. The other hand fingered the fletching of an arrow. Each he had made himself; they were old friends.

'You are small, Welshman,' said the giant. He looked at Culhwch, throwing his spectacles and the paper aside. 'Bring him a table so at least I can see this would be son-in-law.' Two servants carried a large wooden table between them and set it down in front of Ysbaddaden. Culhwch stood on it. Now he was level with the giant's eyes, a good ten feet from the ground, Ysbaddaden squinted at Culhwch, shoving the forks under his eyes again so that his lids moved up enough for his pupils to be visible. His eyes were the same grey shade as Olwen's.

'Fa fe fi fo fum,' said Ysbaddaden. 'Are you sure you are not English? You smell like you would make a good meal. I only have a liking for English flesh. My fellow Welshman make bad eating. Not enough fat on their bones.'

Culhwch looked down at his waistline. 'My mother is Welsh; she is kinswoman to your brother Custennin's wife. I am also kinsman to the Pendragon through my father's line. My blood is mixed, as is my allegiance.'

'Hmm,' said Ysbaddaden. 'But today, you stand with the Pendragon. You have chosen your side I think.'

'He has chosen mine,' Culhwch replied.

'And me?' said Olwen. She lifted her eyes to Culhwch's. 'Whose side would you have me choose?'

'My lady,' said Culhwch. 'I hope you will find me an acceptable choice. As for me, the choice is already made. I am yours for as long as you breathe.'

'If I choose you, then I will lose my family. I cannot be my father's downfall,' said Olwen.

'Then you must be mine,' Culhwch replied. Culhwch knelt on the table in front of Olwen. He took her hand. Standing at ground level, she was a good foot taller than he; now they were equal height. 'My lady, he cannot keep you here forever. You deserve more than the life of a prisoner to his rage and loss. You cannot bring your mother back by staying.'

'I ease his sadness,' said Olwen.

'And who will ease yours?' A single tear rolled down Olwen's cheek. Culhwch gently wiped it away with the back of his finger. 'If you will allow, I would like to try.'

Olwen smiled.

'Enough of this,' Ysbaddaden growled at them. 'She will go nowhere without my blessing and my blessing you will never have. Puny human. How do you think you could achieve what has defied many a more worthy suitor? That you have even dared come here is an embarrassment to me. My daughter is of giant's blood. A regal line stretching back through many an age of humankind. What makes you worthy of her hand and my death?'

Culhwch stood again and looked Ysbadadden in his one good eye. 'Because I love her. I want nothing more from her. You can keep whatever else is in her dowry. It holds no interest for me.'

Arthur stepped up until he too was facing the giant. 'There you have it, Ysbaddaden Bencawr,' he said. 'Tell us what we must do, and it will be done. We have wasted enough time in this place.' Arthur drew Caliburnus from its hilt and pointed it at the giant's chest. 'If you do not wish to feel the sting of the steel, speak your tasks.'

'The list is long,' said Ysbaddaden.

'Then tell us so we can get started,' said Mawgan. He had joined Arthur and Culhwch on the table. Ysbaddaden looked at the three men before him, then down the hall towards Darcy, Simon, Glewas, and Gorau. He smiled.

Ysbaddaden got up from his chair and walked to a window on the far side of the hall. All eyes followed him. 'Look over to the far horizon there,' he said.

Ysbaddaden pointed through the window. In the distance, some sort of vegetation covered the ground. It had thorns so long; they were visible even from this far away. 'I want that field cleared.'

'That is easy,' said Culhwch. 'We will go and start while the day is young.'

'Not so fast, son-in-law,' said Ysbaddaden. 'I have not finished. It must be done before the sun sets on this day. The thicket must be cleared and burned to ash to feed the soil.'

'That is easy,' said Culhwch. 'We will do it.'

'Not so fast, son-in-law,' said Ysbaddaden. 'I have not finished. I want the field ploughed when the thicket is burned to the ground, and only the ash remains. It must be tilled and turned so that the ash and soil mix. It must be ploughed before the sun sets on this day.'

'That is easy,' said Culhwch. 'We will do it.'

'Not so fast, son-in-law,' said Ysbaddaden. 'I have not finished. That field is as old as time itself — the thicket, only slightly younger. The soil is as hard as rocks in the mountains and as barren so that only the thicket will grow in it. There is only one ploughman on this earth who could do it; Amaethon son of Dôn, and you will never get him.'

Darcy turned to Simon next to her, shaking her head. 'We must all be insane,' she said.

CHAPTER NINETEEN

PLOUGHING DIFFICULTIES

'Where do we start?' said Darcy.

She stood alongside Mawgan. They looked into a mass of tangled branches that formed the tight thicket. Some were the circumference of an arm, and the thorns; the shortest was longer than Caliburnus, and as sharp.

'Think, Mawgan. Think,' said Mawgan, tapping his head. He kicked at the dirt. Not a speck of dust rose. It was like a rock under his feet, just as Ysbaddaden had said.

'That is easy,' said Simon. He mimicked Culhwch's accent and slashed at a branch. His knife stuck fast in the flesh, so he pulled. It wouldn't budge.

'There is no way to cut it down,' said Arthur. 'It must be burned where it grows.'

'It is too green,' said Gorau. 'A fire will not take when there is so much water in the stem. It must be dried first.'

'We don't have time for that,' said Simon. He still hadn't retrieved his knife and continued to pull on the handle.

'No,' said Mawgan. 'But the boy has a point.'

Darcy recognised the look on Mawgan's face. 'What do you know?' she asked.

'I know how it can be done,' he said. 'Glewas, I shall need your assistance.'

Glewas and Mawgan walked the perimeter of the field, each in the opposite direction until they stared across the vast growth of thorns, one at the other. They raised their arms, stretching out fingers over the mass of the thicket. Each closing their eyes.

'*A'drygan*,' they said together.

Nothing happened.

'What?' Darcy said.

'Just wait,' said Arthur.

Simon was still pulling unsuccessfully on his knife. It moved slightly. 'At last,' he said. He pulled a bit more, and the knife slid out of the branch. As it did, the branch powdered where the knife had cut into it, and a warm wind carried the dust away. A smell tickled at the back of their throats and Gorau sneezed.

'Bless you,' said Simon.

'What is that?' said Gorau. He wrinkled his nose, frowning.

The wind was growing stronger. It was hot like a fan oven and blew in their faces, stinging their eyes. Glewas and Mawgan still stood over the thicket moving their arms in circular unison. They controlled the hot air and blew it back and forth between them; it stole every drop of moisture out of the branches. Cracks appeared in the long stems, and the thorns fell to the ground like overripe fruit. The heat was unbearable.

'I think I'm passing out,' said Simon. He bent over, pulling the hood up on his hoodie as he staggered and sunk to the ground. Gorau sat beside him with a hand on his back.

Darcy looked at Arthur and Culhwch, both were unconscious on the ground. The dizziness was sneaking up on her too, and a strange buzzing in her ears had replaced all other sounds. The world was fading away. Darcy saw Glewas lower his hands just as everything went black.

*

Darcy woke up. She felt woozy as she sat and looked around.

'Come on sleepyhead,' said Mawgan. 'There's work to be done.'

Glewas knelt beside her. 'Better?' he asked.

'How long was I out?' said Darcy.

'All fainted, but you are the last to wake. Mawgan is impatient to get on. Can you stand?'

'Yes, I think so.' Glewas helped her up. Darcy wobbled and grabbed his hands to steady herself. He smiled before going to help Mawgan.

Simon nudged Darcy in the back. 'What is wrong with you?' he said.

'What do you mean?'

'You're different around him, letting him help you and acting so coy and needy. *Let me hold your hands Glewas, let me lean on you Glewas. Oh Glewas you're my hero.* It's not like you. Have you forgotten you're an emancipated twenty-first-century woman? The suffragettes will be turning in their graves.'

'No, they won't because they haven't been born yet.'

'You're missing the point. You can't be yourself around him, and that's a bit of a problem if you ask me.'

'Don't be ridiculous.'

Darcy stomped off to help the others set the fire under the mass of dried thicket. She picked up a smouldering piece of wood. It glowed red hot at one end and crackled as she moved it. Glewas walked up to her. 'Here, let me help you with that.'

'I'm fine. I don't need help.' Darcy moved away to work beside Mawgan and Gorau.

Simon came up beside Glewas. 'Women,' he said. 'They need us one minute, then the next... we're a nuisance to them.'

'Hmm,' said Glewas. He picked up another smouldering piece of wood and went to the far side of the thicket. Simon watched him go, smiling.

The thicket did little more than smoke at first as the fire

struggled to get going. But their persistence paid dividends, and ever so slowly, an orange glow set in. At the end of the hour, the fire had engulfed the thicket, and the whole field was brightly ablaze.

'Now to seek out Amaethon of Dôn,' said Mawgan. 'We can leave this to burn while we go for him.'

'I will stay and watch the fire,' said Glewas. 'We do not want it to go out or be put out.'

He didn't wait for a response, moving off. Mawgan watched Glewas walk away; frowning, he turned to Simon who shrugged.

'Hmm,' said Mawgan.

'Where will I find this Amaethon?' said Culhwch. 'The family of Dôn is familiar to me. I remember them as tricksters and magicians. If this man is the only hope we have of getting that field ploughed, I doubt he will make it easy for us.'

'He lives in the foothills of the mountains there,' said Mawgan. 'It is a good hour's walk.'

'Then let us not waste any more time,' said Culhwch. He and Arthur walked off without a moment's further hesitation. Darcy, however, looked back towards Glewas.

'Leave him,' said Mawgan. 'If he must sulk, let him alone to enjoy it. I have to admit, I tend to agree with Simon.'

Darcy blinked in surprise. 'What do you mean?'

'I overheard your conversation. I agree; you hide yourself when you are with Glewas. You are a clever, independent girl, Darcy. If he cannot allow you your true nature, then he is not for you, nor you for him. But beware, I also do not believe that Simon's motivation for pointing this out is purely out of concern for you.'

'I know,' said Darcy. 'I hurt Simon's feelings, and now I've done the same to Glewas. It's such a mess, Mawgan.'

'Do not fret child. A mess can always be tidied. What is broken can be fixed when all is said and done. Come, let us catch the others.'

Arthur, Culhwch, Gorau, and Simon were quite ahead as Darcy

and Mawgan set off to follow. Just as before, the magic of Siluræ Insulæ tried to halt their progress. They walked, and it was a tiring trek, but the foothills were no nearer than before they started.

'Concentrate,' said Mawgan.

All talking stopped between them, and they set their minds to the destination. Sure enough, now, when they moved forward, they made progress. As they grew nearer their goal, it became clear that the home of Amaethon was set into the rock of the mountain itself. It also became clear, just from the size of the dwelling, that Amaethon was also a giant. They didn't wait long to have this confirmed. A huge man appeared in the doorway. He lent on the door jam, absentmindedly chewing on a corn stem, picking dirt from his nails.

'What do ya want?' he growled, not looking up from his nail picking.

'We need you to plough a field,' said Culhwch.

'Ha! I know that field. Nothing on this earth or in the heavens above us will encourage me to attempt such a futile task. The field is barren. There is no point in ploughing it. Nothing will ever grow from its empty dirt.'

'We have felled the thicket, and it burns as we speak,' said Arthur. 'It will feed the soil and make it wholesome once more.'

'You have felled and burned the thicket, have you? Hmm. Impressive.' Amaethon smirked. 'It is not enough. I will not come unless you have Gofannon of Dôn set the irons of the plough. My brother is the only smith I trust to do the job right.'

Culhwch clicked his tongue against the roof of his mouth. 'And if we find your brother and ask him to do this thing, will you then plough the field?'

Amaethon thought for a moment. 'If you can persuade my brother to stir his stumps and come down the mountain to help such a feeble band in this fruitless task, then yes, I will come and plough that field for you.'

Mawgan looked up at the steep path from the rear of Amaethon's home up into the mountain. It looked so narrow that it was barely there at all in places.

'We can't all go,' said Simon. 'It's too dangerous for so many. I have climbed before; I should go and maybe a couple more, but that's it. The fewer risking themselves, the better.'

'I can do it,' said Gorau. 'I want to go.'

'No, you don't,' said Darcy. 'You're too young for that. And Mawgan, before you suggest going, you're too... old.'

Steam rose out of the top of Mawgan's head at Darcy's suggestion that he was not in the peak of physical fitness.

'I will stay with the boy... and Darcy,' he eventually said. Now it was Darcy's turn to be offended. But before she could object, Mawgan continued, 'And just how much climbing have you taken part in recently?' Mawgan looked down his nose through the half-rimmed spectacles he wore more often than not these days and winked. 'So, we have our climbing party,' he said. 'Culhwch, Arthur and Simon. Our three knights. It is a true quest.'

*

Simon, Arthur, and Culhwch had only been gone an hour, but Darcy was already impatient to be moving on.

'What's taking so long?' she asked. 'I feel like I'm always waiting for something or someone these days.'

'Ha,' Mawgan shuffled himself into a more comfortable position on the dusty ground. 'You sound like an old soul Darcy, yet your life has barely begun. I would say to you; What are you waiting for? Mawgan removed his spectacles and rubbed the smudged glass on his coat before slipping them back on his nose. 'If the age I have attained has taught me anything at all, it is that life is short. However long it turns out to be, there is never enough of life to accomplish everything you feel like doing. There is always something more.'

Mawgan stood now, swaying from side to side to ease the stiffness in his joints.

'My body is failing; I feel it every day that passes. Stop waiting for life to come to you. Work out what it is you desire the most. Not the trivial or fleeting. Something hard, something that has worth. Pursue it as if your very life were dependent upon it. Because in the end, we are all just intelligent dirt, and one day, the wind will take us away.'

Mawgan shivered. He sat once more and pulled his cloak around himself, closing his eyes. Darcy looked at his craggy face, taking in every line and wrinkle. She realised how much she had missed him the last three years. He looked fragile there on the ground. She didn't usually think of him in that way. He had been so strong. Now she saw the man he was, and it worried her.

'Is he sleeping again?' said Glewas. Darcy jumped, not hearing him approach. 'He has been doing that a lot recently. I believe he is finally feeling his years.'

'Do you know how old he is?'

'He would never say, but I have heard the stories, the things he has witnessed. He is older than most. A little younger than the giants maybe, but for a human, his life is exceptionally long.'

'He said something strange to me a moment ago. I think he might be dying.'

'If he is, it is the longest death in history. He has been talking this way for years and is especially melancholic when he feels his body has let him down. What happened?'

'The boys went on without us.' Darcy's mouth pursed to one side.

'You are upset about that too.' Glewas smirked.

'I don't see why I'm left here to mind a child and an old man.'

'You do not believe that was their intention any more than I do.'

'Just because I haven't climbed before, I could learn.'

'You were not needed.'

Glewas' words were like a slap on the face.

'Then why am I here?'

'To be honest, I am not sure I know the answer to that question. I am discovering it is certainly not for me.'

'Don't sulk.'

'What am I supposed to do? I have not hidden my feelings or intentions, yet you are indifferent. Cold even.'

'Cold? Because I don't throw myself at you or do what's expected? I can't be that girl. I can't just smile and be submissive. Simon saw I was starting to act that way. He's right; I'm not myself around you.'

'Simon! Why is his opinion so important to you?'

'Because, he's my friend.'

'Friend!' Glewas laughed, but the sound was harsh. 'Oh Darcy, you are blind. He wants you for himself.'

'I'm not blind. I know how he feels, and this isn't about that. It's about you and me, and the fact that I can't be myself with you because you can't handle who I am.'

Glewas looked at the ground, trying to hide the anger in his eyes. Gorau looked up at him and saw it, quickly turning away and returning to the picture he was drawing with his finger in the dirt.

'And who is that, Darcy?' said Glewas. Perhaps if you gave me the chance to see you clearly, you might find I like you very much as you are.'

'What is all this shouting and carry on?' Mawgan scratched his head and rubbed his sleepy eyes.

'They are having a lover's tiff,' said Gorau. 'It is very funny.' The boy covered a giggle with his hand.

'We were having a conversation,' corrected Glewas. 'A much-needed discussion as to why I am not good enough for Darcy. She was enlightening me, and now I believe we are done.' Glewas stomped off in the direction of the burning field.

'Well, do not stand there, girl,' said Mawgan. 'Go after him.'

'But the last time he did this, you said I should leave him to his sulking.'

'That was before he came all this way to bare his soul to you and before you proceeded to stomp all over it. You wanted to know why you had come here again Darcy. I believe this may be your opportunity to find out.'

*

Glewas was poking a long stick at the smouldering ash that now covered the whole surface of the field. The dirt was a deep red and smoked with heat.

'Glewas,' said Darcy. He turned to look at her. His beautiful dark skin was covered in soot, making his eyes shine even brighter. He smiled at her, and their fight faded as she saw who he truly was, perhaps for the first time.

It was the most natural thing, to walk up to Glewas and slip her arms up around his neck. She kissed him, and he returned the kiss. In that moment, she knew how she felt about him. She was here for him. She had known this to be true, even before stepping back into Dumnonia, and the realisation surprised her. But as she kissed Glewas, there were no more doubts in her mind. His own feelings were clear in the way he kissed her back.

CHAPTER TWENTY

THE PLACE OF THE RED SOIL

Darcy knelt by the small stream and scooped up water in her hands. She drank then sloshed the remainder over her flushed face. The sharp coolness was refreshing. Glewas moved behind her. Picking up her discarded top, Darcy dried her face on it before slipping it over her head. She pulled her hair back and threaded it through the scrunchie, looking at her reflection in the water.

I don't look any different. She had expected she would. As if the world had shifted a fraction.

'Are you alright?' said Glewas.

'I'm not sure.'

Glewas smiled and with his hand on her cheek he kissed her. 'Your lips are cold.'

'The water's freezing.'

Someone stood on a twig behind them. It split sharply, making them jump. It was Simon. He was close enough that Darcy could see the expression in his eyes. It was the same hurt she had seen the night he had kissed her at the festival. The night she had pushed him away. Darcy knew now that Simon finally understood; she would never be his.

He walked away without saying a word. Darcy wanted to follow, to explain, but something held her where she stood. She hadn't done this to hurt him, but it was inevitable. They were on separate paths.

⫯

Amaethon and his brother stood tinkering with the plough. They had pulled it between them from Amaethon's house. Culhwch, Simon, and Arthur had successfully persuaded Gofannon to come down the mountain and help his brother set the irons, and now they stood impatiently waiting for the plough to be ready.

'You are missing something,' said Gofannon.

He cranked a hunk of metal with a spanner, tightening the bolt.

'What are you talking about?' said Simon.

'You have a plough, that was clever of you. But you are lacking in locomotion. It will not pull itself.'

Amaethon smiled at his brother's craftiness. A stem of corn still hanging from his mouth.

'There are only two oxen that can pull that plough, Nynhyaw and Pheibiaw; they are cared for by the Bannog and must be retrieved from there. If you want the field ploughed, you must get the oxen and bring them here.'

'Darcy and I will go,' said Glewas.

'It is our turn to be useful.'

Glewas looked at Simon, Culhwch, and Arthur.

'We cannot let you have all the glory. Besides, I have seen the Bannog before.'

A few fields over, just as the ground started to rise into the foothills again, there was a fenced paddock. Nynhyaw and Pheibiaw stood on the side furthest away from Darcy and Glewas as they approached. The creatures resembled bison in their size with massive, humped shoulders. As Darcy and Glewas reached the fence, the oxen strolled towards them. Their large, hoofed feet sank into the soft ground under the weight of their bodies, shoulders rolling side to side.

The oxen swung their heads over the fence and blew out their nostrils. Darcy rubbed at the soft patch just above a nose. The beast closed its eyes, enjoying it.

There was a small cottage behind the paddock. Darcy had the strangest feeling of dèjá vu. The cottage had only to change its location, and it was the exact likeness of Kea's home. Right down to the flowers in pots on the doorstep.

'Glewas?'

'I know,' said Glewas. 'I did not say anything because I thought you might be upset. No, you are not imagining things. I said I had seen the Bannog, and so I have... and so have you. The Bannog is Peter Willow.

*

Kea's father was the same as Darcy remembered. As they approached the gate to the cottage, Peter met them there.

'Come on in,' he said. 'Kettles on the fire.' He turned back through the door, Darcy and Glewas followed him. Inside, Darcy felt the clock had wound backwards. She was sure that Kea would burst in at any moment, shouting and boisterous, his happy self.

Unlike Trecath-en, with its permanently bustling kitchen and constant stream of visitors, the cottage was quiet. When they entered the living room, it was empty of any ornaments or pictures. There were four old armchairs, worn and tired from long use. Someone had lit the fire unnecessarily as the day was warm. Peter joined them in the living room. He carried a tray with tea, setting it down on the floor.

'Tea?' He looked at Darcy. There was not even a hint of recognition.

'Yes please,' said Glewas.

'That would be lovely,' said Darcy.

Peter poured the liquid from the pot into the cups. The tea had not brewed; the liquid was almost clear instead of brown. Peter handed Darcy her cup.

'Thank you,' she said.

'Where is Gwen?' asked Glewas. 'I thought she would be with you.'

'Na, not this time. She's home, on the mainland. I thought it best this year. She's not so good still. You know how it is.'

Peter took a long sip of his tea. Screwed his nose up. Looked at it, then chucked the remainder in the fire. It sizzled, the steam rising in little puffs that wafted around the room.

'Yuck, gnats piss. I can't make it like Gwen does.' His voice trailed off, and he hung his head.

Darcy placed her hand over Peter's. 'Would you like me to make you a fresh pot?'

'No. No need. I don't even like tea really.'

Darcy forced herself to drink the horrible liquid. Glewas placed his cup back on the tray untouched.

'So, ya back then?' Peter lifted his head. Darcy noticed the dark circles under his eyes. His face had always been so jolly. It was gaunt now, stretched over the bones in his cheeks. He wasn't the same.

'I didn't think you recognised me,' said Darcy fidgeting. 'I'm sorry, Mr Willow. I know it doesn't change anything, but I want you to know that.'

'Kea was a good lad,' said Peter. 'Strong, could pull up a turnip with his bare hands.' Darcy remembered the first time she met Kea in the turnip field. '... And thoughtful to his mother.'

Peter stared out of the window for a moment. 'He chose to help you. He loved a challenge, and farm life was sometimes a bit dull for him. He chose to go knowin' it would be risky business. It was an adventure, and I'm glad he had the thrill of it.' Peter got up and stood in front of the window, looking out at the oxen.

'Looks like rain's comin' at last. We need a bit o' rain. Been too dry this summer.'

'I didn't think... after what happened, that you would keep this place on,' said Glewas. 'Do you still come here every year?'

'Yeah. The beasts still need carin' for. Who else will see them in for the winter? It's me job after all, n' they need me. It's good to be needed.'

'Can we borrow them for a while?' said Glewas.

'Borrow 'em? What eva for. They're only good for ploughin' an' it's too early for that.'

'We are attempting to win the favour of a lady.'

'What? You're jokin'. Who would want a field ploughed this time o' year? Doesn't make any sense.'

'Her father was very insistent. And we must get it done before sundown today.'

'You've got a job on your 'ands. It's already afternoon.'

'Then, if it is alright with you, we will get going.'

*

Peter grabbed up the yoke lying at the side of the cottage. He carried it as if it were only the weight of a feather. Nynhyaw and Pheibiaw threw their heads around at the sight of it. Closing the space between them, they stood as Peter laid the yoke across their shoulders and secured it around their necks. Threading a rope through the centre ring, he led them out of the paddock and handed it to Glewas.

'All yours,' he said. 'Take care of em', they're very special.'

'We will,' said Darcy.

She tiptoed and kissed Peter on the cheek. He smiled at her.

'Take care of yourself,' she said. 'We'll have them back to you soon.'

'I'm holdin' you to that, girlie.'

As Darcy looked into Peter's face, he winked at her.

Forgiven.

Her heart did a little leap as she returned the wink with a smile.

Glewas led the oxen away from the paddock, back towards the field.

'So, what's the story with these two?' said Darcy. 'Why are they so special?'

'There is an old story of two brothers, Nynhyaw and Pheibiaw, who were wicked through and through. They plagued the town and its inhabitants, and even though they had great wealth and power, they chose to spend their time teasing and tricking the inhabitants for their entertainment. One day, a saint visited the town and seeing the misery of the people, decided to do something to help them. He sentenced the two brothers to a life of servitude. As they had bullied and teased the townsfolk, the brothers would serve the people for the rest of their days. And to make sure, he turned the brothers into oxen, to plough the town's fields every year and learn humility in the process.'

'So, these two creatures are the brothers in the story.'

'So legend has it. The Bannog has custody and care of the beasts. Peter's family have always been Bannog. It passes from father to son.'

'Not anymore.' Darcy stared at the ground.

'No. There will be a new Bannog appointed after Peter, and I hope that will not happen for a very long time.'

It was mid–afternoon when they finally reached the field. The dirt still smouldered a little. Amaethon touched the earth; placing his palm flat to judge the heat in the ground.

'It is cool enough.'

He hooked up the plough through the central ring of the oxen yolk. Standing to the rear of the plough, he pulled on the guide straps. Gofannon led Nynhyaw and Pheibiaw by the nose onto the red dirt and straightened their position to a perfect parallel with the side of the field.

They began. Walking slow and steady, they pulled the great weight of the plough through the soil. It cut like butter, turning the dirt over on itself, revealing the fertile dark red layers.

By teatime, they were halfway done. By supper time, two-thirds were ploughed. As the last rays of sunlight dimmed behind the horizon, Amaethon and Gofannon brought the plough to a stop on the far side of the field. Finished.

Culhwch paid the brothers their due. 'Thank you,' he said, handing them their coin.

'We have done as we promised,' said Amaethon. 'For what, I do not know. But we wish you well.'

The brothers left with the plough to return home.

'We should leave too,' said Arthur. 'We must go back to the hall and collect your prize Culhwch.'

'Before we do that, I must take the Oxen back to the Bannog,' said Glewas.

'We will do that on the way,' agreed Mawgan.

Peter was waiting at the gate to the paddock when he caught sight of the party leading his oxen home. A smile crossed his lips as he watched Glewas, Darcy, and Mawgan approach. Then his heart skipped a beat. Simon walked on the other side of Darcy. His tall build and thick curly hair, the first features that Peter noted. Was he looking at a ghost? The blood drained from his face.

Darcy rushed to his side. 'Mr Willow! Are you alright?' She held his hand. 'Do you need to sit down?' Peter shook his head. As Simon came to a stop in front of him, Darcy realised the problem. 'Oh, of course. This is my friend Simon. He's from my side. He came through with me. I'm so sorry, Mr Willow, I should have warned you.'

'Warned him?' said Simon.

'I thought it was Kea,' said Peter. His voice croaky.

'For a moment, I thought I was lookin' at a ghost, but I can see, you're no ghost.'

They all retreated to the comfort of the cottage, where Peter made tea once again. This time though, it was entirely drinkable, and after the long day, they all enjoyed being revived by the mugs of hot liquid handed to them. They toasted muffins in the fire and plastered them with butter before gratefully stuffing them, almost whole, into their mouths.

It was not quite the same, but Darcy had the feeling she was back in that cottage in Willow Wood three summers before. Peter kept looking at Simon, trying not to stare. He couldn't help himself. Simon's quick wit and keen mind could not be ignored. But for a moment, he was sat in his living room with Kea again.

CHAPTER TWENTY-ONE

HONEY WITHOUT BEES

The hall was dark. The lamps around the walls had been lit, but the tallow candles were dim and smoky, and made the room smell of bad meat.

It was closing on midnight as they stepped up to Ysbaddaden's chair. As usual, he was sleeping. When Simon reached the steps, he stomped on each tread. Ysbaddaden stirred, rubbing at his eyes.

'So, you have returned, have you? I suppose failure is a lesson you needed to learn. Never mind, you will make good eating if I cook you all up together.'

'Not so fast, giant,' said Culhwch. 'Failure is not for us today. We have ploughed your red field. The brothers of Dôn were easily persuaded with the right motivation.' Culhwch jingled the coins in his pocket. 'The task was completed by sunset, and we are returned to claim the prize.'

Ysbaddaden smiled. 'You are a clever one, son-in-law. You persuaded the brothers of Dôn to plough for you. That was most ingenious. But... you are not done. I will not let my Olwen go so easy. I need the field planted. If you would marry Olwen, she will need a veil, and only the finest flax will make a veil fit to adorn her head. If you would marry my daughter, then plant that field. When I first met my girl's mother, nine trusses of flaxseed were sown in the field. But not an ear of black or white has come out from it since, and I still have that measure. Nine trusses of flax must be grown for her daughter before sundown tomorrow.'

'Before sundown,' said Simon. 'That's ridiculous; it can't be harvested before sundown tomorrow if we are only planting that same morning.'

Before Simon could continue, Culhwch once again stepped forward. 'That is easy,' he said. 'We will do it. You will be ordering the weaving of a flaxen veil by tomorrow's evening.' Culhwch turned to Simon and shook his head. Simon held his tongue and stomped back down the steps with the others.

When they were outside once more, he couldn't hold it in any longer. 'Are you mad?' he said. 'There is no way to make flax grow in a day.'

'Not normally, no,' agreed Culhwch. 'But that is no ordinary field, and we have wizards.' He looked in Mawgan and Glewas' direction. The wizards nodded.

*

They spent the night back at the field, ready for an early start. They noticed nine large baskets of seed had mysteriously appeared.

Darcy tossed and turned in her sleep. After her visit with Peter Willow, she had been happily engulfed in a warm sense of well-being. She had seen Peter relax and enjoy Simon's company, and it had once again cemented for her that Simon was the true reason for her second journey into Dumnonia. Nevertheless, she was troubled by a thought that she was losing him. The thought would not leave her, it niggled and festered in the darkness. She didn't know how or when, but she felt sure the loss of Simon was inevitable. As she floated in and out of dreams, she knew she would never be ready for it, not even if she had a lifetime to prepare herself.

Gorau tapped her shoulder. 'Darcy, you must wake up,' he said. 'We need to start sowing, and Arthur wants to show you what to do.'

With so little sleep, Darcy struggled to get herself moving.

'Come on, sleepyhead,' said Glewas. He had been to the stream to wash. He looked fresh and clean. Glewas bent and kissed her, then wrinkled his nose. 'You need a wash,' he laughed.

Darcy's mouth felt dry and furry under her tongue. She nodded and pulled a face before heading down to the stream herself to swill her mouth and splash her body with the cold water. Simon was already there.

'You're late up,' he said.

'I didn't sleep well.'

'Want to talk about it?'

'No, it's nothing.'

Simon finished washing and shook himself dry with a dramatic body jiggle that made Darcy laugh.

'Do you think we will get this done today?' she asked.

'We'll sow the flax seed no problem. That doesn't take long, and there are seven of us doing the work. The hard bit is going to be growing and harvesting it by tonight. I don't know what sort of magic it will take, but I hope Mawgan and Glewas are up to it.'

'They are.' Darcy was confident. She had seen Mawgan work magic many times before, and Glewas was very competent now. She nodded and set her chin firmly outwards. Simon admired her confidence but didn't share it.

Back at the field, they were ready to start. Darcy and Simon were the last to arrive. Arthur instructed the latecomers in the art of seeding the ploughed earth. Darcy thought it ironic that the man who would be king one day knew the finer points of such a mundane task. But Arthur seemed to revel in the simplicity of it, his face carefree, all worries gone. Gorau walked behind Darcy, turning the clod back on itself once she had placed the seeds in the furrow. One row, then the next. And so, they went until midday.

The sun, directly above them was hot on their backs and made the work uncomfortable. Simon stood upright, leaning backward, stretching his muscles. He was surprised to see just how little they had left to do, and this gave him the burst of energy he needed. Less than an hour later, they were done as Culhwch threw the last of the seed onto the ground, and Arthur turned the clod to cover it.

'Now, my friends, it is over to you,' said Arthur. He patted Mawgan and Glewas on the shoulder. 'If we are to harvest this flax before sunset, you had better not hang around.'

Mawgan looked at Glewas. 'What do you think?' he said.

'I've been contemplating this all night,' said Glewas. 'We need a combination spell, one that incorporates speed and action.'

'Good, you are on the right track. I thought to use *'ā'spryttan' and 'snūd.'* A combination of these two spell words will encourage quick growth.'

'We will need to encircle the field for it to work evenly. Once will not be enough. Constant chanting will give a much better result.'

'Please,' said Arthur. 'We must hurry.'

Mawgan did not appreciate being harangued. He cast a look, his mouth pursed and his eyes narrow that made Arthur take a step backwards. 'Come Glewas, let us begin.'

Glewas and Mawgan jogged around the field in opposite directions, crossing over at intervals. All the while, they chanted their incantation, 'ā'spryttan snūd', over and over as they ran. The ground quivered and rumbled. Tiring, both men slowed. By the third circuit, tiny shoots peeped through the red soil.

'Keep going!' Darcy shouted from the other side of the field, 'It's working.'

Unable to stop and check their progress, Glewas and Mawgan pushed on. By the fifth circuit, the flax was a good foot tall. Seven times around, and the tiny blue heads lifted to the sun, drinking in warmth. Nine times around and flower heads showed the promise of seeding. On the thirteenth circuit, as Mawgan and Glewas reached the point of exhaustion, the flax was ready. They had done it.

Darcy ran to where Glewas lay on his back, heaving in great gulps of air. She offered him a cup of water, and he drank it in seconds. 'Careful, you'll choke drinking it like that.'

'I need more,' said Glewas. His voice was a dry croak. Darcy refilled the cup and handed it over again. He drank it all.

'Are you alright?'

Glewas' usual colour was tinged with a strange purple in his lips and under his eyes. His breathing was strained and a bit irregular.

'I will be fine. Just give me a moment.' Darcy looked across the expanse of the flax and saw that Mawgan was also on the ground. Simon and Gorau were helping him to his feet. 'He is at least three times my age, and he is already standing.' Glewas reached a hand to Darcy. 'Help me up, please. I cannot let the old man think he has the better of me.' He winked at Darcy as she pulled him up to stand on wobbly legs. 'Darcy, you need to get everyone moving and harvest this flax. Time is running away from us.'

'If I let you go, you're not going to fall over, are you?' She looked at him, concern showing in her eyes.

Glewas smiled. 'I am fine now. Go. I can make my way back.'

Darcy ran towards the main group, not wasting a second.

Once she was gone, Glewas sank to his knees. Confused at what was wrong, he felt an uneven thumping in his chest. He put his hand over it and could feel his heart banging against his palm. He had experienced the same sensation many times before. The most notable time had been when he was no more than a boy, being chased by Imps; he had run until his sides had ached so much, he had no choice but to stop. Expecting to be pounced upon at any moment, he remembered the fear that had him quivering on the ground, but no attack came. There was however, the same thumping in his chest. It had taken an age for his body to recover, and he had sat on the ground for a couple of hours just breathing until his heart had slowed again.

Come on.

Frustrated, Glewas was determined not to let the others see. He got to his feet again. It took every ounce of strength he had.

One foot, then the other.

He made his way towards the rest of the group, pushing a smile onto his face as he got nearer. After checking that Mawgan was none the worse for his efforts, Darcy had rallied the rest into picking the flax in an organised manner. She had set Arthur and Culhwch at opposite ends on the far side of the field. She and Gorau matched them on the near side, and with Simon working the middle rows, they moved up and down towards each other.

When Mawgan and Glewas had regained their strength, they worked the middle rows with Simon. And so, they went on, cutting neat lengths of flax and bundling the lengths around the middle until just as they cut and bundled the last stems, the sun set and darkness came.

*

A line of torches were approaching from the town.

'Whatever they are, they're coming this way,' said Simon.

They watched as the torches grew bigger. In their light, the shadowy outlines of people were hurrying towards them. Arthur pulled Caliburnus from its hilt, while Culhwch drew his bow.

'I don't think they mean us any harm,' said Mawgan. 'Look at them. There are children.'

Arthur and Culhwch stashed their weapons again as a large, jolly-faced woman approached. She held the hand of a young girl. The girl had the same jolly features, her daughter perhaps.

'I see you made a good go of the flax crop then.'

The woman continued smiling; her voice carried the usual burr of the West Country.

'It will make beautiful linen for Olwen's gown and veil. The very finest it will be, you wait. She will make a beautiful bride. The most beautiful ever.'

'I'm sure she will look lovely,' said Darcy. The woman's smile widened. '... All brides are beautiful on their wedding day.'

The woman's sideways look disagreed with Darcy's last sentiment.

'Well, me dearie, our Olwen will outshine them all.' Darcy nodded. 'We linen weavers of Silurœ Insulœ are the very best there is. Give us the flax, and we will be away to our weaving. Ysbaddaden Bencawr has ordered it, and so shall it be.'

'There is no need for you to take the flax back,' said Culhwch. 'We will deliver it when we come to collect my bride.'

'Not so fast Welshman, you are not finished in your tasks. There is more you must do before Olwen of the giants would be yours.'

'I don't believe it,' said Simon. He sunk to the ground hanging his head. The amusement on the woman's face at his frustration did not go unnoticed.

'Speak your task woman,' said Mawgan. 'What else must we do?'

The woman straightened herself further as she prepared to recite. 'Before the sun sets on tomorrow's eve, you must collect the sweetest honey ever tasted, made without the touch of any bee. Only this honey will be good enough to make the Braggart for the wedding feast.'

'That's easy,' said Culhwch.

'What's Braggart?' asked Darcy.

Simon, looked up at her. 'It's a drink made by fermenting honey and ale.'

'Trust you to know.' She smiled and pulled him to his feet. 'Come on,' she said. 'In for a penny, in for a pound.'

Simon laughed. 'You sound like your dad now.'

The townspeople collected the flax bundles between them and left as quickly as they had arrived. Their torches trailing away into the night.

'So, where do we find this honey? Any suggestions?'

Arthur was impatient to be going.

'None,' said Glewas. 'But I know who to ask. If we are fortunate, we may also find a comfortable spot to sleep tonight.'

'I could live with that,' said Simon. He smiled his agreement.

Maybe he is not so bad.

Glewas hoped it was true.

*

They approached the cottage. It looked different with only the moon's soft light bathing its stone walls, peaceful. Warm light flowed out of the windows onto the paddock where Nynhyaw and Pheibiaw stood swaying in their sleep.

'I hope Peter's not going to mind us all turning up again like this,' said Darcy.

'I think he will be glad of our company,' said Glewas. 'Especially Simon's.'

'Yes. He did take to him, didn't he? It's understandable. Just look at him.'

Darcy and Glewas both turned in Simon's direction.

'I cannot see it myself.'

'Oh Glewas. You're joking, surely? He's the spit of him.'

'If you say so.'

Mawgan knocked on the door. It was opened a few moments later. 'Gwen! It is good to see you.'

'Peter sent fer me. I arrived this afternoon.' She looked past him at the rabble on her doorstep. Her eyes rested on Darcy. She moved forward and grabbed her up into a hug. 'Oh, darlin' girl.' She held Darcy's face between her hands and squeezed it gently before returning to her vice-like hugging. 'Come in, come in. Don't stand there catchin' cold in this night air.'

She bustled them through the door. When it was Simon's turn to enter, she smiled. 'It's Simon, isn't it?' she said. 'Peter told me about you. I'm happy to meet you, dearie.'

Once inside and settled around the fire, Gwen made them a supper to rival any of the meals Darcy had experienced at Trecathen. They ate until they couldn't take another bite. Kea would have been proud of their efforts. They settled down to spend the night in front of the fire, resting comfortably in the well-worn sofas and chairs.

'Peter, would you know where we could put our hands to some honey made without any bees?'

Unlike Glewas, Mawgan did not hold out much hope that Peter would know of any such thing, but the question was worth asking.

'I think you mean to ask how it is made, Mawgan,' said Peter. 'Not where do you find it?'

'What do you mean?' Mawgan's forehead lined as it always did when he heard something he did not expect to.

'Gwen, I think you need to come here and explain something,' said Peter. Gwen popped her head around the door from the kitchen.

'How do you make honey when you don't have any bees?'

'You need some poor man's honey,' she said.

'Poor man's honey?' Darcy had never heard of such a thing. She looked at Simon, but he too had a blank expression.

'We make it all the time to sweeten food and drink. Honey is not always easy to get hold of. It's made with apples, lemon juice, sugar, chamomile, and water. Tomorrow we will all make it together. Ysbaddaden will have his braggart for the feast.'

She looked at Culhwch and winked. 'You knew!' said Darcy.

'Of course. Why do you think I'm here? Peter had a feelin' you'd be needin' more help. Ysbaddaden will not make this easy fer you, but it'll be in all our interests if you can win Olwen's hand. The end of Ysbaddaden Bencawr will be a fresh start fer us all.'

*

They spent a peaceful night in the cottage. Morning arrived bright and clear, the earth steaming in the early sun. Peter, Darcy, and Glewas were busy in the shed rooting in a barrel of last year's apples. Most of them were old now and on the turn. Peter sniffed the air and smiled.

'Mmm, smell that. Sweet and juicy. These will do fine.'

They picked up as many apples as possible and carried them into the cottage. In the kitchen, Gwen was selecting copper pans from the store. Gorau carried them to the stove arranging them on the hot plates. Simon, Culhwch, and Arthur entered carrying chamomile in a crockpot, a bowl of lemons, and a large bag of raw sugar.

'Where do you want all this?'

Simon looked around the kitchen, but every surface was cluttered with something or other.

'Put it on the dining table,' said Gwen. 'There's nowhere else. Well don't just stand there...'

Gwen scowled at Peter, Darcy, and Glewas as they stood in the hallway. Their arms full of ripe apples.

'... get those peeled, cored, and in these pots. There's a lot to do.'

A snore rumbled along the hallway from the sitting room.

'Has anyone seen Mawgan?' Darcy hadn't set eyes on him at all that morning.

'Shhh,' said Peter. 'He's still sleeping.'

Darcy popped her head around the door. Mawgan stirred and scratched his head. 'How are you doing?' she asked.

'My brain is a fog this morning. Where is everyone?'

'We've been up and about for hours. Sleepyhead.'

'I am nothing of the sort.' Mawgan's face creased into a frown. The twinkle in his eye remained.

'Are you sure this isn't all too much?' Darcy squeezed his hand. Mawgan rose out of the chair.

'Absolutely not. I am as fit as I ever was.'

'Good. Because there is one huge pile of apples to get ready for the pot, grab a knife and let's get to work.'

All day they worked, mixing and cooking, sieving, and potting until they had made honey mixture for more Braggart than any party animal could drink in several nights. By sundown, they were done. They walked the road again to deliver Ysbaddaden the fruits of their labours.

CHAPTER TWENTY-TWO

THE CUP OF LLWYR

They each carried two baskets of honey pots between them. As they drew closer to the hall, the lights of the village below shone out a welcome. Peter and Gwen trailed behind with an enormous basket. Gwen being much shorter than Peter, struggled to hold up her share of the weight.

Once at the hall they waited, listening to what was going on inside.

'Olwen, you cannot leave me!' Ysbaddaden bellowed across the hall at his daughter. He took the cup he had been drinking from and threw it against the wall. Shards of glass and chips of wood showered the floor. The puny servant scurried from his hiding place with a brush and pan, sweeping erratically as he went. 'Leave that, fool.'

'Father, calm yourself. You will be ill.'

Ysbaddaden's face was blotted with beetroot patches. His anger was a whole other presence in the room. 'I cannot be calm. What will become of me if you go? I am all alone.'

'That is because you choose to be alone. You push everyone away. You rid yourself of friends thinking they will take advantage. Nobody comes near for fear of your temper. Your anger terrifies the villagers, who would be your closest companions if given a chance to see what I see. There is nobody left because that is how you like it.

And soon I shall be gone too.'

'Not if I have anything to do with it. He will not win. The tasks I have set would floor the greatest of men, and this boy is no great man.'

'No Father, he is not. But he keeps company with greatness. He will be your undoing.'

Arthur swung the door wide.

'Oh, here he comes,' Ysbaddaden called. 'The great man himself, our would-be king. What else would you take from me lad? The shirt off my back?'

'Your daughter will be enough,' said Arthur. 'We come bearing the honey you asked for.'

The rest of the party entered carrying their baskets. Peter and Gwen came through the door last of all, Ysbaddaden called out again waggling a finger.

'Treacherous do-gooders. How dare you!'

Peter puffed his way across the hall with the heavy basket. Gwen was nearly underneath it now, swaying with the weight.

'You didn't say we couldn't help the lad,' said Peter, swinging the basket up onto the seating platform. It skidded across the wooden surface and banged into Ysbaddaden's great chair. The bottles inside rattled, blobs of honey sprayed the giant's face. His tongue licked up the sweet drops as he ran it around his lips.

'That has to be some of the best honey I have tasted in many a long year.' Wiping another spot of honey from his face, he turned to Gwen. 'Woman, your skill is legendary.' Gwen smiled despite herself. Ysbaddaden searched the group for Culhwch.

'So, son-in-law, you have brought me honey as I ordered.'

'Yes,' said Culhwch. 'And finished by sundown. Make your braggart, and we will have a feast to celebrate my wedding day.'

'Not so fast, Welshman. Your tasks are not yet completed.'

'You've got to be kidding me,' said Simon. 'What else could you possibly want?'

Ysbaddaden smiled. Or was it a grimace? On his face it was difficult to tell.

'There is only one cup that can hold the braggart I will have made for the feast. It is the strongest brew made from the sweetest honey. Bring me the cup of Llwyr so that I might drink to my daughter's beauty and toast her happiness. Only then will I allow her to leave.'

'Who is this Llwyr?' said Simon. 'And what's so special about his cup?'

'Llwyr is a knight,' said Arthur. 'In my father's guard.'

Ysbaddaden sat in his great chair, listening, and smiling.

'You have until sundown tomorrow to bring me the cup. Fail, and I will grind your bones for bread flour.'

'There's nothin' more to be done tonight,' said Peter as he led them all from the hall.

'Come on back to the cottage. Have somethin' hot to eat and a night of good sleep. It'll all be clearer in the mornin'.'

'I wish I shared your optimism Peter,' said Mawgan. 'Tasks rarely get lesser on the arrival of daybreak; we just look on them with fresh eyes.'

'What's wrong with that?'

Peter patted Mawgan on the back.

'Fresh eyes are sometimes all it takes.'

They returned to the cottage. Darcy was so tired, she sunk into the armchair in the living room; falling asleep almost as soon as she closed her eyes. Her dreams full of sounds and disturbing images.

She stood alone in the forest of Lyonesse, listening to the waves lapping against her feet. Cold; she was numb.

She heard a strange sound. It had physical substance; she felt it penetrate her bones and zing through her body. As she listened, more sounds came. Like learning a language, the first were meaningless to her; as she listened more intentionally, they took form, she understood. It was Morwenna, weeping. And they were the most heart-wrenching cries she had ever heard.

Darcy felt tears on her face; hot against her cold skin. She reached up to wipe them away but they evaporated. Her feet were now uncomfortable as water ran into her boots and rose over her ankles. Following the sound of the cries, she saw a dark figure resting against one of the water-logged trunks. She moved towards the figure. As she drew nearer, it turned. Instead of Morwenna's lovely face, peering out from underneath the black cloak, was the bleached bone white head of Narcasta.

The crying stopped. Darcy heard nothing more.

A laugh split the air between them. It grew louder and took over Narcasta's whole body. Darcy looked down her legs. The water was at her knees. The cloaked figure swayed with growing hysteria.

'I am coming for you girl; now all obstacles are removed, there is no one left to stop me.'

Darcy saw he was holding something wrapped in a blanket. It wiggled, and out popped a tiny, pale foot. It took her a moment to realise what Narcasta was holding. She heard a shout. Turning, Darcy looked for someone else, then realised she was shouting. Narcasta threw his head back, laughing again.

'I have all I need. Dumnonia is mine once more.'

Narcasta disappeared into the dark holding the baby to himself. The water was now around Darcy's neck. It moved up over her mouth and nose, she fought for air. The water was over her eyes, the top of her head. Everything was dark and silent.

*

Darcy woke with a start. She coughed and spluttered. Glewas stirred next to her.

'What's wrong?'

Still choking, it was a few seconds before she could speak. 'It's

Morwenna; something terrible happened. I saw it. I don't exactly know what it means, but I'm sure we're all in danger, Morwenna most of all.'

'Of course, it's terrible Darcy, Morwenna will be heartbroken at losing Cadan.'

'No!'

Glewas recoiled at the sharpness in her voice. 'What is it? Please tell me.'

She tried to calm her thumping heart and steady her voice. Darcy took a deep breath and released it slowly. 'He's back.'

'Who?'

She could feel her heart speeding again, pounding. *Breathe, just breathe.* 'Narcasta.'

Mawgan jumped up from his chair and rushed to where Glewas was standing. 'What have you seen, Darcy?' he asked, rubbing his eyes to rid them of the last remnants of sleep.

Simon stirred where he lay on the floor. He raised his head, immediately slumping back and closing his eyes once more.

'I saw him,' whispered Darcy. 'Back in that sunken forest. I heard Morwenna crying.'

'Morwenna?' Mawgan turned to Glewas. They shared a look that Darcy didn't understand. 'What else?' said Mawgan.

'When I got close, I realised it wasn't Morwenna; it was him. He laughed at me.'

'Laughed?' said Glewas.

'Yes, like he thought the whole thing was amusing. He was carrying something in a blanket. I only saw a little bit, but I know what it was.'

Again, Mawgan and Glewas looked at each other.

'Darcy.' Glewas' voice was soft. He picked up her icy hand. 'Was it a baby?'

'Yes!' Darcy snatched her hand away. 'How did you know?'

Glewas looked at Mawgan for a third time. Mawgan nodded.

'Because we have seen it too,' he said.

*

Breakfast was a big deal in the Willow household. Gwen insisted it was the most important meal of the day. She had been in the kitchen since sunup, and now the dining table groaned under the weight of its contents. The smell was heavenly.

Simon and Gorau were awake, their noses prickling. They followed the aroma to the table and tucked in. Darcy was pleased to see that Gorau looked much better, almost happy. It was remarkable what a wash, fresh clothes, and a few good meals could do.

'Do you think Gorau should stay with Peter and Gwen?' Darcy whispered as Simon stuffed a warm buttered roll into his mouth. After quite a lot of chewing, he swallowed hard.

'I think that's a great idea,' he said. 'Though I'm not sure Gorau will agree. He's very taken with you.'

'He should be looked after; he's just a little boy. He needs to be at home.'

'He's only a little younger than you were when you first came to Dumnonia.'

'Yes.' Darcy shivered. 'I remember.'

Darcy decided to speak with Gwen and Peter after breakfast. She wasn't sure if they would want to have another child around. It might be too painful. She broached the subject as she helped them clear the used dishes away in the kitchen.

'Course he can stay with us,' said Peter. 'He can help me get the oxen ready for winter. There's always so much to do before we head back to the mainland.'

Gwen stood looking out of the kitchen window, continuing to rub at a cup that had been dry minutes before. 'Gwen, love.' Peter took the cup from her hands and placed it on the dresser. 'What are you thinking?' He gently ran his hand across her forehead and tucked a wisp of hair behind her ear.

'I'd like it if he stayed,' she said. 'It'd give me someone else to think about.'

*

Gorau stamped his foot.

'You are trying to get rid of me.'

'No, I'm not,' said Darcy. 'I wouldn't do that. But I think you would be better off here with the Willows, and they could do with the help. Their son died a few years ago, you know.'

'Yes, I know.' Gorau studied his feet as if they were the most exciting thing in the world.

'What do you think?' said Darcy. He continued to stare at his feet. 'You really could help them a lot, you know. More than just with the work.'

Gorau lifted his head. 'You will come back for me?' His eyes were almost pleading. Looking at him Darcy felt the breath catch in her throat.

'Yes, we will. I promise.'

*

Llwyr lived in a fortress.

'This is Karregi Gorlewen,' Simon whispered to Darcy as they stood on the rocky shore. 'The islands are uninhabited in our time. But just look at it. Incredible.' Great stone walls rose meters into the air. Cut from the rock, the black tower dominated the view as the sea pounded its foundations without effect.

'How do we get there?' Darcy looked along the shoreline. There were no coves or bays to draw up a boat, and the sea angrily beat the land into submission, spraying white foam over its rocky surface. Around the smaller islands, the remains of shipwrecks were visible. A shiver made its way down Darcy's spine. She did not love boats on calm days; just the idea of sailing in this made her queasy.

As the rest of the group looked around for a boating solution, Arthur worked his way along the rocks in the other direction. Turning the smaller ones over and wiping the surfaces of others. Systematically he checked every one until...

'Got it!'

'Got what?' Culwhch shouted back.

Arthur cleared away sand and seaweed from a rock's surface until he uncovered a smoothed-out section. He followed the mark of a roughly scratched rune with his index finger, reading it. His free hand rested on a lever down the side of the rock. Fingers clasped around the handle, he pulled until his arm felt like it might break. At last, straining, he planted his feet against the rock's surface and pulled with every ounce of strength he could muster. The lever moved a millimetre. Then it moved a centimetre. Then it continued to move until, to his left, an opening appeared. Down it went, deep into the ground.

'What is it?' said Mawgan. 'I do not remember this being here.'

'That is because no one is supposed to know about it,' said Arthur, wiping the sweat from his eyes.

'If that is the case, how did you know?' said Culwhch.

'It is a long story,' said Arthur. 'I came here many times as a boy, but not for a long time. I was hoping it would still be here, and here it is. We must keep moving if we are to do what is to be done.'

A set of steeply carved steps led down into the ground. Walls dripping in condensation close on either side. There was so little light at the bottom of the steps that it was impossible to see the way forward.

'*Beorht*,' said Mawgan, and he held his hand up. As he did so, a phosphorus globe suspended in his palm pulsed with light, throwing shadows onto the walls and revealing a long tunnel.

'Let us go,' said Mawgan. He led them along the dark passage, the globe continuing to pulse above him. Darcy wrapped her light jacket tighter around her bare arms, and Simon blew warm air into his cupped hands. The air was frosty, their breath suspended around them for a few seconds before drifting away.

At the end of the tunnel, a heavy door blocked their way. Mawgan ran his hand over its surface; there was no handle.

'What now?' Simon said. He turned expectantly to Arthur, who was farthest from the door. Arthur pushed through and laid both his palms against the carved surface. Feeling with his fingertips, he followed the tiny grooves until he found eight indentations. Placing a fingertip in each dent, he pushed the door. A series of clicks were heard from inside as it shifted backward on the ancient hinges and slid away into the wall cavity.

Arthur smiled as he turned to answer Simon's question. 'Is that good enough for you?'

Simon slapped Arthur on the back. 'Perfect.'

CHAPTER TWENTY-THREE

THE IMPORTANCE OF TABLES

Darcy peeped through the slit window opposite the doorway, down to the sea below. White spray whipped her face with icy specks. She could smell the tang of salt and seaweed.

Mawgan tugged her arm. 'Come, Darcy, this is not the time.'

They hurried along an empty corridor. Simon scanned left to right and back again.

'Do we even know where we're going?'

'Not exactly,' said Mawgan. 'But other than head back down the tunnel we just came through, there is only one other direction.'

They crept under an archway at the end of the corridor to find themselves opposite a wall of armed knights. Their heavy chain mail clinked as they moved their visors down, covering their faces. Long poleaxes lowered so that the sharp, pointed ends were inches from the travellers' faces. Simon lifted his hands into the air.

'What are you doing?' said Darcy.

'I don't know; I can't think of anything else.'

Arthur pushed his way through the group for the second time. 'Put up your weapons; there will be no fighting.' He unsheathed Caliburnus and held it high. The light caught its finely worked blade. A thousand diamonds of reflection sparkled over the walls of the room.

'Welcome Arthur Pendragon,' said Llwyr. 'I see you have found your sword.'

Arthur smiled as the knight nearest to him lifted his visor and put up his poleaxe. He laughed, a great, full belly chuckle.

'Gawain, Tristan, take our friends through to the great hall.' Llwyr gestured towards another door on the far side of the group of knights. 'Let us be comfortable. Today is a feast day.'

Darcy would never forget the first time she set eyes on it. Her breath caught and then slowly hissed out.

The table dominated the room. Inlaid with gold and walnut, fires lit in all four walls threw a glow across its carved surface. Around its perimeter were many chairs. Darcy wanted to count them, but kept losing her place. This table had no sides, no head, or foot. It was perfectly and legendarily round.

'What is wrong with the two of you?' Arthur nudged Simon as he took a seat to his left. 'It is a table. A beautiful one, I will acknowledge that, but still only a table.'

'You don't understand,' said Darcy. 'It's…' She saw Simon shake his head out of the corner of her eye. '… lovely.' She ran her hand over the surface before taking a seat on the other side of Simon.

Llwyr was true to his word. He had his kitchens prepare a feast fit for a king. The servants laid it out on the round table and gave his guests the choicest cuts of meat, the juiciest fruits, and the most delicious bread. They were served the best of the summer wine in tall, stemmed glasses, cut so that the light fractured and danced across the table's surface.

Darcy ate until she was so full she had to lean back in her chair. It allowed her to watch the room's other occupants. The knights had removed all their armoury before coming to table. She looked for the men Llwyr had asked to show them through to their places, Gawain and Tristan. Names almost as familiar to her as her own.

On winter nights as she and her parents had snuggled up on the sofa together, the fire lit and the cosy lamps throwing an amber glow over the walls of their cottage, they had read the stories of Arthur and his honourable knights. Their daring deeds and swashbuckling adventures, which now, as Darcy sat across the table from them, seemed so contrived. These were real men. They laughed, got angry, horsed around, and even bled when punched on the nose, as Bedivere soon found out when Bors hit him for stealing a chicken leg from his plate.

The knight that sat on Darcy's left was looking at her. At last, he spoke. 'Your clothes. They are not usual attire for such occasions.'

Thinking that she had no idea what the appropriate dress might be for dinner with a rowdy gang of soldiers, Darcy smoothed her hands over the jeans and jacket that Gwen had insisted she take for the cold. 'Am I underdressed?'

'No, just unusually so. I am Lancelot. Pleased to make your acquaintance.' Darcy gulped in a breath as Lancelot held out his hand to her.

'Darcy,' she said, taking his hand and hoping that hers wasn't sweaty.

'You were taken aback by our fellowship here.' He continued to look at her with concentration. 'But I do not believe you were surprised?' His eyes searched her face. This was an interrogation.

'How do you come to be a companion of the young prince?'

Darcy looked at Arthur who was deep in conversation with Llwyr. *What could she say? She couldn't tell the truth.* She felt Simon's hand on her arm.

'We are old friends of the Wizard,' he said. 'Here for a visit and roped into a quest to find Culhwch a wife. It's been quite an experience so far.'

Nice save.

'And where are you visiting from, pray tell?'

Lancelot's eyes now looked at Simon with equal intensity.

Come on Simon. Think of something.

'Overseas.'

'I see,' said Lancelot.

No, I don't think you do.

'Let us return to my first question. You know more than you will own to, I am sure of it.'

Darcy hoped yet again that her face would not let her down.

'Okay. You got us,' said Simon.

What are you doing?

Darcy turned to face Simon fully to keep her surprise from Lancelot.

Simon grinned. Leaning across Darcy, his voice low and serious, he said, 'We have come from another place to help Culhwch win his bride, and Arthur take his throne. He will be king in Dumnonia. Once, and for all the times to come.'

'You jest with me,' said Lancelot. 'This boy could never be the king you speak of.'

'Don't underestimate the power of good friends and wise counsel.'

'Indeed.' Lancelot drained his glass and looked around the table. 'My fellow knights and I are sworn to serve the king. Ours is a life of sacrifice. My father...' He looked across at Llwyr. '... has been in the king's service since he was no more than a boy. I, the same. This fortress protected the royal house in exile until Narcasta was removed. Now it stands as a bastion against all such evil. So, I find myself wondering why a girl, a man, a couple of wizards, the king's nephew, and the prince himself would wander about the countryside when such dangers abound.'

'But you said it yourself,' said Darcy. 'Narcasta's gone. Any danger from him must have gone too.'

'I never said the danger was from Narcasta. The Pendragon throne has more than one enemy.'

'Yes,' said Simon. 'The giant Ysbaddaden Bencawr. We've had some experience of him.'

'Hmmm,' said Lancelot. 'The giant is nothing to worry about. His self-interest will be his downfall, and it keeps him more than occupied in the meantime. I was thinking of Arthur's sister Morgause and her son. That is where the real danger lies.'

'Mordred,' said Simon. Lancelot sat forward in his chair.

'You know of him?'

Realising his mistake, Simon scrabbled to correct himself.

'I... er... I have heard of the boy.'

'He will soon be a man. He has his mother's craft.' Lancelot rubbed his forehead. 'He shares his mother's hatred of Arthur. The king does not see it, but mark my words, Morgause has plans involving the throne for her son. With Arthur so restless, it would not be so difficult for her to change the course of what should be.'

Darcy and Simon managed to steer the conversation to safer ground for the rest of the dinner.

Llwyr pushed his chair back from the table as the last of the meal was cleared away

Getting up, he lifted the cup in his hand.

'To old friends and new, welcome to our fellowship. At this table, we meet as equals; we sit alongside princes, nobles, and country folk alike.' The nods around the table shared their agreement. 'We share food and opinions, and we are all the better for it. Today we are called again into service.' The knights leaned in, anticipating new orders. 'The cup in my hand is the cup of friendship. We have often passed it amongst ourselves and drunk deeply of its rewards. Now another needs it, and I have no grounds to refuse his request. Except to say that I cannot give away something so important without your blessing. So, I ask you all, do I have it?'

Mixed voices rose as the knights around the table shared their opinions, concerns, and consent. Llwyr listened to each argument until he had his answer.

'So, we are agreed then. Arthur will take the cup for his cousin's wedding feast.'

Turning to Culhwch, he lifted it once more.

'I hope the braggart will taste all the better for it.'

He took a long sip and passed the cup to Arthur.

*

Ysbaddaden paced the hall.

'You are back again, Welshman. I am looking forward to a good stew tonight.'

'I hope you do not mind disappointment, giant,' said Culhwch. 'We have brought the cup of Llwyr so you can drink your fill of the strongest Braggart at my wedding feast.'

The giant made a ball with his fist and smashed it down on the table, breaking it in two; it crashed onto the floor.

CHAPTER TWENTY-FOUR

BLOOD OF A WITCH

'So, here you all are,' said the giant. 'And much too soon for my liking. I am wasting away for want of a good casserole at my table.'

'There will be no meat stew today, giant,' said Culhwch. 'We have done all that has been asked, and now, once more, I request the hand of your daughter.'

'There is another thing that must be done before you can wed.' Ysbaddaden rubbed at the whiskers on his chin. 'I must shave. It would not be right to appear so unkempt on such an occasion.'

'Off you go then,' said Culhwch. 'We will wait.'

'Ah, not so fast, son-in-law. Shaving is difficult with whiskers as tough as mine. They must be softened, or the blade will not cut. I will need a large amount of blood taken from a dark witch. It is the only thing to work.'

Darcy's hand shot up to cover her mouth.

Ysbaddaden laughed. 'You are a squeamish girl.'

'Where do we find this witch?' asked Arthur.

Ysbaddaden paused, his finger resting on his lips as a smile moulded his rugged face.

'The Valley of Desolation, in the Uplands of Hell.'

Arthur looked at his cousin and then back at the giant.

'Then that is where we are going,' he said.

They hurried back down the hill, through the town, and onto the thin strip of beach.

'Do we have a plan?' asked Simon. The blank faces that met his were not what he was hoping for. 'Does anyone know this place? What did he call it? The Uplands of Hell... what kind of place is that, anyway?'

'I have never heard of it,' said Glewas.

'I believe it may be metaphorical,' said Mawgan.

Darcy kept silent as the others discussed the situation. She felt the anger growing in the pit of her stomach until she couldn't hold it in. 'Has anyone thought about what we're about to do? I don't want any part in hurting another person.'

She was close to tears. 'No one said anything about hurting anyone, Darcy,' Mawgan said.

'Then how exactly are we going to get enough blood for that beast to shave?'

'If you will pardon the expression, I have heard it said many times, "there is more than one way to skin a cat." I still believe this Valley of Desolation in the Uplands of Hell is a metaphor. It is a state of mind and heart, not a place. There is a witch we know well, who at this moment is all too familiar with it, I am sure.'

Recognition flickered across Darcy's face.

'Morwenna,' she said.

'We will need to get off these islands,' said Mawgan. 'Wherever Morwenna is, it is not here.'

'What if she has gone to The Vale of Secrets with Nix and Hicca?' said Darcy. 'If I had found out that the father of my baby had died, I would want to be with my family.'

Mawgan nodded. 'There is an excellent chance that is where she will be, but one thing is certain, we will not find her standing about here.'

Night descended, and everything was swaddled in a frosty blanket.

The world sparkled in the full moonlight. It was beautiful and cold.

'What's on your mind?' Simon sat next to Darcy and looked at the shiny black sea.

'I was just thinking about Morwenna.'

'What's she like?'

'Amazing. She's the main reason I wanted to come back.'

'What, not Glewas then?'

'Yes him. Of course, him. He and Mawgan, Nix, Hicca. All of them. It's just Morwenna... well... it was like discovering I had a sister. We connected.'

'She's special?'

'Yes, she is.'

'Someone as special as she is would help her friends in whatever way she could. Right?'

'Yes... I suppose so.'

'Then stop fretting. Nobody's going to hurt her. Mawgan hinted that there's a way to get what's needed without doing that. You forget what you brought me here to see.'

'What?'

'The magic.'

*

They crossed the sea floor, through the long-dead trees of Lyonesse. It seemed quicker this time; before the tide turned back, they were once more safely ashore on the mainland.

'We are going to need some help,' said Mawgan. 'Glewas, we need to work.'

Mawgan and Glewas followed the outer wall of the caer along the thin strip of the beach until they were far enough to be out of earshot.

'What are they doing?' asked Arthur.

'Whatever it is, they do not want us to see.' Culhwch tapped his friend on the shoulder and sat on the cold shingle. Simon plopped down next to them.

'You know how it is,' said Simon. 'Magicians never reveal how they do it. It's part of the trick.'

'I do not understand your meaning,' said Arthur.

'No, I don't suppose you do. But it's like Darcy's always telling me... we just have to trust them. Mawgan seems to know what he's doing.'

'That is true, my friend.' Arthur smiled. 'You are proving yourself to be good council.'

Simon felt a rush of satisfaction.

*

Darcy watched Glewas and Mawgan as the others talked. The wizards were further down the shore, hands folded in their laps, heads bowed. Looking at them, you would think they were practicing some form of meditation.

The sun was visible on the horizon now. It sparkled off the sea, eating away at the frost. Darcy's concentration was drawn to its warmth; it promised a bright day. As she watched the amber light spread across the sky, it acquired a green tinge. The green spread. As though a giant paintbrush had swirled it across the sky, it seeped into the sunrise.

Mind twinning.

Darcy was already standing when Glewas and Mawgan re-joined them.

'I had forgotten until now,' she said. 'It was how you talked to me back home. They're coming, aren't they? The pixies? You were mind twinning.'

'What's mind twinning?' asked Simon.

'It's how Mawgan first spoke to me three years ago. It's a kind of telepathy, only it's like the other person is there with you, but in reality, they could be hundreds of miles away.'

'Or worlds away,' said Simon.

'Yes, exactly.'

The morning sky was filled with green lights. A hundred shooting stars at dawn.

'They are here,' said Glewas.

*

Nix hugged Darcy to herself, stroking her long red braids.

'How are 'ee, my lovely? You could do with a brush I see. We've been wonderin' if 'ee is gettin' on.'

'I'm well, Nix. And you?' Before Nix had a chance to respond, Mawgan was between them.

'I have been discussing with Hicca how we can get to Morwenna.'

Darcy touched Nix's arm. 'How is she?'

'Not good, lovely. Not good at all.' A single tear wandered down Nix's cheek. 'We found her at the cottage in Piddleton. She went there… well, you know we can't go into Fae lands.

'We told her about Cadan and how he had died. We took him and buried him up by the stones, at the edge of the wood where they had first met. She wouldn't leave him; she laid on his grave for days. We tried to get her to eat; she wouldn't. She was wastin' away. We were worried about her and the baby. In the end, we forced her to come with us. She had the baby that night. A girl. With all the upset, she came early. Morwenna had a bad time of it. Then *they* came for the baby.'

'Who?'

'The Fae. They took our tiny girl from us.'

'Did Morwenna go with them?'

'No. They don't want her no more, not now Cadan's gone.'

'Mawgan, they took her baby,' said Darcy. 'It's just like my dream.'

'Yes,' said Mawgan. 'And if that part of your dream has come to be then...'

'Then the bit where I saw Narcasta with the baby.'

'Yes, that could well come to be too. Nix, we need to see Morwenna.'

'Yes, that's why we came. All of us.'

A hundred pixies stood in the morning sun.

'We have come to take you through the Vale.'

*

Morwenna likened the sensation to burning. Darcy thought her skin was evaporating. At the point just before it became unbearable, where she gave in to the pain, it stopped, and she was through. They soared above houses and streets arranged in neat, little rows. A world hidden away from outside troubles. It was a haven that had saved Morwenna as a young girl; now perhaps, it could do so again.

Landing in the front garden of a pretty cottage. Darcy and Simon waited until the whole group was reunited. They were none the worse for their trip through The Vale of Secrets; the only sign was a pinkish tint on their skin. They all looked a little sunburnt.

'Your nose is red,' said Glewas. He ran his finger down Darcy's nose before planting a little kiss on the end of it.

'Are you alright?' asked Darcy. Cocking her head to one side, she looked at him.

'I must admit I do feel a little strange.'

'It'll wear off,' said Hicca.

'It's given you a beautiful glow, Glewas,' said Nix. 'You look like a bronzed statue standin' there. We better all go inside out of this air before Glewas 'ere gets completely carried away.' She winked at Darcy, who blushed.

Simon, unimpressed, led the way inside. They made themselves comfortable in the tiny living room while Nix and Hicca went to find Morwenna.

*

Simon felt that he had been struck over the head with a heavy object. His brain was in a funk. Every thought was just out of reach, every word jumbled. He had heard about this sort of thing happening, but it was usually reserved for Hollywood movies or corny romantic novels. Never once had he thought such a thing could happen to him, but that was until he set eyes on Morwenna Tredinnick.

She walked into the sitting room flanked by her pixie parents. Darcy immediately noticed the change in her friend. Her eyes didn't have their usual sparkle, her skin was sallow, and her jet hair fell lifeless and dull.

'Morwenna!' Darcy couldn't keep the tremor out of her voice.

'It is alright, Darcy. I am alright.' Nix helped Morwenna into a chair. Darcy knelt and took hold of both Morwenna's hands.

'What can we do?'

Morwenna closed her eyes. Darcy could feel her shaking, and when her friend looked out again, she was shocked to see anger of such intensity, it made her back away.

'Firstly, I want to deal with whoever killed Cadan. Once I have done that, I want to get my baby. Can you help me with that?'

Morwenna looked unwaveringly at Darcy. The question hung between them. Simon, not knowing what else to do, stepped forward.

'We can,' he said.

*

Darcy and Simon sat on a bench, enjoying the late afternoon sun. The smell of the herbs and flowers growing in Nix's garden was a heady combination in such warm weather.

'Simon, she's in pain. And in no fit state to go rambling around the countryside looking for a murderer,' said Darcy.

'Maybe not. But sitting around here isn't helping her either. You said yourself; she's not the same person she was three years ago. Well, the only way we will be able to bring that Morwenna back is to find some restitution for her. Some closure. She's not going to find that here in this cottage.'

Glewas was heading in their direction.

'I'll leave you to it,' said Simon. 'Three's a crowd, and all that.'

'You don't need to run away.'

'I'm not. I'm going to talk to Arthur and Culhwch and see if we can come up with a plan. We still haven't discussed this blood thing. I'm not sure whatever Mawgan was planning is even safe now. I don't think Morwenna is up to it.'

'You believe she's up to dealing with Custennin. If she can do that... well, you'd be surprised how much she can deal with. You reminded me of something I had forgotten. She's stronger than we think.'

Glewas sat on the bench beside Darcy, his eyes on Simon's back as he retreated to the cottage.

'He does not like me.'

'Who, Simon? You're imagining things.'

'I do not think so.'

'It's not that he doesn't like you. It's just that we make him uncomfortable.'

'Oh?'

'He and I... well, he, he thought there was something between us.'

'And is there?'

'Not like that, no. We both realise now that what we have is more like brother and sister. He's family.'

'I see. And as your brother… Simon does not approve of me.'

'I don't need his approval. I don't need anyone's. But yes, he has his reservations. We're different, you and I, from different worlds. He worries about me, that's all.'

'I don't want to be his enemy.'

'Then don't be.'

'I am not sure I know how to be his friend.'

'He's a good person. Give him a chance.'

*

'So, what's the plan?' said Simon.

He was sitting opposite Culhwch, Arthur, and Mawgan at a small dining table inside the cottage. Hicca had prepared a salad with fresh leaves and flowers. Arthur held up a forkful, looking at it doubtfully. He sniffed at it, nodded, then popped it into his mouth, chewing.

'Mmm. Who would have thought this would be so tasty?'

'The pixies eat very well,' said Mawgan. 'For vegetarians.'

Culhwch chased the greenery around his plate with a fork, unconvinced.

'This is all very interesting,' said Simon. 'But it doesn't get us what we need, and it certainly doesn't help Morwenna.'

Arthur smiled. 'Morwenna's welfare is important to you. Why is that, I wonder?'

'It's important to Darcy, so it's important to me.'

Mawgan thumped his hand down on the table.

'Enough. Simon is right; we do need a plan. I will work with Glewas on our little blood issue. You three put your heads together and think of a way to transport us all back to the islands safely.'

'All of us?' said Culhwch.

'Yes,' Mawgan replied. 'We will not be able to leave Morwenna behind. I am certain of that.'

CHAPTER TWENTY-FIVE

FOR OLD TIMES' SAKE

Glewas and Darcy sat with Morwenna in the living room. Morwenna's face was grey in the afternoon light. All her vitality had gone; replaced by a despondency that tore at Darcy's heart.

'I don't understand what you are asking me to do,' she said.

The flatness of her voice struck Darcy. 'We need to borrow some of your blood,' said Darcy. 'Well, not borrow; take.'

'Yes,' said Glewas. 'We only need a little. Mawgan and I have been working on something that will quadruple whatever you can provide.'

'And it has to be my blood?'

'Yes,' said Darcy, 'we're sure about that. 'He didn't say your name exactly, but Ysbaddaden knew about you. Mawgan guessed that bit. Regardless, it's got to be your decision, Morwenna. Everyone would understand if you didn't want to do it.'

'No, it is fine. I want to help,' she said, rolling up her sleeve.

'That is good news,' said Glewas.

'I do have some conditions, though.'

Glewas nodded. 'What conditions?' he said.

'I take it to the giant.'

'Why would you want to do that?' asked Darcy.

'Because his arm is far-reaching. He may not have killed Cadan himself, but he as good as did the deed. Custennin's wife is just as much a victim in all of this as I am. She has lost her family too. None of us will ever be free until he is gone, and I don't plan on staying here and waiting around for that to happen. I will make it happen.'

*

Morwenna rested her arm over the bleeding bowl. She'd nicked the vein just under the bend at the elbow with her knife and the blood dripped freely.

Darcy watched Morwenna's face for signs that she was in distress or pain, but she needn't have worried. After a few minutes, it was over, and Morwenna held a white cloth over the wound to stop the blood as she rested in her chair.

Mawgan and Glewas took the bowl into the kitchen and closed the door. After a deal of time had passed, they came back into the living room.

'It is done,' said Mawgan. 'There is enough for the giant to shave a few times over. He will be satisfied; I am sure of it.'

'Morwenna, you should rest now,' said Nix.

'Stop fussing, Mother. I am better now than I have been for weeks. Do not take this away from me.' Darcy looked at Morwenna's face. It was true; she did look a little brighter. Maybe this was exactly what she needed.

Hicca and Simon appeared at the door. 'We have a plan,' said Hicca. 'If anyone would like to hear it?'

In the dining room, Culhwch and Arthur were seated at the table.

'Please, everyone, sit down,' said Arthur. 'This table may not be round, but it will serve. We have an idea to get this done, but we will need your help Morwenna, and that of the pixies. We must all work together if we are to finish this, for Culhwch here, for you Morwenna, and for the person we have all forgotten to mention since we left him behind with the Bannog.'

'Gorau,' said Darcy.

'Yes,' replied Arthur. 'For the boy.'

'So, what is the plan?' said Mawgan.

'It's simple really,' said Simon. 'We get back to the islands as fast as we can, get the girl, stop the giant and leave before anyone realises what we've done and gets upset about it.'

'Simple,' said Darcy.

'The best plans always are,' said Culhwch.

'So, you've been in here for hours,' said Darcy. 'And this is all you've come up with?'

'It is a start,' said Arthur. 'The rest will come to us, I am sure.'

'We are going to need your help again, Hicca,' said Mawgan.

'That you will,' said Hicca. 'And a few more besides if 'ee are all goin'. It's a long way for us to carry you. We will need help.'

*

Nix and Hicca spent the rest of the day going door to door, gathering their friends and shoring up support. It was a big ask. Generally, pixies were wary of involving themselves in the matters of humans. It usually always spelled trouble, and they avoided it. The pixie-Fae wars had taken their toll on the peace-loving species. Before those times, the only bad things the pixies had been guilty of was a bit of mischief when the mood took them. Now, they longed again for the simpler times of leading travellers astray and losing children in woods. But the hint of a menace that would change their world was always with them, and their fear was growing. They could not stand by and get lost in the crossfire.

'We'll help,' said Tub.

He was a rotund pixie that suited his name. His round face

shone with a rosy glow that heightened the shock of red hair receding from his forehead.

'It'll be difficult,' said Hicca. It's a long way to fly 'em.'

'Nothin' we haven't done before. That girl of yours isn't well, Hicca. If this'll help her, then it's the least we can do. You know we all think of 'er as one of our own.'

'I know that Tub 'n thank you.'

*

They left the next morning, each of them carried by a pixie through The Vale and over the countryside until they reached the southwest coast. There was no need to wait for the sea to pull back and reveal Lyonesse; they flew over the waves to the islands and the beachhead. Up, over the town they went. The hall at the top of the hill looked small from so high above. Onwards, past the fields where the flax had grown and been harvested in a day until the paddock of oxen and the little cottage with the thatched roof and the roses around the door was below them. They were back, and Peter, Gwen, and Gorau greeted them at the gate.

Morwenna rubbed at her face. The journey had been difficult. She had seen the Caer as they flew over it and the walled yard, knowing that was where Cadan had died, and she hadn't been with him.

The last time they'd been together, they had argued. She'd been angry that he was leaving her to follow some silly notion, so close to the time she was due. She felt alone in that enormous house with just the guards and servants for company. It had never felt like home to her; she was always the guest, even after three years. Home was the cottage hidden by The Vale or the house at the end of Piddleton Village, but this was where her heart was now.

Darcy helped Morwenna into the cottage.

'You must rest,' said Darcy.

178

'I will do no such thing. You are as bad as Nix. I do not need to be mothered.'

'No, but you do need to be sensible and keep yourself well for your baby. You'll be no good to her sick.'

Morwenna had no comeback. Darcy was right. She did need to be strong; Cadeyn needed her strong.

Morwenna had settled on the name last night. It had come to her in between brief bouts of sleep. The name honoured both the child's father and her hope of who this little girl would become; her warrior baby and all the promise she held. For old times' sake and the times yet to be.

Cadeyn, wherever you are, please know this: Mama loves you. I will find you and bring you home.

CHAPTER TWENTY-SIX

DEATH OF A KING

Morwenna and Nix sat in two chairs in the bedroom while Darcy made the bed for Morwenna, insisting that she get some rest.

'I don't think 'ee should be comin' with us today,' said Nix. 'Why don't we stay here? You, me and your father. We can do somethin' nice.'

Morwenna looked at her. 'Mother, I know you mean well, but even you must know how ridiculous that sounds.'

Nix sighed. 'I don't think you need all this extra worry; you 'ave enough.'

'I must go. Ysbaddaden is the reason Cadan was killed. I want to be there when he gets what is coming to him. It is my right. I will have retribution.'

Nix nodded. 'I understand. I wish you wouldn't, but I won't stop you.'

Darcy smoothed the bedcovers for a final time and stepped outside onto the landing, closing the door behind her. Simon was there, leaning on the banister, wearing the usual look he had when trying to appear disinterested.

'How is she?' asked Simon.

'Surprisingly determined.' Darcy smiled to herself. 'You like to put yourself through it, don't you?' she said.

'What are you talking about?'

'Or it is that you just hate the easy life, so are always drawn to the most difficult options?'

Simon's face was blank. 'I don't know what you're implying.'

'Oh, stop it. This is me. I know what those looks are. I've seen them before. Just take it easy. I don't want either of you to get hurt.'

'Darcy, nothing is going on.'

'Keep it that way. Whatever may be in your mind, she's not ready for it and may never be. Remember that.' Darcy pushed past him and stomped down the stairs, leaving Simon alone on the landing.

*

They set off to the great hall for the last time. A large group now, Darcy and Simon, Nix, Hicca, Morwenna and Glewas, Mawgan, Arthur, Gorau, Peter, and Gwen. Not forgetting Culhwch, the reason they had come to the Isles.

Darcy thought back to that morning in Jenna's shop in Bude. It had been weeks ago in Dumnoinan time. Had the same amount of time passed in Cornwall? But she knew it didn't work like that. Time wasn't a constant between the worlds. As Simon had said in Mawgan's cave, not long after they had met Arthur, "It was like an undulating stream that never touched in the same place twice." It was the reason the gateways moved. The reason they needed the compass. They had come such a long way since she and Simon had decided to go into Dumnonia, and things were still far from concluded. This trip had not been what she had expected. But who was she kidding? Things rarely were.

Glewas walked beside her. He slipped his hand into hers, intertwining their fingers together. They had not spent much time alone since those hours by the flax field. They walked without speaking; it was a comfortable silence full of understandings. They had found each other again. Neither of them knew how things would work out, but now was enough. It was all they were guaranteed.

*

The hall looked the same. It was mid-afternoon when they entered through the enormous wooden door with its metal strap and stud work. The door creaked as it swung inwards, and they all knew their arrival had been announced.

Ysbaddaden Bencawr sat in his great chair, his daughter on one side, his younger brother Custennin on the other. The shepherd was hunched over, chained by his hands and feet. Bloody welts were visible where the shackles dug into his skin.

Gorau looked at his father wide-eyed. Apart from a growing redness spreading across his cheeks and up his neck, his face was pale. Morwenna glanced at the boy by her side. Their eyes held each other, an unspoken understanding passing between them.

Ysbadadden rose from his chair. He stepped down from the platform and rolled several glass balls towards Morwenna. Darcy had seen apotropaic witch balls when she had visited Shelburne Museum. She had travelled to Vermont with her parents as her mother was speaking at an event there. The highly coloured balls on display had intrigued her with their beauty, much the same way they had been designed to distract and captivate a witch. She remembered her father had jokingly called her a witch that very day.

The moment the giant released the glass balls, Morwenna knew she had the advantage. He was afraid. She took the bottle of blood from the pocket in her cloak. It had cost her more than she had let on at the time, but it would be worth every drop if the plan she had designed the night before played out.

Much to Ysbaddaden's disappointment, the glass balls did not affect Morwenna. Mawgan picked them all up. He held one to the light and allowed the brightness to shine through the particles of coloured glass.

'Very pretty,' he said, popping them into his pocket.

Morwenna approached the giant. Ysbadadden jumped back onto the platform and down into his chair.

'Are you afraid of me?' asked Morwenna. She moved nearer to the giant's chair. Standing in front of him now, Morwenna looked small and fragile, but her voice had a strength that belied her appearance. She held up the bottle of her blood.

'I have brought you blood to shave your wretched face,' she said. 'It holds enough despair and sadness to soften the hardest of bristles. Let me apply it for you.'

'No!' Ysbaddaden looked like he might disappear into the chair fabric if he could. Morwenna took no notice as she poured the blood into a shaving bowl held out to her by the puny manservant. The servant's hands shook, and Morwenna grabbed one of his wrists with her free hand. 'Steady now; we wouldn't want to spill.'

She continued to pour until the bowl was filled almost to the brim. All the while, the group watched on, unable to move. All that was, except for Gorau. He moved from his place, up the steps, and onto the platform beside Morwenna. The rest of the group did not know what was happening; they also had no notion that Morwenna had contrived to disable them with a freezing charm. They couldn't move even if they wanted to. She had planned this. It was her moment, and nobody would interfere. She'd made sure of that.

Gorau grabbed the shaving brush from the puny servant and dipped its bristles into the bowl of blood. He handed it to Morwenna. She took it from him, slipping her ebony-handled knife into Gorau's fingers.

'Ready?' she whispered.

He nodded. Morwenna climbed up onto the arm of Ysbaddaden's great chair. The giant didn't move a whisker. Gorau climbed onto the opposite arm. Morwenna dipped and pasted, dipped and pasted, until the giant's entire face was smothered in her blood. He didn't make a sound. No one did. The entire hall was silent.

Morwenna reached into her pocket. Looking down at her bloodstained hand, she saw that it now held a long razor, the blade hidden in the handle's recess. She flicked it, and the shiny blade was free.

Morwenna carefully drew the blade across the giant's chin, bringing a mass of bloody bristles with it. She wiped it with a towel and began the next sweep. Ysbaddaden closed his eyes and breathed out slowly. Even through his fear, the sweet sensation of the blade smoothing his chin of the itchy bristles relaxed him. Morwenna looked across at Gorau. Their eyes locked as Gorau raised the black knife he was holding, and with the next sweep of Morwenna's razor, he dragged it across Ysbaddaden's throat from ear to ear. The blade was so sharp; the giant didn't feel the cut until the blood gushed from the wound, and he gurgled and spluttered.

Ysbadadden fell forward, knocking Morwenna and Gorau from their perch on either side of him. They fell onto the floor of the platform. The giant toppled over them. It was only then that the rest of the group could move again.

'Morwenna!' Nix screamed.

Arthur and Culhwch ran up onto the platform, pulling at the giants flailing limbs, they tried to lift him off the boy and the witch trapped beneath him. Mawgan raised both his arms, mumbling incantations as he did. Sure enough, the giant's body lifted for Gorau to roll out from under him. The boy sprang to his feet, the knife still in his hand; he jumped onto the giant's back, slashing at the neck.

'This is for my brothers, dead every one.'

Slash.

'This is for my father, I now his only son.'

Cut.

'The next is for my mother; her love makes all things die.'

Slash.

'The last is mine and mine alone. Forever, all know why.'

Cut.

The head of Ysbaddaden fell from his shoulders and rolled along the platform, down the stairs, and out of the hall. It continued rolling down the street, through the town. As it did, the townsfolk followed, congregating to watch the spectacle. It rolled over the sand and into the waves until it was swallowed by the sea. And so it was, that the giant Ysbadadden Bencawr met his end at the hand of his brother's youngest son—the best and bravest of boys ever to have lived.

CHAPTER TWENTY-SEVEN

THE WAY OF THINGS

Morwenna crawled out from under the giant's dead body. Her breath was laboured as she struggled to get her diaphragm to expand. Still holding up the dead weight of the right arm, Simon stood over her.

'Are you alright?'

Morwenna was still panting. Nix and Hicca were on the floor of the platform beside her. Nix stroked her hair. 'C'mon my darlin',' she said. 'Let's get you on your feet.'

Hicca lifted her himself and gently placed her down, feet first. She held on to him until her legs steadied.

On the other side of the giant body, Olwen cried quietly for her father.

'You are free now, Olwen,' said Culhwch, taking her hand. 'Do not be sad. This was always how things were to end. Your freedom had a price. It would either be his death or mine. I, for one, am glad it was the former.'

'As am I,' she whispered. 'But he was still my father for all the terrible things he has done. I wish it could have been different.'

'That was unlikely,' said Arthur. 'He could not change who he was.'

'I always hoped he would find a way,' she said.

Gorau slipped a giant set of keys from Ysbaddaden's trouser pocket. A smaller key hung from a heavy ring. He went to his father and inserted it into the shackles at Custennin's ankles; the key turned, and the metal fell away. Custennin held out his wrists so that the boy could do the same with them. Once free, the shepherd grabbed his son.

'My boy.' The burly man wept quietly, cradling Gorau in his arms. Darcy was surprised. Custennin had never appeared to her the slightest bit sentimental.

As the father and son continued to hold each other, a strange darkness rose out of Custennin's chest, hovered for a moment above them, before vanishing.

'What was that?' said Darcy.

'That, dear girl, was the spectre that has plagued the shepherd for longer than I care to remember,' said Mawgan. 'There is no room in him for it any longer. The space has been filled by something else.'

'Love,' said Darcy.

'Yes, love,' Mawgan replied. 'Now the true healing of this family can begin, and an island people will have a king worthy of them.'

'What do you mean?' said Darcy.

'The king is dead. Long live the king.' Mawgan nodded towards Custennin, and Darcy at last understood. The large man was the guardian of the Caer no longer. On the death of his brother, the pathetic, downtrodden shepherd had become king.

Simon sat with Morwenna on the floor of the platform. He knew there was nothing he could do; all he wanted was to be near her. It felt like the right thing. Her breathing had eased, and a little colour had returned to her face.

'Better?'

'Yes.' She looked across at the lifeless mass. 'Much better now. I feel an immense weight has been lifted.'

As they talked, the hall started to fill with townspeople. They crept in warily, one by one at first, then in groups, until there was no more room. And so, they filled the forecourt, then a line stretching down the cobbled street. They had all come, every man, woman, and child, and when they were all assembled, Arthur addressed them.

'You know who I am. I came with my kinsman to claim a bride worthy of him. A marriage that would unite the islands and bring our kingdoms together under the Pendragon banner.

You have been freed from the tyranny of the giant. His brother, the shepherd Custennin, will be a very different king, one that will cherish and care for you, much like the flock he once watched over.

May this kingdom prosper all his days and those of his offspring.'

A cheer went up in the hall, and the crowd chanted, 'Long live the king. Long live the king.' Over and over.

*

Leaving Custennin and Gorau in the hall with their people, the rest of the party moved outside, pushing through the crowd. They made their way down the hill towards the beach.

A hand grabbed Darcy's arm. It was the woman who had collected the flax that night at the field. She handed her a parcel.

'Tis beautiful, it is,' she said. 'Fit for the head of a princess, as was meant to be. Make sure she has it, won't 'ee?'

'Yes,' said Darcy. Realising that the woman had handed her the flaxen vail they had worked so hard to produce. The woman smiled into Darcy's face. She lifted her hand and cupped Darcy's chin with it.

'All is well, dearie, don't fret. Tis the way of things this is. New times come, and old ways pass.' The woman reached down and picked up the hand of the child next to her. Moving off, they were swallowed by the crowds once more. Darcy looked at the parcel she was holding.

'I'll take that if you like?' said Nix.

Nodding, Darcy handed it to her. As Nix took the package, it shrunk to the size of a fifty pence piece, and she popped it in her pocket. She winked.

'That's a handy skill to have,' said Darcy, smiling. Her face became serious. 'Do you think Gorau will be alright? I'm not sure we should just leave him with Custennin. He didn't look after him before.'

'That was because the family was cursed, Darcy. Curses can make people behave very differently from their nature. Back in the hall, we saw Custennin for who he is. He did his best for the boy even under the curse, didn't he? He gave him to you. Now you have given him back. The boy will be fine; Peter and Gwen will keep an eye on him. That was a kind thing you did, Darcy, asking 'em to care fer him.'

'I thought they could help each other.'

'They did. You've grown up thoughtful and kind. Magic is clever, but it's nothin' compared to that.'

They made their way through Lyonesse. As this was the third time they had crossed, it did not hold the same uncertainty, and the crossing was uneventful.

When they came to the Caer, a new shepherd had been installed. He and his family of six sons watched on as they passed through. The place was changed, almost welcoming and homely now. Custennin's hound was nowhere to be seen. The new shepherd had an English Sheep dog that nuzzled them each in turn and laid belly up, hoping to be fussed over.

*

What is it about journeys home? The miles pass quicker somehow.

Two days after leaving the islands, the party was at Piddleton Village. They had said goodbye to Gwen and Peter at Willow Wood and continued on. Now, they stood outside the pub in a deserted square with only the clock tower to acknowledge their arrival.

'Anyone fancy a pint?' said Simon.

Mawgan's brow furrowed so deeply that Simon took a step backward.

'I just want to get home,' said Morwenna. Hicca was already holding the door open for her, and she gratefully walked the last few steps to her cottage. Darcy hadn't been in Morwenna's home since her first visit to Dumnonia. It was unchanged. There were herb jars all over the kitchen where Morwenna practiced her craft. The living room was small and cosy, if a little dusty. Darcy remembered the night Morwenna had told her story. How Kea had warmed to her after a frosty start.

Darcy smiled at the memory.

'We're leaving,' said Simon.

Darcy turned from the fire she had lit in the tiny living room. Even though it was just autumn, the evening was cold, winter was on its way. 'What?' said Darcy. 'We've only just got here. Morwenna needs to rest.'

'I didn't mean that Morwenna should go anywhere. Or you, for that matter.'

'But you just said, "we're." Who's "we" then?'

'Arthur, Culhwch, Olwen and... Me.'

Darcy's jaw dropped. 'You're leaving me?'

'No... not leaving for good, anyway. Just to help sort out this wedding thing. After Morwenna's a bit better, you'll follow, and we'll meet up again.'

'Jenna told us to stick together.'

'And we are. I'm just needed elsewhere for a bit. Anyway, you have Glewas watching out for you now. You don't need me.'

'What I don't need is people thinking they have to protect me all the time. I can look after myself.'

Simon's jaw set in a way Darcy hadn't seen before. He'd decided;

she could see that arguing would be useless, and that wasn't how she wanted to leave things, if he'd decided they had to part ways. 'Be careful. You're my best friend; I wouldn't know what to do if anything happened to you.'

Simon's face softened. 'I'll always be here.' He bent and kissed her forehead before walking out into the evening. Darcy watched him leave, not knowing when she would see his face and hear his voice again. The tears flowed freely down her face..

*

'So, they have gone,' said Mawgan the next morning

Darcy looked up from the herbalist book she had been reading. Morwenna had quite a collection. 'Yes. Though I don't understand why Simon had to go.'

'Do you not?'

Darcy shook her head.

'I have been watching him for some time. When he arrived with you all those weeks ago, it was as though he had no direction. Over the weeks since, he has been changing. Or rather, he has been gaining a purpose; talking with Arthur and Culhwch, using his knowledge to plan and solve problems.

I've also seen Arthur's growing liking of him. That young prince has been friendless in the old castle for too long. Culhwch will soon be married and gone to his new life, and Arthur will be left to his estranged father and mad sister once again. He will need a friend.'

'Mawgan, you talk as if Simon is staying. He'll be going back to his own life too... eventually.'

'Hmmm.'

'Mawgan. What's going on?'

He didn't answer because Hicca walked into the living room carrying a plate of sandwiches at that exact moment. 'Ah, Hicca, just what we need,' said Mawgan. Taking a sandwich, he munched away on the lettuce and cucumber, ignoring Darcy's look of frustration, and leaving her question hanging in the air.

*

Simon walked beside Arthur in silence. He could smell and hear the sea now. In the dark, it was a warning that they were close.

'Where's the gate?' said Simon. 'Why aren't there any lights?'

'Father likes to make things challenging,' said Arthur. 'This way. It is not far now.'

Arthur ducked into an almost invisible gap in the wall. They had secured the use of a couple of ponies in Piddleton Village and packed up all the wedding gifts. Culhwch led them through the gap while holding tight to Olwen's hand.

Olwen hung back.

'It is alright Olwen, do not be afraid,' said Culhwch. 'They are my mother's family. They will love you as much as I do.'

'I would not hold your breath,' said Arthur.

Culhwch frowned. Olwen looked horrified. Arthur winked at her, turned, and marched into Tintagel.

CHAPTER TWENTY-EIGHT

THE SWORD BEARER'S CHARM

Arthur walked into the throne room. As a child he had played amongst the chairs, pretending they were trees and rocks, and that he and his horse leaping over them could escape to safety, far from here.

Tonight, the room looked as he remembered it. The lit torches in their sconces threw long shadows across the floor. Up on the platform, his father's great chair stood empty. The gold dragon sewn into the fabric glinted in the flickering light, as if alive. But the night was full of tricks.

Morgawse watched Arthur from behind the great chair. His very existence violated her, and she couldn't look at him without the familiar feeling of nausea. She had set her heart against him. It was her way of coping with the knowledge of what they had done.

'You are back then?' said Morgawse as she stepped into the light.

'Yes, sister. I am.'

Morgawse sniffed the air and wrinkled her nose. 'I smell pigs. Have you been mixing in low company, dear brother?'

'If you mean have I been with our mother's nephew? The answer is yes. Culhwch is to marry.'

'Is she beautiful?'

'Very.'

'As beautiful as me?'

'Dear sister, did no one ever teach you that self-praise has no worth?'

Morgawse smiled and stepped down from the platform. She sidled up to Arthur and stood so close, he could smell the faint perfume of soap. Lilac and heather tickled his nose, and his head spun.

She was beautiful. A face that could send his mind into free-fall and turn his heart to mush. He often wondered if it was just her beauty or was her craft as much to blame for how she made him feel?

Arthur took a step backward, putting space between them. He must keep his head.

Simon hid at the back of the room watching Arthur speak with a beautiful woman.

'Who is that?' said the woman, her eyes on the spot where he hid.

Simon stepped forward and she glided towards him. Her deep purple robe highlighted the milkiness of her skin. It draped elegantly from her shoulders and swished across the floor in her wake. When she had reached Simon's side, she raised her eyes to his. They were the same colour as the dress.

The woman lifted a hand and gently brushed Simon's cheek.

'This is my sister, Morgawse,' said Arthur.

'I'm Simon.'

As they walked from the throne room, Arthur pulled Simon aside.

'Watch yourself with her,' said Arthur. 'She is dangerous. Men have lost themselves in those eyes.'

'I can see why.'

'My father is bewitched.'

'And you?'

Arthur nodded. 'Once. Long ago. It was a mistake, and I have paid dearly ever since.'

*

The next day, Simon and Arthur went riding, leaving Culhwch and Olwen to their wedding planning.

Simon was a fair horseman, having learned to ride as a boy. It had been his joy. A chance to escape from the tension at home. An hour of freedom every Saturday morning at the local riding school. He had mucked out stables and poo picked paddocks to pay for his lessons. Back in the saddle, he felt the familiar elation return as the horse powered beneath him, lengthening its stride as it gained speed.

Arthur was pleased to find Simon enjoyed a ride as much as he did. They galloped onwards through the countryside, only stopping when they found themselves at the well.

'How did we get here?' said Simon.

'I do not know,' said Arthur.

The water was the same murky rust colour that Simon remembered from the dig. Until now, he hadn't thought about his life back on the other side of the gateway. He felt suddenly heavy.

'What is wrong?'

Arthur was frowning.

'Nothing. It's not important. Why have we come here?'

'I am not sure. I had it in my mind to ride to Piddleton again to see your ladies, but I am drawn to this place.'

Ignoring the comment about Darcy and Morwenna, Simon looked into the water. A ripple radiated from the centre and splashed against the sides of the pool.

Arthur slid from his horse.

'I have seen this before,' he said.

A second ripple. Arthur stepped into the water and walked to the centre. As he did, a hand rose, quickly followed by its owner, until Arthur and a woman stood together in the pool.

'Jenna!' Simon shouted, sliding off his horse and hobbling it to a tree branch.

Jenna smiled at him. 'You have found yourself, I see. I knew it. Each of us has a destiny. This is yours; I am pleased for you. And for you, Arthur Pendragon.' She turned back to Arthur. 'Yours is a path I do not yet see clearly. Beware of those closest to you. They do not have your best interests at heart. Look to the strength of friendship and follow what is in here.' She placed her hand on his chest. 'It will lead you to the truth.' She stepped back and extended her hands. 'Give me your sword.'

Arthur passed Caliburnus to Jenna. She closed her eyes and held the sword high above her head. 'I name you Excalibur.'

As she called out its name, the sword lit up. Sparks flew off the surface. Arthur fell backward into the water and slipped under.

Simon splashed through the pool, reaching down, searching. He felt the limp body beneath him and hauled Arthur to the surface. The prince spluttered and coughed.

Jenna handed Excalibur to Arthur. The sword had changed. As the light caught its wet surface, he could see more engravings than had been there before. A lion had joined the others. It looked out at him, wearing a crown on its large head. A serpent-like tongue tasted the air from its open mouth. Arthur's attention was drawn to its large and extended claws.

'This is your destiny, Arthur Pendragon,' said Jenna. 'Claim it.' Turning again to Simon, Jenna took his right hand in hers and placed something in his palm. As she took her hand away, Simon immediately recognised what it was.

'A compass!'

'Yes. A traveller like yourself should have a compass of his own to keep him true. Keep it safe. It will always show you the way home.' Then she disappeared.

'Where did she go?' said Simon.

'Back the way she came. You knew her?'

'Yes, she's a friend of Darcy's.'

Arthur looked at the compass still in Simon's hand.

'I have heard of these charms leading travellers to other worlds through moving gateways, here one moment, gone the next.' He studied Simon's face. 'You came from somewhere other than Dumnonia. You and Darcy... you are travellers from another world?'

Simon nodded.

'I suspected as much,' said Arthur. 'You are both very odd and speak strangely. Still, Mawgan trusts you, and I trust him.'

'I hope you'll grow to trust me for myself.'

'Teithiwr, you may well get your wish.'

'What did you call me?'

'It is your name now. Get used to it. Quickly, hide that before anyone sees. These forests have eyes.' Arthur looked into the trees around the perimeter of the pool. The horses were still hobbled there, eating grass. 'Come, let us return before we are missed. I do not want to explain what has happened here to anyone.

Back at Tintagel, Uther Pendragon stalked the halls of his ancestors like an evil-tempered cat. He had not seen his son since Arthur's return to the castle the night before. Morgawse had relished telling him he was back with the swine herder and some girl in tow. He could not understand why Arthur gave Culhwch so much of his time. He was family, yes, but some connections are better ignored. At least the wizard had not returned with him. Uther had no time for those that practiced the craft.

Arthur walked along the hall, stripping his riding gloves as he went; he slapped them rhythmically against his leg, whistling to himself.

'There you are, boy,' said Uther. 'I have spent half the morning looking for you.'

'Father, I have not been a boy for at least ten years. I do not understand why you persist in calling me so.'

'Because your ability to act like a child has not diminished.

Where have you been?'

'Out riding.'

'For the last six weeks? It must have been a good ride.'

'No, Father. I only rode this morning. For those weeks, I have been on a quest to secure Culhwch a wife and his future happiness.'

'And what of the kingdom's happiness? Does that not need your attention? Do you think your position here does not require you to be present? Perhaps I should give Morgawse her wish and name her son king on my demise.'

'You should do what you think is best, Father.'

'What I think best is for my son to be about the business that is his to be about. And stop shirking his responsibilities.'

'I was shoring up our relationship with the southwestern isles. Is that not my business?'

Uther stopped pacing and fell silent. Arthur had a point. Eventually, he started to pace again. 'And has that been accomplished?'

'The giant is dead.'

Uther swung round and looked directly at Arthur. 'How?'

'By the hand of his nephew and a witch.'

Uther shuddered. 'The treachery of family is the hardest betrayal to bear.'

'I do not think there was any love to lose between the giant and his kin, Father. They were not close.' There was a hint of defiance in Arthur's tone. It was not lost on Uther. He frowned.

'So, a new king for the Isles then. What is he like?'

'Different from his brother. As for the rest, only time will tell us that.'

'Who is the stranger you travelled with?' Uther pointed behind Arthur to where Simon was busy trying to make a stone wall look interesting.

'He is Simon. I am considering adding him to my household. A man needs good council.'

'A king even more so. He is dressed strangely.'

'Yes, he is strange, but he is also honest, and I like him.'

'Hmmm. What is he doing?'

Arthur turned to see that Simon was still studying the wall. 'That, I do not know, Father.'

'As I said...' Uther's eyes narrowed, '... strange.'

CHAPTER TWENTY-NINE

A KING IN THE MAKING

Simon sat in the great eating hall of the castle, turning the compass over and over in his hand. It was different from Darcy's; his had none of the glamour of hers. It was crudely engineered, with a plain brass casing that had the tool marks of its maker scratched over every surface. There were no runes to read around the dial, just a N, S, E, and W, and a pointer that spun incessantly.

He knew that to make it work, he must wear it, but he couldn't bring himself to pull its chain over his head.

Why was that?

'You should keep that hidden,' said Arthur. Simon jumped. He hadn't noticed Arthur enter the hall. Quickly, he shoved the compass back in his pocket.

'They are sought after and should not fall into the wrong hands.'

'How do I know mine are the right hands?'

'It was gifted to you by the lady. That is proof enough that these things are meant to be.'

Arthur looked at his sword. It was also a gift of the lady in the lake and felt like an extension of his own body. It had to be right that the sword had found its way to his hand.

Who else could she have given it to?

A young woman waddled into the room from the nearby kitchen, carrying a couple of bowls. She slapped them down on the table in front of Arthur and Simon, slopping some of the contents over the table.

'This must be lunch,' said Arthur. He sniffed at the soup. 'Leek and potato, I think.'

The woman returned with two hunks of roughly cut bread. Arthur pulled a grub out of his piece and threw it away. 'Not exactly like eating with the Willows, is it?'

'No,' said Simon. 'Not exactly.'

Olwen entered the hall, followed closely by Morgawse.

'Afternoon ladies,' said Simon.

Olwen smiled, slightly dipping her head in acknowledgment of Arthur. Morgawse, ignoring everyone, went to sit to the right of Uther's chair at the head of the table.

'She has got some nerve,' said Arthur.

'Shouldn't that be your seat?' asked Simon. Arthur only nodded in reply.

A young boy of no more than ten or eleven entered the room. He was small with delicate features, dark hair, and a long sad face. Arthur visibly stiffened.

'Mordred?' whispered Simon. Arthur nodded again. The boy moved gracefully down the table to sit with his mother. Culhwch entered. He stood for a moment assessing the table before squeezing Arthur's shoulder in consolation as he passed and sat opposite Olwen.

The last to arrive for lunch was Uther. He clattered through the door nearest the table's head. On seeing where the rest of the party had positioned themselves, he shook his head but sat anyway, with Morgawse on one side and Mordred on the other. Uther stared down the table, not taking his eyes off Arthur, who sat quietly eating.

'Your father looks furious,' said Simon.

'That is because he is. He insists on this hollow ritual. That we all should know our place and stay in it. I want a different life. One with people I respect for who they are, not what they were born to. My father disagrees. He calls it "newfangled," and by that he means dangerous. He dislikes anything he does not understand. He is old and afraid, and I scare him most of all.'

'By the sounds of it, you would prefer a table like Llwyr's where everyone sits equally.'

'Yes, exactly like that. And equal in more ways than just at the table.'

'I think you're going to have a battle on your hands.'

'Perhaps.'

Uther banged his fist down on the wooden surface. The table rattled and upended his goblet, spilling its contents. 'Get out of that chair,' Uther yelled.

Morgawse dabbed at the corners of her mouth before putting her napkin gently down and sliding her chair away from the table. She walked to the other side of Mordred and sat next to him.

'If he refuses to sit in his proper place, then the chair will remain empty until such time as my successor fills it. Whether that be him,' Uther pointed at Arthur, 'or another.' Uther turned on Morgawse, pointing. 'It will never be you.' The words stuck in his mouth. Uther went to breathe but couldn't.

'Father!' yelled Arthur. He ran the length of the table. Uther still couldn't breathe, and Arthur grabbed him up in his arms. 'This is you doing this.' Arthur spat the words at Morgawse. She offered a sickly sweet smile, got up, and left.

'Simon, what do I do?'

Simon was by Arthur's side in an instant. 'Loosen his collar.' No change. 'Lay him flat.' Uther was limp and unconscious now. Simon tilted his head back and felt if anything was blocking the airway. 'I think it's his heart,' he said, reaching to check Uther's wrist. 'I can't feel anything. There's no pulse.'

Simon started CPR, but it wasn't working. He was at the point of giving up when he noticed that Uther's colour had changed and the bluish tinge, although still on his lips, had lessened. Simon leaned over Uther, putting his ear up against his mouth, and listened. Uther was breathing. It was shallow and very faint, but he was alive.

'He's breathing. Let's move him to a bedroom.'

They hadn't noticed in all the commotion that the room had filled with people. They lifted Uther and carried him away.

'Careful,' said Simon. 'He's frail.'

As soon as Uther had gone, Arthur sprung into life.

'I will kill her. Where is she? This was her doing, the evil witch.'

'Don't say that,' said Simon. 'Not all witches are bad; we choose who we are.'

Culhwch came back from helping with Uther.

'She has run. The boy has gone too, and horses are missing from the stables.'

'Where would she go?' asked Simon.

'She will try to get back to Orkney, to that husband of hers,' said Culhwch.

'King Lot?' said Simon.

'You have heard of him,' said Arthur. 'He is not a good man. We have him to thank for the Imp invasion. He sent them to Narcasta. It took an age to rid the countryside of them after he went back to the Fae.'

'I've never seen an Imp,' said Simon.

'Then you are the luckier for it,' said Culhwch. 'They are evil. Many have been injured, and worse, by them.'

'Yes...' said Simon, remembering what Darcy had told him about Kea. '... So, what do we do then?'

'We go after her,' said Arthur.

'Simon and I will go after her,' said Culhwch. 'Your father is on his death bed. You cannot leave now.'

'I cannot stay either. There is nothing I can do here. A good son would avenge his father.'

Simon put a hand on Arthur's arm. 'I know you don't believe it, but you're a good son. You have nothing to prove.'

'You are wrong. I have it all to prove. And catching that woman will be my first act.' The three men flew out the door, leaving poor Olwen alone with the servants.

CHAPTER THIRTY

DARKENING TIMES

The best horses had been taken. Arthur, Culhwch, and Simon had to make do with the three remaining nags.

'These look like they are ready for the dogs,' said Culhwch.

Simon quickly covered the ears of the nearest horse. 'Don't listen to him. You're perfect.' He stroked the old horse's mane, whispering in its ear as he did. The animal's ears pointed forwards excitedly. It was feeling the old rush of adrenaline. 'I bet you've seen your fair share of excitement, hey girl.'

'That she has,' said Arthur. 'This is Hester. She was my mother's favourite mare.'

'Your mother's? If you'd prefer, I took a different horse...'

'No, no. I can see she likes you.'

'She's beautiful.'

'That she is.'

They rode out through the castle gates once more. This time, it felt like they were crossing a line that couldn't be uncrossed. Olwen had clung to Culhwch as if she would never see him again. 'Watch over the King,' he had asked her. And she went willingly to her duty, glad to have something to occupy herself.

They headed north, stopping at intervals only long enough to rest the horses.

'This could take weeks,' said Simon.

They had found a small copse of trees that formed a sheltered canopy and unloaded and rugged the horses for the night. Culhwch built a fire, and they sat huddled around it, poking at a pot of stew and a kettle of water that never quite reached boiling point.

'I could eat a rotten badger,' said Arthur. 'Let me dish this up before hunger takes us all.'

Culhwch sighed. 'If we end our days with the gripe, it will be your doing.'

Arthur spooned stew into bowls and handed them out. 'See,' he said, handing Simon his bowl, 'it did not take as long as you thought.'

'I wasn't meaning the stew,' said Simon. 'Do you have any idea how far north Orkney is? We will need to use a boat for the last part of the journey.'

'Who said anything about going to Orkney?' said Arthur.

'You did,' said Culhwch.

'No, I said that Morgawse would try to get back to Orkney. Not that she would ever make it or that we would be following.'

'So, where are we going?' asked Culhwch.

Arthur put down his stew and looked at both men. 'We are going to see the Fae,' he said.

'Well, we cannot ride onto their lands,' said Culhwch. 'They guard all the borders. We will need a plan to get past the sentries.'

'There will be no need for stealth. We will not arrive in secret. I am going to see the new Lord, whomever that is,' said Arthur.

'Why?' asked Simon. 'From what I know about them, and that isn't much, they're not the friendliest of folk.'

'No, but Morgawse will need to pass through their lands. So, if we can convince them to help us, we might catch her and the boy before they reach the Pictish borders. Once they get up there, they will be lost to us.'

'It's a good idea, but why do you think they would help us?' said Simon.

Arthur looked at Culhwch. Simon couldn't read what passed between them. The moment was over quickly. Arthur picked up his stew again and swallowed a mouthful.

'Because the enemy of my enemy is my friend. They have as much reason to want her gone as we do.'

*

The border to the Fae lands is inconspicuous. You wouldn't even know you'd crossed except for the nasty surprise on the other side.

Arthur, Culhwch, and Simon crossed at dawn the following day. As they rode under a tree canopy, Culhwch's horse stumbled, completely losing its footing. Its legs buckled, and it rolled over onto the grassy floor, asleep. Behind him, as they crossed, Arthur's and Simon's horses did the same. Simon knelt beside Hester.

'What do we do? What's wrong with her?'

'She is asleep like the others,' said Arthur. 'No harm will come to them. We only have a few seconds before the same happens to us. Keep your wits about you and do not say anything. You will want to. By gods, they have a way of wheedling information out of a person. You must be strong and fight it.'

Simon felt like his arms and legs were suddenly weighed down. He couldn't move. Rolling onto his side, his vision blurred. The last thing he saw were two men standing a little way off. He tried to stretch out his hand to them. 'Help me... please.' He lost consciousness.

*

Later, they woke to the sound of bells. Slowly opening his eyes, Simon found himself in a large room. He was laid on a chaise. His vision was still blurry, and his head banged like it usually did the morning after a night on the town. He sat up with his head in his hands and groaned.

'What's that awful noise? Someone make it stop... please.'

'My stomach tells me it is the dinner gong,' said Arthur.

'Your stomach is usually correct,' said Culhwch.

He rubbed at his forehead and squinted.

'You are right.' The voice was high and melodic and had a softness that was soothing against the harshness of the gong. The three men sat upright at her entrance. 'I am Finnabair, lady of these lands since the death of one brother and the incarceration of the other. Please make yourselves comfortable and relax; no one here wishes you harm.'

She was spectacular. Tall like her brothers, but that was where the similarity ended. She was pale as a ghost. Her long, red, waist-length hair brought out the striking green of her eyes.

'They have rung the gong for dinner. Will you join me?' The three men nodded acceptance and followed Finnabair into another room where a table had been set and laid with food.

'Eat whatever you desire,' she said.

'There is so much to choose from,' said Culhwch.

'We aim to please.'

'Not usually,' said Arthur. 'But the change is refreshing.'

'We have come far since my brother took a human wife.'

'I understood that they never married,' said Simon.

'You think because they did not take vows in public, the vows they made in private were not binding? We do not share that belief. Their daughter is evidence enough of their commitment.'

'The daughter you stole,' said Simon.

'We did no such thing. She is where she belongs.'

'She belongs with her mother.'

'One day, all this will be hers. What could her mother possibly teach her about that?'

Arthur rested his hand on Simon's arm.

'Lady, we have not come here to argue this point.'

'Then what have you come for?'

'The lady Morgawse and her son will cross your borders, if they have not already done so.'

Finnabair visibly stiffened.

'Why would they risk coming here?'

'Because they are trying to get north, and there is no way of doing that by land without crossing your borders. They will not risk sailing; the merfolk are too dangerous.'

'They have not crossed yet. Our sentries have found no strangers on our lands recently. Apart from you, that is.'

'She is strong in the craft,' said Culhwch as he munched on a strawberry. 'She could have found a way. And you would have been none the wiser but for us.'

Finnabair rose from her seat and paced the floor.

'There, you are wrong in your assumptions.'

The door opened at the far end of the room, and Mawgan appeared.

'What are you doing here?' said Simon. 'Where's Darcy? Is she okay?'

'Enough of the questions. I am not here to be interrogated. Darcy is fine and well and still in the home of Morwenna. I have left Glewas in charge, and he is more than capable. I came here to speak with Finnabair; I see that you have had the same idea.'

'You lied to us, Finnabair,' said Arthur, 'saying that no others had crossed your borders. What else have you lied to us about?'

'I did not lie. I said no strangers had been on our lands. Mawgan is no stranger. He was my brother's friend.'

Mawgan nodded. 'I hope to be your friend as well.'

'I could do with a friend or two,' whispered Finnabair. 'Especially now. I must hold these lands until such time as my brother's child is old enough to take his place. Being older than I, my other brother has ideas of his own.'

'You mean Narcasta,' said Arthur. 'Over my dead body.'

'He would like nothing better than that,' said Finnabair.

She studied Arthur closely, but his face was blank. She had heard many things about the young prince; none of them rang true now that she had her opportunity to see him for herself.

*

Mawgan and Finnabair walked in the garden. It was evening, and the smell of jasmine hung in the air.

'Oh Mawgan, how will we stop them? I do not share the optimism my brothers had. Our world is dying a little more with every passing year. The humans have strong magic and big ideas. How will the old ways survive in their new world with a new king?'

'My lady, you are strong as well. Your magic will not fade, and neither will mine. He is a good man, you know, Arthur. He will make a great king in his time.'

'His father is weak, and the witch Morgawse has taken advantage of that weakness. Now we are left to pick up the pieces.'

'You should know first-hand the burden of a problem unresolved. How long was it that Narcasta was allowed to cause havoc before your brother saw fit to fix it?'

'You do not mince your words, do you, Mawgan?'

'That is the thing with friends. They remind you of your faults as well as your strengths. Speaking of such things, I want to discuss Morwenna and Cadan's daughter.'

'There is nothing to discuss.'

'Not right now, maybe. But you cannot put it off forever. What you are doing is wrong.'

*

In the early evening hours of the following day, the alarm went up. Morgawse and Mordred had crossed over.

CHAPTER THIRTY-ONE

TO STAND WHEN OTHERS FALL

Finnabair sat by a jasmine tree, enjoying the smell of the tiny white flowers carried on the night air. She picked one, absentmindedly twirling it in her fingers, then lifting it to her nose and closing her eyes. She loved this garden. It filled her with a peace she found nowhere else. It was her secret place to be alone.

'My lady.' Arthur stumbled into the tiny space.

Finnabair sighed. 'What is it?'

'Word has come of a sighting. We know where they are.'

'Why all the hurry? They cannot get away. Sit with me.'

Finnabair patted the spot beside her. Arthur sat on the stone bench. It was a squeeze on the small seat, his leg brushed against her robe, and he felt the warmth of it through his clothes. It was unexpected.

'Tell me, Arthur. What do you believe is the greatest quality of a king? Is it nobility perhaps? Or is it lineage?'

'It is neither of those things, my lady,' said Arthur shaking his head. 'Birthright does not guarantee greatness. I believe the quality a king should possess over all others is service.'

Finnabair smiled, surprised by his answer.

'There is more to you than I thought, Arthur Pendragon.'

'I am glad you think so, my lady.'

'Come,' Finnabair got up. 'We have a witch hunt to attend.'

*

'I don't like that talk,' said Simon. 'Not all witches are bad. I've never met anyone kinder than Morwenna.'

Culhwch and Arthur shared a smile.

'Yes, yes,' said Mawgan. 'We know all that. But this is no hedge witch we are dealing with. No, Morgawse is a sorceress, and her powers are extensive. Do not underestimate her or think for one moment she is anything like our dear Morwenna.'

Mawgan patted Simon on the back, nodding before clipping the top of Culhwch's head with his hand. 'I am also concerned about that boy of hers,' Mawgan continued. 'He is strong in the craft too.'

'That does not surprise me,' said Finnabair. 'I have learned that magic amongst humans is passed down the female line. If a mother has it, then her offspring almost always follow.'

Simon looked towards Arthur, who was concentrating on his feet.

So, you are still not owning up to your part in Mordred's lineage.

He was only too familiar with the story of Arthur and Morgawse.

*

On his sixteenth birthday, twelve years earlier, Arthur was given to Sir Kay to be his squire. If you think that sounds important or exciting, it wasn't. Being a squire is about service. Fetch his breakfast, polish his armour, pick the weevils out of his bread.

All these things Arthur did daily and more. And although it doesn't sound pleasant at all, there were some redeeming features to the life. Sir Kay was the consummate soldier. His sword skills were second to none, and he knew his way around a battlefield. As his squire, Arthur trained with him every day, and every day he grew stronger, faster, and more confident. He was a favourite among the other knights, and Sir Kay liked him a great deal, although he would never admit it.

Years before, Sir Kay had been Grand Officer in Gorlois, Duke of Dumnonia's army. The position of Grand Officer was the highest rank for a knight. And at the time, Sir Kay, and anyone who worked for him, enjoyed a particularly enviable lifestyle. That was until Uther Pendragon set eyes on Igraine.

Igraine was Gorlois's wife when Uther fell in love with her. He pursued her with a passion that few could ignore, least of all Gorlois, who took his wife and young daughter Morgawse into hiding.

Keeping Igraine safe from Uther was not easy. Uther was clever and creative.

One night he asked Mawgan, the wizard, to make him look like Goloris. He sent the Duke away to fight a battle in the neighbouring Shire, and while he was gone, he snuck into Igraine's bedroom. Their son Arthur was conceived, and conveniently for Uther, Goloris was killed.

Uther was plagued for many years by the guilt of what he had done. So much so, that when he took Igraine as his wife on the death of her husband, he also brought Morgawse to live with them. He kept her hidden away, and none of the royal household knew who she was.

Igraine gave birth to a son, Arthur, but she died soon afterward, never recovering from the traumatic birth. Uther was devastated. For many years he was unable to forgive Arthur, and sent him away.

Morgawse's bitterness at losing her mother and father grew inside her.

For years Arthur had been kept away from Morgawse; he didn't know who she was when he saw her watching him brush down Sir Kay's horse. Usually, one of the grooms would take care of Jago, but they were all elsewhere today. Sir Kay had ridden him through mud; there was a lot to do.

Morgawse watched as Arthur cleaned out the horse's feet. He was a few years younger than she was but muscular, and he had a friendly face. Arthur smiled at her. Morgawse blushed. Annoyed at herself, she stormed away.

He saw her again later that same evening. She was sitting in the kitchen talking with the cook. A large mixing bowl with the remains of a cake, now baking in the oven, was being meticulously licked clean; the bowl almost swallowed her head. Morgawse's face was splattered with the mixture when she finally emerged, licking her lips luxuriously.

Arthur burst into giggles. Morgawse was mortified, the splatters of the cream-coloured mixture now sharply contrasting with the redness in her cheeks. She ran from the kitchens, the sound of Arthur's laughter ringing in her ears.

CHAPTER THIRTY-TWO

MY SISTER'S SON

Over the following weeks and months, Arthur saw Morgawse more frequently. She had come to live in the castle. The servants talked, and Arthur overheard that she had lived here once before when his mother had been alive. After Igraine's death, she was shipped off to stay with her father's family.

Morgawse intrigued Arthur. Something about her compelled him to find out more, but she remained a mystery, and that made him seek her out at every opportunity. She was pretty, and that in itself was all the incentive Arthur needed.

*

After six months in each other's company, Arthur and Morgawse were inseparable. They ate their meals in the kitchen together. Nobody seemed to care that much, two unwanted strays blown in by the wind.

Morgawse was manipulative; Arthur mistook it for cleverness. She also had magic but hid that from everyone, deciding it was an advantage keeping it a secret. She didn't even let on to Arthur. She was sure he was falling under her spell, and she liked how that felt.

Morgawse decided she would give Arthur a present he would

never forget on the night of his seventeenth birthday.

She had long ago discovered her power.

As a child, she had been ordinary, invisible. Yet in Goloris' household, there lived a sorceress who saw in Morgawse the awakenings of a spirit that might one day avenge her family's misfortune. The sorceress trained and educated Morgawse until the spark of spirit had been fanned into a furnace. With the help of her craft, she made herself beautiful to look at, tall and athletic, a Grecian statue come to life. Morgawse's looks, coupled with her magic, made her an irresistible force. No one had been out of her reach.

Sneaking into Arthur's bed-chamber had been easy, and to her delight, he was no different than all the others. She revelled in her power. Men were so easy to control if you knew how.

As dawn broke and Arthur moved in his sleep, Morgawse slipped away before the rest of the household stirred from their beds, blissfully unaware of what she and Arthur had done.

CHAPTER THIRTY-THREE

THE ONCE AND FUTURE

Later that morning, as Morgawse helped cook in the kitchen, Arthur staggered in for breakfast. He hardly looked at her. He ate then he shuffled out to the stables to begin his day.

It was typical. Morgawse had been treated this way many times. Arthur was embarrassed now and full of regret. It had been different the night before.

Sir Kay was in the stables when Arthur arrived.

'Not today, boy.'

The knight finished saddling Jago and pointed to the horse in the next stall.

'We have somewhere to be.'

Sir Kay and Arthur rode out towards Piddleton Village. As they drew nearer, the knight slowed, and dismounting, he hobbled his horse. Arthur did the same.

Entering a clearing, they walked towards the large standing stone marking the village's outer boundary. As they did so, twelve knights stepped up and took stationary points around the perimeter. Arthur recognised Llwyr and Bors. This was the castle guard.

Why are they here?

Beside the stone stood the wizard. Mawgan beckoned Arthur to stand beside him.

'Yesterday you became a man.'

Arthur blushed and looked at his feet.

'Today, you will take your rightful place as a prince.'

'What?' said Arthur, his embarrassment immediately forgotten.

Mawgan pointed to the stone. As he did so, a haze appeared above it, and in the haze, an object was just visible. The haze cleared, Arthur saw his father's sword buried to the hilt.

Arthur looked at Mawgan in confusion.

'What am I supposed to do now?'

'Take the sword.'

Arthur still looked blankly at Mawgan.

'Get on up there, boy. Grab that thing and pull it clear.'

Arthur clambered up the side of the stone. It was smooth, and he struggled to get a purchase. Mawgan moved behind him. Embarrassed, he gave Arthur a shove, pushing him upwards with both hands on his backside. Eventually, Arthur stood on top of the stone with his hands around the hilt of the sword.

'Pull it boy. Pull as if your life depends on it. It very well might.'

Arthur looked at the hilt in his hands. He wiggled it a little, but it didn't budge. It was stuck fast.

'You must believe, boy,' Mawgan whispered below him. The wizard's eyes pleaded for Arthur to try harder. 'The power comes from inside. Believe you can, and you will.'

Arthur closed his eyes.

He had never felt anything resembling confidence, particularly not in himself. His father despised him for living when his mother had died. So much so that he had sent him away, abandoned and relegated him to the life of a servant.

He had begun to feel he had a place in the world in Sir Kay's service, but even now, after a whole year, Arthur waited for the inevitable end. Nothing good ever lasted.

Arthur tried to push these thoughts aside and focus on the sword.

Believe... Believe... Believe what?

'Believe in who you are,' whispered Mawgan. 'You are for now and all the future to come. The once and always. It was foretold. Take the sword; it is yours and only yours.'

Arthur wrapped his fingers firmly around the hilt, wiggling them, finding his grip. He planted his feet on either side. Closing his eyes once more, he focussed all his intention on the blade. All his past had brought him to this point. Everything that had happened, even the night before, he was here, now because of it.

Arthur forced all his energy, hurt, every feeling that came to him, down his arms and into the blade. When at last he couldn't stand it any longer, he pulled. He pulled with every ounce of being, every fibre of his body. The sword slipped from the stone like a warm knife dragged through butter.

The sword came loose so quickly; it took Arthur entirely by surprise. He stumbled backward off the stone and landed in a crumpled heap on top of a very inconvenienced wizard.

Around them, the shout went up.

'Huzzah! Huzzah!'

Arthur scrambled off Mawgan, quickly righting himself and lifting his prize. Caliburnus sparkled in the morning sun. Arthur laughed and thrust the sword point first into the air.

'Huzzah!'

*

Morgawse cleaned dishes at the sink. Her hands were sore from too much scrubbing at blackened pots.

'The king wants to see you.' The boy dumped another stack of unwashed dishes on the bench beside her. 'I would hurry if I were you. He is as grumpy as a wet cat this morning.'

Morgawse carefully dried her hands. She didn't have the anxious bustle of the other servants. Laying the drying cloth down on the bench, she walked from the room down the corridor and headed towards the dining hall and whatever awaited her there.

'Where have you been?' said Uther. 'I sent for you an hour ago.'

'You exaggerate, sir. It has only been minutes, and I have been about my work, as you well know.'

'You do not fear to defy me, girl. You are as unlike a servant as it is possible to be.'

'You are mistaken, sir. I am completely your servant, as my shredded hands attest.'

'Hmmm. I have heard a disturbing report circulating the castle concerning you and my son.'

'Your son? To my knowledge, you do not have a son.'

'I can assure you, I do. He is in this very castle.'

Morgawse thought for a moment, but no one sprung to mind that could fit the description of a prince.

'I do not know who it could be you are referring to.'

'Arthur!' Morgawse froze. She couldn't even take her next breath. Her mind was racing as the realisation dawned on her.

She wanted to run, anything than be in this room with this man. But she couldn't go until she was excused, so she stood frozen and red-faced, looking at the floor. Uther enjoyed her discomfort.

'You were seen leaving his chamber this morning. What have you got to say about that?' Morgawse was still silent. 'You disgust me. I always knew you to be a witch. Now it is confirmed.'

'I did not know. If I had... I would never... Why were we never told?'

'It was not important you should know you have a brother. You are both on very different paths. I intended to marry you off to some nobleman or other in a few years. You are pretty enough a prize with which to beat any would-be challenger into submission. But I can see now that I must move on the matter sooner than later.'

'I am not your possession.'

'That is exactly what you are. And you will do as you are told. Now get out of my sight. I do not wish to see hide nor hair of you until I have decided what is to be done.'

Morgawse ran from the dining hall, her face flaming and tears free-flowing down her cheeks. Her room was her only sanctuary. She closed the door and pushed a chair-back under the handle to secure it. Leaning back against the wall, Morgawse closed her eyes. Her shame and self-loathing were only diminished by her fear of what the future might hold. Whatever was coming, she probably deserved it.

Uther was right. She was a witch.

The moment the thought was in her head, it was too late. She had pushed it down somewhere inside, determined it would not show. But it was no good.

The chair lifted itself from under the door handle and flew across the room, shattering against the opposite wall. Morgawse hadn't realised how strong it had become. She only need to think a thing now for it to happen. There was a strange satisfaction in knowing something that no one else knew. And no one else knew she had magic.

*

Arthur and the castle guard rode through the gates in triumph. He held the sword high as the servants and other workers cheered them on. Reaching the stables, they dismounted and headed to the great hall. Uther was in his chair. His face all lines, and his eyes were so dark they looked like holes in his face.

'Look Father, the sword has come to me.'

'So I see.'

Mawgan positioned himself next to Arthur. 'The boy is correct Uther. He is your heir. It is time.'

'Time for what? He is a child. The kingdom needs leadership from someone who has reached the age of reason.

'It is time to begin Arthur's preparation. I agree, he has a great deal to learn, but he will not do that, mucking out stables and cleaning armour. You must take him back.' Uther looked like a balloon that recently had all the air squeezed out of it. Being with Arthur reminded him of his own weaknesses; he did not want him close.

Mawgan stepped up to the great chair and leaned into Uther.

'You must do this, Sire. What the kingdom needs is stability. The line of succession must be preserved, and you do not get any younger.'

Uther looked down at his wrinkled hand. The rough skin reminded him of his own father's. He did not feel that these hands should belong to him. He frowned.

'We all must face our mortality, Sire. You are a great king, but you are also a man and cannot live forever. You must prepare the boy for what comes next.'

Nodding, Uther beckoned Arthur forward to stand beside him. The weight of the sword made Arthur stumble as he climbed up to his father. Uther smiled.

'You still have some growing to do.'

'Father, I am seventeen and over six feet tall. A good half foot taller than you ever were, even in your prime. The sword is heavy, and I am unused to such a cumbersome weapon. That is all.'

Uther thought for a moment. Then a smile spread across his weathered face as he saw his next move.

'Your sister was in the castle today.'

'Sister? I have no sister that I know of.'

'Of course you do, boy. Morgawse. She is your mother's daughter from her marriage to Goloris.'

Uther kept his face inscrutable as his eyes held Arthur's. He still had power here, and that pleased him.

The realisation of what they had done flickered like a broken lightbulb in Arthur's mind. The more he thought about it, the more inconceivable he found the idea. Morgawse, his sister? It couldn't be true.

'Arthur. Are you alright?'

Mawgan put his hand on his shoulder. But Arthur shrugged him off. 'Why didn't you tell me?'

'Arthur... I...'

'Do not bother to think of a suitable lie. I will not fall for them again.'

With that, Arthur threw the sword down onto the platform before leaving the room. All the while, Uther smiled. He bent and picked up the sword, hiding it in his robes.

*

Three months later, Morgawse sat on the bed, hands resting on her growing belly. The serving girl she shared her room with bustled in.

'The king wants you. 'E's in the throne room.'

Morgawse stood, smoothed down her dress, and left. She would not be able to keep the baby a secret for much longer.

On entering the throne room, she noticed the king had company. The two men were talking, but stopped when she entered. On seeing her, the stranger nodded, satisfied.

'She iz prettier than I expected Uther. I accept your offer. Her dowry will be welcome.'

Morgawse looked at Uther.

So, he has sold me.

'There are conditions, Lot. You will not move against me or the south lands. Do I have your word on that?'

Lot thought for a moment. Studying Morgawse once more, he

thrust his hand at Uther, and the men shook on the deal.

I am a bribe.

'Morgawse, go and pack. You leave tomorrow.'

*

The next day Morgawse left with the party from Orkney. Arthur watched from a window, unobserved. He had not seen her in months, and now she would be gone from his life and with her, he hoped, the guilt he had carried since the morning he discovered who they were.

Arthur had kept away from everyone who reminded him of that day. He continued in Sir Kay's service, even though the knight insisted that a prince should not. Caliburnus, his sword, his inheritance, was nowhere to be found.

*

Although Simon knew Arthur's story, he would never admit as much to him. Arthur must never know. The temptation to tell him information about his future would be too great. Besides, Simon had promised.

*

Two sentries stood under a yew tree listening. It was the smallest of sounds, but there it was again... and there, again. It wasn't a natural forest sound, so it could only mean that it was made by something or someone.

The two Fae pushed their backs into the old trunk, melting into it. Bark grew across their bodies and faces until they became part of the tree. All that remained visible were four amber eyes following the travellers as they passed.

Morgawse wore a dark cloak, the hood drawn up, covering her head and face. The boy walked awkwardly beside her. Unused to his adolescent body, he stumbled, falling over his feet. His mother tutted.

'Be more careful Mordred,' she whispered. 'You will give us away. These trees have ears and eyes.'

She couldn't be more right. As soon as Morgawse and Mordred had passed, the Fae extracted themselves from the tree and with metamorphic precision, changed into a pair of tawny owls, flying off in the direction of the palace.

On the arrival of the sentries, the palace inhabitants flew into a fluster of activity. Humans and Fae rushed here and there, giving and following orders and instructions, until the whole place broke down into a chaotic mess.

'Enough!'

Finnabair's voice rang out through the halls and rooms. Everyone stopped, not making another movement or sound.

'I will have order,' Finnabair continued, 'We will not dissolve into disharmony. Captains of the Guard, I will see you in the great hall. We shall have a plan to deal with this witch before the hour turns.'

Mawgan had been in the hall before. The last time, the ceiling had cracked and fallen in a magical earthquake, engineered to frighten unwanted guests. Now the hall was serene. A cloudless sky soared above them in the vaulted ceiling space. Birds spun and somersaulted over their heads, alive in a biosphere confined to the boundaries of the room.

'This is amazing,' said Simon.

'You have not seen what it can do when it does not want you here,' Mawgan replied. 'It can conjure up a storm to frighten the stoutest of hearts.'

Finnabair seated herself on the chaise in the centre of the room.

Her guard positioned themselves around the perimeter, and the others found space to sit where they could.

'Mistress, they are well within our borders now,' the Fae sentry confirmed. 'They are moving quickly northwards. The boy slows their progress, giving us some time to act, but not much. They will be at our northern border by the end of the tomorrow.'

'Yes,' said Finnabair. 'And if they reach it, they will be lost to us. We cannot venture onto the hinterlands.'

'Why?' asked Simon.

'Trolls.' Mawgan shook as he spoke. 'They are spawned by hate and fed on greed. Alongside the imps, they roam over the hinterlands, destroying anything that crosses their path.'

'And she is choosing to go there?' said Simon. 'She must be desperate. No one in their right mind would take their child to a place like that.'

'There you have it,' said Mawgan. 'Morgawse does not have a right mind. Not as we would think it.'

'Yes,' said Finnabair. 'Who knows what she would do or risk. We must intercept her and the boy immediately. Sentries, where were they last seen?'

'Just south of the castle, half an hour past.'

The palace broke into a frenzy again; the Fae moved as one this time. A murmuration of coordinated orderliness. It was incredible to watch.

Arthur, Culhwch, Simon, and Mawgan were swept along. In a jiffy, they were all outside, heading in the direction of the last sighting.

'It strikes me,' said Culhwch. 'We would be better served searching a little closer to the palace. She will have to pass this way. The other paths are too difficult for a child.'

'The Fae know what they are doing,' said Arthur.

They were moving faster now.

'Come, we are being left behind.'

'Arthur,' said Simon. 'Culhwch's right. It's pointless rushing off to try and catch them. We should stay here. Let them come to us.'

'Wise council again, Simon,' said Mawgan. 'We cannot go as fast as the Fae, anyway. With any luck, they will drive the witch and the boy right to us.'

The party watched the hunters disappear into the woods. Many changed their form as they ran. Birds and animals scattered in amongst the trees, silent and invisible.

'Yes, you are right.'

Arthur looked at the other men and the wizard.

'I know what I must do. You three go back into the palace. It is me she wants. If I am out of the way, she can finish what she started.'

'We won't leave you,' said Simon.

'You must. It is the only way. She must believe I am alone. If I am vulnerable, Morgawse will not be able to help herself. She is arrogant, and her overconfidence will be her mistake. This is when you will attack. Mawgan, can you do it?'

'She is strong, but I can.'

'Wait for my signal,' said Arthur. 'Then take her.'

'And the boy?'

They all turned to look at Culhwch.

'You can leave the boy to me,' said Simon. 'I'm sure I can manage a child.'

They left Arthur on the path in the trees. It was no more than a hundred feet from there to the palace's outer wall. Hiding behind the iron gates where tiny grotesques clambered up and down metal vines, spitting and pulling faces.

'I don't like this at all,' said Simon. 'We can't see him from here.'

'Maybe you cannot,' said Mawgan. 'I see him clearly.'

Seconds seemed to last for hours. The woods were quiet. Any movement sounded like thunder as it echoed off tree trunks and buildings. Two hours passed, nothing stirred. Simon could no longer feel his toes as he crouched behind the gate. A little grotesque spat, and a tiny iron ball pinged off his nose. He screwed up his face and bit his lip silently. Even that had Mawgan putting a finger up to his mouth.

*

A twig snapped as Mordred's foot touched it. His mother swung around, scowling. He cowered slightly, waiting for a blow, but it didn't come. He opened his eyes, expecting to see his mother leaning over him, but she looked at something further along the path. Mordred moved to get a better look himself. It was a man.

His mother's face was set, contorted in a painful grin. He had seen that look on her face before. It made him afraid. He took a better look at who stood ahead of them.

I know you, Arthur Pendragon.

He looked at his mother again. She was statuesque, more still than a lead block. The only part of her that moved was a shadow behind her eyes. It hazed its way across the cornea. Mordred caught it for a second, then it was gone, and she sprang into life.

Morgawse was suddenly behind Arthur. She had him pinned and tied in an eye blink. Her left hand cupped his chin as her right held the wand to his head. Arthur's knees buckled and hit the ground hard.

'What are you doing here?' she spat into his face. 'You fool! Do you think you can challenge me? You are just a man.'

'That I may be, lady,' said Arthur. 'But he is not.'

Morgawse swung around, but she wasn't quick enough. Mawgan snatched the wand out of her hand. It disintegrated, falling in a cloud of black dust before scattering on the breeze. Her arms snapped to her sides, and her feet slid out from under her until she was floating on her side a few feet above the ground. With a flick of

Mawgan's wand, Morgawse spun mid-air as a silver rope bound her from neck to toe.

'Go!' she screamed. Mordred turned and ran.

Simon raced down the track with Culhwch. Mordred was fast for a child, and Simon wondered if he was channelling some magical power, as the faster they ran, the faster he went.

'It is hopeless,' said Culhwch slowing. 'We are losing him.'

He drew his bow and sent an arrow down the path. It never reached its target. Mordred smashed it into a million splinters without turning or slowing his pace.

'We can't let him get away,' said Simon.

They ran on. Eventually, Culhwch grabbed Simon's arm and pulled him to a stop.

'That is it. No further,' he said.

'Why?'

'We are at the northern border.' An axe whistled past Simon's ear and embedded itself in the tree next to them. Then another.

'Get down!' Culhwch pulled Simon onto his knees next to him. 'Trolls,' he explained, expression grim.

'I don't see anything,' said Simon.

'You will.'

Simon scanned the bare scrubland ahead of them. Nothing moved. Thwack!

Another axe hit the tree behind them.

A shape moved ahead; a distortion in the air, the same as its surroundings, but different.

'You have it. I can see that you do,' said Culhwch. 'That is a troll, my friend.'

'They're invisible.'

'Not invisible, but they do take on the essence of their surroundings.' Culhwch put an arrow to his bow and pulled back, letting it fly at the troll. The arrow sank into soft flesh. Black blood oozed out of the place where the arrow struck and ran across an arm, leg, and some torso, revealing the shape of the injured troll as it staggered about, clutching its shoulder.

'There,' said Culhwch. 'See.'

The troll ran off across the scrubland, howling.

*

Lot waited just out of the woods and out of sight. He would not cross onto the Fae lands. It was forbidden. Mordred ran towards him. He smiled at his son clambering onto a horse.

'Where iz ya mother?' said Lot.

He looked back down the path but could only see the two men and the trolls he had sent, allowing Mordred to make his escape.

'They have her,' said Mordred, hanging his head. 'She will be in a Fae cell by now.'

Lot made three clicks on the roof of his mouth and shook his head.

'She iz losing her touch. I dinna have the stomach for battle today. A few weeks enjoying the hospitality of our faery friends will soften her, I am sure.' Lot turned his horse to stand directly in Simon's and Culhwch's path. 'Anotha time perhaps,' he shouted, turning his horse north again. 'When I can be bothered with the effort of it.'

They rode away.

CHAPTER THIRTY-FOUR

THE CALL OF HOME

The cell walls dripped with a lime green ooze that smelt of age and prisoners long forgotten.

Morgawse licked at the moist drips. Since being thrown into the cramped space, she had been offered nothing to drink or eat. She was sure it was over a day now, and thirst made her mind fizz and her muscles ache.

'I need a drink,' she shouted at the walls. Unsure if anyone was listening.

Morgawse got up and grasped the bars at the entrance to the cell, rattling them back and forth.

'Listen to me!' she shouted into the darkness.

A door opened somewhere above her, and she heard footsteps descending. They were light and soft.

A woman is coming.

A brightness flickered at the end of the long corridor leading to the cell. As her eyes grew accustomed, Morgawse could see Finnabair coming towards her. She carried a lantern in one hand and a tray in the other. On reaching the cell, Finnabair slid the tray of bread and water under the bars and into Morgawse's hands who gulped at the water.

'Slowly,' said Finnabair. 'You will choke if you drink like that.'

'What do you care? It was you threw me in here. Starved me half to death. Left me nothing to drink this whole day. Is that how you treat your guests?'

'Guests are invited. You were not. It interests me that you have the bare-faced gall to show yourself in these parts at all, given our current state of war with your husband.'

'My husband's wars are none of my business and therefore none of my concern.'

Morgawse stuffed a large chunk of bread into her mouth. Chomping down hard on it, her cheeks puffed out like a squirrel's. Finnabair smiled. She would have to watch herself. This witch was tenacious, much like herself. Their similarities were not lost on either, there in the semi-darkness.

'You realise, I think, that we cannot allow you to leave.'

'Then what is to become of me?'

'That is up to you. Being a prisoner here can be easy, or it can be hard. The choice is entirely yours.'

'And if I choose not to be here at all?'

'Then you will stay in this cell until you wither away, and your bones join with the dust that formed them. Time is of no consequence to us. But for you, a human woman, time must be the gravest of all opponents.'

'And a welcome friend. The greatest of all friends. I am sorry for you.'

Finnabair leaned her head to one side.

'Why?'

'Because you will never know the joy of things passing and the peace of endings. You roll on through ages, seeing all and feeling nothing. What a dull existence that must be. It is no wonder your brother Cadan sought a different life with a human. Even if it was brief by your standards, at least he had one.'

Finnabair turned away for a moment.

I must be careful. This witch sees. She must not know how right she is.

The Faery got up from the stone floor and walked away. 'The choice is yours,' she shouted back into the darkness. 'Choose wisely.'

*

'Are you ready, Darcy?' Glewas stood at the bottom of the hall stairs, peering up at the landing.

Morwenna walked out of the tiny living room. 'Is she coming? We will miss the whole thing if we do not leave soon.'

Darcy looked around the bedroom one last time. She had everything packed in her backpack. 'I'm coming,' she called down, turning for one last look.

'You are welcome back any time, you know that, right?' said Morwenna as Darcy joined them. 'Just do not leave it so long next time between visits.'

Darcy, Nix, Hicca, Glewas and Morwenna headed outside. The village was quiet at this time of day. The pub and the church closed, shutters latched, and curtains drawn. The clock striking the sixth hour, reminding them how early it was.

'It's times like this I could do with a pixie lift,' said Darcy.

'Stuff 'n nonsense,' said Nix. 'The walk'll do 'ee good. 'Ee's been cooped up in the house fer days.'

'It was worth it though, wasn't it?' said Darcy, looking at Morwenna. 'She's much better.'

'Yes, darlin' girl, that she is. Somethin's changed in her, and it is good to see.'

Nix was right. Darcy could pinpoint the exact time it happened. The air in the cottage sweetened. It felt like a great weight had lifted off them all. Every action was easier. Standing, sitting, walking, they all felt lighter, free. The most noticeable change happened in Morwenna herself. Darcy saw the grey pallor lift from her skin and the deathly tiredness fade. Nobody in the house knew why, but they had each embraced it for what it was.

It would take a good few hours to walk to Tintagel. They moved at a comfortable pace to not get too hot and sweaty. Nobody wanted to arrive for the wedding in a hot mess. Darcy had walked this track twice before. As they passed the turnip field, she couldn't resist peering over the hedge; knowing Kea wouldn't be there, she looked nevertheless and drew back disappointed.

'I always feel the same passing this spot,' said Glewas. 'He was a good friend.'

'Yes,' said Darcy. 'He was.'

Nobody spoke for a while. A respectful silence, each caught in their remembrances. Glewas slipped his fingers through Darcy's. His hand was warm and soft. It felt like an extension of her own; his closeness, more than comforting, was now necessary to her.

She was overcome by a sadness that had been creeping up on her. Darcy knew she would be leaving soon. She had felt that this journey was coming to an end for some time. Home was calling through the gateway, and inevitably she was drawn towards it and to when she and Glewas would say goodbye again.

They fell into step. Glewas conscious that what troubled Darcy was more than just the missing of friends departed. But he had a plan.

CHAPTER THIRTY-FIVE

THE WEDDING

The castle was strewn from turret to cellar in white flowers, delicate as snowflakes; they hung in chains from almost every surface. Servants scurried through the rooms fetching and carrying and depositing guests, hoping everyone was where they were supposed to be.

Olwen oversaw it all. She had waited for Culhwch to return, and two days earlier, he had, along with Arthur, Simon, and Mawgan. And most unexpectedly, the Fae queen Finnabair herself.

Olwen stood now in her suite; a young girl tied the laces on her calico bodice, embroidered with a delicate buttercup design that continued down the skirt in little falls of the tiny yellow flowers. The creamy fabric laying in folds from Olwen's waist, right to the floor. It was the most beautiful of dresses, fit for the daughter of a king on her wedding day. Olwen's wheat coloured hair was dressed around her oval face. The girl swept a couple of escaping tendrils back and secured them with a pin before lifting the flaxen veil and draping it over Olwen's fair head.

'You look beautiful, my lady.'

Olwen examined herself in the dressing mirror.

'I will do, I suppose,' she said, twirling on her toes.

The serving girl giggled as she picked up the remaining clothes from the floor and scurried from the room.

'Alright. Time for the show,' said Olwen to her reflection.

*

Darcy, Glewas, Nix, Hicca, and Morwenna walked through the castle gates. Darcy shivered.

'It's fine, darlin' girl,' said Nix. 'He's not 'ere.'

Darcy could still feel the chill of the cell she was held in when Narcasta had imprisoned her. There were times, even when she was back home, where she would feel the walls closing in around her, and for a moment, she would be back, huddled in a corner, trying to keep warm.

Nix was right though; Narcasta was gone. Instead, Simon was running towards her.

'I missed you,' said Darcy.

'You look amazing,' he said. Stepping back to admire the dress she and Morwenna had spent several hours altering for the occasion.

'So do you.'

Simon wore a blue tunic with matching breeches. A sword was belted at his waist and his long legs were encased in black boots polished to a shine.

'Very medieval.'

'Why, thank you, my lady.'

Simon bowed affectedly. He looked at Morwenna out of the corner of his eye. Darcy caught it.

'She's much better,' she said. 'Much more herself the last few days.'

'Really? That's odd. It could just be a coincidence.'

'What?'

'Oh, you'll see.' Simon took Darcy's hand and led her away from the crowded reception hall. Darcy remembered how rambling the castle was. Corridors led off corridors, rooms off rooms. It was very disorientating. When they finally arrived at a small wooden door, she was almost dizzy. Turning the handle, they went inside.

'What are we doing here?' Darcy asked.

They stood in a nursery. A breeze lifted the thin linen hanging over the window, which was open a crack to let in the fresh air. Under the window was a crib. A baby stirred as the breeze passed over. Darcy looked in. The baby was only a few weeks old, but she was unmistakable.

'Is this who I think it is?' Darcy ran her hand over the soft fuzzy head, as dark as her mother's.

'Finnabair has brought Cadeyn back to her mother,' said Simon.

'This is your doing, isn't it?'

'She took some convincing, but in the end, she saw sense. The little girl belongs with her mum. We persuaded Finnabair of that a couple of days ago.'

'That's the same time Morwenna started to get better.'

'I thought as much. It's good to see. Let's get her.'

Darcy ran into the reception hall, scanning in all directions for Morwenna. There she was, standing head and shoulders above Mawgan in conversation.

'You need to come with me. Sorry Mawgan...'

'I will recover, I am sure.' He smiled and winked at Darcy.

*

Morwenna cried silent tears as she held Cadeyn to her, kissing her soft head. She reached and took Simon's hand. Kissing it, her tears running over his skin.

'I do not know how to thank you,' she said.

'You don't need to do anything. Seeing you happy is enough,' he said.

Morwenna released his hand again and stroked Cadeyn's soft head once more. 'I had forgotten how beautiful you are,' she said to her.

Simon looked at Morwenna holding her daughter.

So had I.

*

The chapel ceiling was groin-vaulted, like many great churches Darcy knew well. As she sat in her pew next to Simon and Morwenna, she leaned back, lost in the space above, and was suddenly thinking of her parents. They had dragged her around so many places like this one over the years. She suddenly felt the pain in her chest. It was the first time since coming here that she had. She knew then that it was almost time.

The musicians played a delicate melody, and the congregation turned. They had all come: kings and knights sprinkled amongst servants, Fae, pixies, and country folk. All alike and caught up in the beauty of it. Custennin's wife, who was now unrecognisable from the pitiful creature she had been and Gorau, with Peter and Gwen, Finnabair, even the flax weavers from the islands, and the brothers' Dôn.

Arthur and Culhwch turned from the altar to look back along the aisle as the great doors opened once more to let in Olwen on Custennin's arm. Uther still being very unwell and confined to his bed.

The crowd sighed collectively as Olwen reached the alter and Custennin placed her hand in Culhwch's.

'There you go, lass,' he said, kissing her on the forehead and stepping away.

Culhwch kissed Olwen's hand.

'Ready?'

She looked down into his face and nodded.

'Yes.'

CHAPTER THIRTY-SIX

THE CHOICE

The wedding feast was a sumptuous affair. The Braggart flowed freely, Culhwch and Olwen sharing from Llwyr's cup, enjoying the guests' company as they received well wishes and gifts. Looking across the hall, Culhwch saw his cousin watching them. Arthur smiled and nodded, and Culhwch lifted the cup in a silent toast to his best man.

Arthur turned to Simon sitting next to him.

'Well, that has done it, I suppose. What will we fill our days with now?'

'I don't expect your days are dull, Arthur. A prince must have a lot of responsibilities.'

'Some, but they never seem enough. I am constantly waiting.'

'That won't always be the case. You will be king.'

'Yes, but for that to happen, I must first lose my father. It is the oddest conundrum, longing for the day and yet dreading it.'

'You feel like that even though Uther mistreats you?'

'I cannot blame him. I am a reminder of his mortality. My purpose is to succeed him, and my job is to be better. It is not a good foundation on which to build a loving relationship.'

Simon thought about his parents. They had divorced when he was young. Leaving home as soon as he could, for college and then university, he only saw his mother occasionally, his visits strained and less frequent in the last few years. He never saw his father. Simon understood those feelings very well.

'What will you do then?'

Arthur stared at the empty glass in front of him.

'Tonight, I will drink. The rest can wait.'

Simon filled Arthur's glass again from the pitcher on the table.

'Cheers,' he said.

Arthur's eyebrows drew together.

'I have not heard that before. What does it mean?'

'Good health and happiness.'

Arthur nodded, raising his glass.

'Cheers.'

*

'Darcy, have you seen Arthur?'

Simon walked into the hall where Darcy was eating breakfast. It was a little past midday. She rubbed at her temples, her eyes were closed, and the furrows across her forehead deepened as her frown strengthened.

'Do you have to be so loud?'

'Oh. Ha ha. Feeling a little delicate today, are we?'

'Don't. I'm never drinking again.'

Yeah, I've heard that before.'

'I've not seen Arthur since last night.'

Darcy rubbed her head again. A bottle slid towards her across the table. Sitting opposite, Morwenna smiled. 'Drink it; you will feel better.'

'What is it?'

'Feverfew tea. It is good for hangovers.'

'I don't have a hangover.'

'Really? Then I must be imagining the look of pain on your face.'

Darcy smiled despite herself. She picked up the bottle and drank. 'Yuck! That's awful.'

'I said it was good for your sore head; I never said it would taste good.' Morwenna turned her attention to Simon. 'Arthur is in the stables. Walk there with me. I have something to discuss with you.'

As he left the table, Simon looked back at Darcy. She had the most extraordinary look on her face. He couldn't read it, but he felt his heart squeeze. He didn't enjoy the sensation at all.

'What do you want to talk about?'

Simon and Morwenna crossed the courtyard; their footfalls seemed very loud in the deserted space. Simon stopped. The quiet felt easier somehow, safer.

Morwenna went to speak but stopped herself before the words came. She tried again.

'I am just going to come straight out and say it. You cannot leave Arthur.'

Simon frowned.

'Why not?'

'Because if you do Teithiwr, he will never be king.'

Simon grabbed her wrist. 'Where did you hear that name?' She snatched her hand back, but he persisted with his questioning. 'Arthur's the only one who calls me that.'

'You are wrong, Simon.'

He frowned.

'Arthur is not the only one. Fellow travellers often recognise it in each other.'

'Recognise what?'

'They see the wanderlust. Darcy saw it in Jenna. They did not meet by accident. She also saw it in you. That is why you were drawn to her.'

'No, you're wrong there. Darcy always says I remind her of a guy she knew. Kea.'

'Is that what you think? Yes, you look like Kea, but it is far more than that. You and Darcy are fellow travellers. You recognised it in each other that first summer. The year after her journey into Dumnonia. You knew what you were doing when you stole her compass from the dig storage at Tintagel. You also knew it when you joined the Well dig to be near her and when you bought the extra ticket to the festival. Everything you have done that you thought was to be near Darcy was actually to get you here.'

'How do you know this?'

'Because my sister is not the only one who sees.' Morwenna's eyes suddenly had tears.

'You knew he was going to die, didn't you?'

'What do you mean?'

'When Cadan left you to help Culhwch and Arthur. You knew he wouldn't be coming back.'

'The gift of foresight is often a heavy burden to carry.'

'Why didn't you stop him?'

'Even if you see the future, you cannot change it. Nothing can.'

'So, what do you see in my future?'

'I cannot tell you that. It would be very wrong of me.'

'Darcy sees. She dreams things.'

'Yes. She is getting better at it too.'

'Pity she didn't see this coming.'

'We often do not see things closest to us. But you are wrong again. Darcy knows you are not going back.'

'She hasn't said anything.'

'Just because she knows, does not mean she is ready to face it.'

*

Arthur brushed his horse, enjoying the simpleness of the task. He could lose himself in it and often had done. He found he didn't need to think while he brushed. All stresses melted away. It was him and the horse.

Footfalls sounded behind him, and he turned.

'We've been looking for you,' said Simon.

'I have not been hiding. Any of the servants could have told you where I would be.' There was an edge to Arthur's voice that Simon understood. He had felt fear often enough to recognise it in others.

'What are you afraid of, Arthur?'

He didn't answer. Turning instead to the horse again.

Morwenna put her hand on Arthur's back. 'What is wrong?'

'Culhwch leaves with Olwen tomorrow.'

Now Simon understood. 'You can do this, Arthur,' he said. 'You are not alone.'

'Then why do I feel this is always the case? I am surrounded by people; nobility, servants, knights. All of them constantly my shadow, none of them ever my friend. Truly, I am very much alone.'

'I am not a servant or a knight, and I'm certainly not noble. I don't need anything from you, and I probably don't have any useful skills to contribute. But I can be a friend.'

'You do not belong here, Simon.'

'Not yet, but I choose to.'

'You have decided then?' said Morwenna.

He nodded. 'I'm staying.'

CHAPTER THIRTY-SEVEN

THE DECISION

Darcy woke just as the first light trickled through the windows of her room. She stretched and sat up. Glewas stirred in his sleep next to her. She bent and kissed his head before slipping out of bed and walking over to the window.

Below, Simon and Arthur were in the yard talking.

Why does that make me feel uncomfortable?

'Darcy, are you well? It is very early to be up.'

Glewas rubbed at his eyes. 'It's okay, go back to sleep. I'm fine.'

By the time Darcy had pulled on some clothes and walked to the door, Glewas was asleep again, snoring softly. He hadn't left her side, always her protector, her friend, and she loved him. But there was something she needed to do alone.

Darcy closed the door quietly behind her and made her way out into the courtyard. Simon was still there cleaning a bridle; he was now alone.

Good, this is my chance.

'Hey, Simon, can I speak to you for a moment?'

'What, no Glewas? I thought you two were surgically joined now.'

'Ha ha, you're so funny. He's still asleep, so I thought it would be a good time for us to have a chat.'

'Oh yeah, what about?' Simon rubbed at the bridle in his hand.

'About why you've been avoiding me. You can't even look at me, can you?'

Simon looked up. 'I can look at you just fine, Darcy.' He put the bridle down and sat on the side of the water trough. 'But I need to tell you something,' he said. 'I've been putting it off, not avoiding you, exactly, just waiting for the right moment, but I don't think there is such a thing.'

'What is it?'

'I think you might already know.'

Darcy looked into his eyes. There it was. She had seen that faraway look before. Then it had been just that, far away, hidden at the back. He was always somewhere else in that look. In a different place, until now.

'You're not coming back. Are you?'

'No... Arthur needs me. I don't know what good it will do, but I'll give it my best.'

*

Darcy ran into the room and shut the door behind her, leaning against it, her eyes closed to stop the tears.

'What is it? What is wrong?'

Glewas was by her side in an instant. He took her hand.

'Simon's just told me he's staying. He's not going back with me.'

Glewas dropped his gaze to the floor.

'You knew?' Darcy's face crumpled.

'I have had my suspicions. Simon and Arthur are inseparable. He is his right arm, Culhwch, his left.'

'Culhwch is leaving.'

'Yes, he has a life to return to and a new one to forge with Olwen at his side. Together, they make a strong alliance. One that Arthur will need in the coming years.'

'Simon has another life too. Back on the other side of the gateway. What about that?'

'What about it? Was it a life that made him happy?'

Darcy deflated. 'No. He hasn't been happy for some time. I think that's why he was so keen to follow me here. He needed an adventure.'

'Yes. He has been searching for his place. We all need to find that, and it is not always a simple thing. Many search long years before they come across it; others never do. But for a few of us, we are lucky enough to recognise it when we stumble over it.'

'I will miss him.'

'Yes... but let his happiness lessen your sadness. He has found where he belongs.' Glewas wiped a tear from her cheek with his finger.

'It's not just Simon I'm sad about.' Darcy looked up into his face. His deep brown eyes were full of love for her. 'I need to go home. So many weeks have gone by. I'm sure I'll have been missed by now. My parents will be going out of their minds.'

Glewas nodded. 'Yes. I understand.' He stepped around her and walked out of the room. The time had come, and she was left alone in her sadness.

CHAPTER THIRTY-EIGHT

RE-ENTRY

Glewas made a beeline for Mawgan in the great hall. He was sitting at the window, puffing on his pipe, lost in thought. Mawgan turned to him, sensing his arrival.

'Ah! There you are my young friend.' The old wizard's eyebrows drew together. 'What is the matter? You look as if the world rested on your shoulders.'

'I have something to discuss with you, and it is not an easy thing.'

*

Simon sat alone eating lunch, his mind elsewhere. Arthur had made himself scarce.

'May I sit?' Morwenna carried a plateful of sandwiches. She plopped it down on the table, not waiting for him to answer.

'I suppose you will anyway,' said Simon.

She tucked into a lettuce and cucumber doorstop with all the grace of a starving hog.

'Hungry?'

'Mmm.' Morwenna swallowed hard. 'Darcy came to see me today. You have told her.'

'Yes?'

248

'You do know how to release a cat into the birdhouse, do you not?'

'Are you pleased I'm staying?'

Morwenna stopped eating. 'Yes. You know, I think you will be good for Arthur.'

'And for you, my lady?'

'Only time will tell.'

They smiled at each other before both looking away.

'I am worried about Darcy, though,' said Simon, changing the subject.

'I do not think you will need worry for long.' Morwenna took another bite of her sandwich. 'Mmm, this is so good.'

'What do you mean?' Simon put down his knife and fork.

'I only mean she will be fine. Once she is safely back through the gateway, she will quickly forget about us, about you.'

'You think so?'

'No. But I think that life makes us carry on. Our losses, put to one side in order to live. It is life itself that carries us, that, and others.' A servant brought Cadeyn and laid her in Morwenna's arms. The baby fussed and snuffled. 'Someone is hungry again, I see.'

'Yes, mistress. She is past settlin'; she needs you.'

Morwenna undid the buttons on her shift. 'Stop your worrying, Simon,' said Morwenna. Cadeyn attaching hungrily to her breast. 'Things will be right. You will see.'

*

Darcy was packing. Her rucksack had seen better days; it was now threadbare in a couple of places. She poked a finger through the outer layer.

It's worse than a sieve.

Folding her clothes, she pushed them inside, along with the bottle containing the rest of Morwenna's feverfew tea concoction, and some money Simon had given her from his wallet.

He had no use for it now.

And her compass.

She had worn it up until this point. Checking it this morning, she was certain she knew where that gateway was. This time there was no mystery. The gateway hadn't moved. It was at the Tor, and that was where she was going.

This time there would be no long goodbyes either. Darcy didn't think she would be able to leave if there were. She was going to slip away by herself, and in a couple of days, she would be back home.

She was zipping up the bag as Glewas walked in.

'What are you doing?'

'Leaving. It's time I went home. There is nothing more for me to do here.'

'You were going without saying goodbye?'

'I thought it would be easier that way.'

'Easier? Do you think anything could make this less hard?' Darcy shook her head. Her red hair fell softly over her eyes. Glewas brushed it to one side, along with a tear that made its way down her face. 'Then do not say it.' Glewas smiled at her. 'Not to me anyway. There is no reason to.'

'What are you talking about?'

'I have been speaking with Mawgan, and he is all for it.'

'All for what, Glewas? What's going on?'

'I am coming with you. It is all agreed and organised.'

'Don't I have a say in it?' Her voice quivered slightly.

'Yes... but not today. It is my decision, and I have made it. You cannot change my mind. Come on, dry your tears. This is not an ending, not today.'

On walking into the great hall, Darcy's worst fears were realised. So many of her friends had gathered. Mawgan, Nix, and Hicca. Morwenna, Culhwch, Olwen and Arthur. Finnabair and her Fae guards. Little Gorau with Gwen and Peter. Even Uther, whose health had improved.

Darcy scanned along the line of smiling faces until her eyes settled on Simon. His curly mop of brown hair was long now and stuck out over the collar of his shirt. He had ditched his modern clothes in favour of a more medieval style. He looked good, but to her, he would always appear in her memories dressed in a hoodie and jeans. That's how she remembers him.

'I don't know what to say,' said Darcy, and she burst into tears.

*

They walked along the clifftop hand in hand.

'You look uncomfortable,' said Darcy.

Realising that he now had little use for his modern clothes, Simon had donated them to Glewas. Conveniently, they were about the same height and build. Glewas had never worn a hoodie before and had zipped it right up to his chin. Darcy loosened it.

'Relax,' she said.

'I feel all trussed up like a yule bird.'

'Well, you look fine to me. I like your hair.' He had tied his dreads back with a large band.

'I have seen you do it many times. I thought it would help me to blend in.'

'Don't worry about blending in. You'll do just fine.'

*

They spent the night camping in the woods. It would take a couple of days to make the journey from Tintagel to the Tor on foot. Although Darcy was eager to be home, they were not really in any hurry. Another couple of nights alone together under the stars, before all the questions and interrogations, was a welcome breath before the dive.

Their campfire spluttered occasionally, and little puffs of ash would rise upwards into the tree canopy and on into the sky. The only light was from the fire and the moon. It was a night that would be indelibly inked into Darcy's memory for long years, to be treasured like a fine jewel.

The next day, the rain started. At first, it wasn't too bad, light, and only short showery bursts. But as the day wore on, it settled in. It came down in big drops that found their way into everything.

They built a makeshift shelter from tree branches and canvas that evening and hung their clothes to dry the best they could. In the morning, they had their first sighting of the Tor. By midday, they were at the top staring into the hazy void that stood between them and the Tor of Darcy's home.

'Are you ready?' said Darcy.

Glewas turned the wand in his pocket around his fingers. A tiny bead of sweat appeared on his forehead.

'Are you sure you want to do this?'

'I've never been more sure of anything in my life.'

Darcy smiled

'You used a contraction.'

'A what?'

'When you combine two words into one. I've never heard you do that before.'

'I'm preparing myself for a modern life.'

They stepped up to the void. Darcy felt the first pull drawing her through.

'Just close your eyes and step forward. That's how I do it.'

Glewas slipped his hand into Darcy's, closed his eyes, and stepped.

CHAPTER THIRTY-NINE

HOME; WHERE THE HEART IS?

Jenna sat nursing a hot drink at the kitchen table. She sniffed the dark liquid, and her nose tickled with the rising scents of peppermint and green tea. Picking up her phone, she dialled and listened for the rings.

'Hello,' said the voice on the other end.

'Hullo, Darcy.'

'Jenna! How are you? Is Glewas okay?'

'I am very well; Glewas is too. He is excellent in the shop. We worked on a suitable disguise, and he is getting quite good at transformation. I'll make a wizard of him yet. Anyway, I was calling to speak to your mother if she's there?'

'Yep, hold on. I'll get her.'

Jenna heard Darcy place the handset down; footsteps fading away, then more approaching.

'Jenna?'

'Yes, hi Pippa. Is Darcy within earshot?'

'No, she's gone outside.'

'Good. I wanted to let you know the venue for next weekend is confirmed. Glewas has organised the cake, and I've booked the band. We are go.'

'Great. Thanks for helping me with this. Organising events isn't my thing. I want this birthday to be special for Darcy, it being her eighteenth. It needs to be perfect for her.'

'She will love it, trust me.'

'Thank you, Jenna, you're amazing. We couldn't have done it without you.'

'Bye Pippa.'

'Bye for now.'

Jenna placed the receiver back in the cradle and smiled to herself.

This party was going to be epic.

*

Glewas dusted the jar of Codswallop carefully, not wanting any of the contents to leak out and accidentally befuddle some unsuspecting shopper.

There had been some unusual visitors to the shop this week. Firstly, there was the surfer who had inadvertently stumbled over them. Then, the woman looking for washing powder who had first thought they were a supermarket, only to run out again when Jenna scared her half to death. And just a few moments ago, a child had wandered in and knocked over the bottle of Fae dust that now coved everything on the shelf in a fine, glittering film.

'Achoo!'

'Bless you.' Jenna grabbed Glewas' arm and held him until the sneezing subsided. 'Fae Dust will float you out the door if you breathe too much of it in. Be careful.'

'Did you call Pippa?'

'Yes, it's all ready. Saturday night will be a night for Darcy to remember.'

'I hope so. I want it to be special.'

'What happened here?'

'Oh, just some kid had an accident with the bottle.'

'Really? Another one? That's three this week.'

'I was just thinking the same thing. Materialists shouldn't be able to get in here. I don't understand what's happening.'

Jenna rubbed at her forehead.

'There were a couple of Materialists that got in here three years ago.'

'Darcy and Pippa?'

'Yes. Then Simon a few weeks ago. Each time it's coincided with someone crossing over.'

'You think someone has gone through a gateway? Who?'

'Well, it's not Darcy. I have no clue. Besides, it may not be someone leaving... it may be someone arriving.'

*

Darcy sat in her room at the student share house. She could hear the comforting doof, doof, of her housemate's music drifting up the stairs. It's ordinariness settling like a blanket over her.

She had been uneasy all week, but there was no reason she could think of for the feeling.

Walking to her wardrobe, she pulled out the black dress for tonight.

Maybe it was this? I hate surprises, and Mum is up to something.

There was a knock on the door, and her heart fluttered a little.

Glewas.

A few moments later, he was there, strong, real. All the uneasiness of before forgotten in a kiss that made her head swim and her toes curl.

'I missed you,' he said against her hair.

'Me too.'

'So, are you ready for dinner with your parents?'

Darcy's head tilted to one side, and her eyes narrowed.

'You are a terrible liar, Glewas. What's going on, really?' Glewas made the action of a zip closure on his mouth.

'My lips are sealed.'

Darcy punched him on the arm.

'Ouch.'

'Don't be a sook. I'll shower and change. And if by any chance you and mum have been lying to me about tonight, you will both pay extensively for the privilege. That's a promise.'

*

The moon was high as he stepped out of the shadow of the ruins. It was not as it was on the other side. There it was, beautiful, whole. Here it was but a flicker of its former glory. He had not meant to do it. The compass had just been sitting there, on the table. He had taken it without thinking. It was instinct, and when he had pulled it over his head... well... destiny?

He heard someone approaching.

Was it this side or back there?

He could not risk being seen, so crouched behind the crumbling wall.

'Where is it?' said a male voice.

'How should I know?' said the woman. 'It's got to be here. It pointed here.'

The two stumbled around, searching for a few minutes before moving on.

They did not find it.

He wiped sweat from his forehead as he stood behind the wall until sure he would not be seen. They had gone; he was alone.

*

As Darcy stepped into the dark room, there was a second when her senses were utterly disorientated. In that moment, she went back three years. Barrowman's hands were on the collar of her coat. She could feel the compass's chain pull tight around her neck and the growing darkness, just before the loss of all feeling and thought. Then the chain broke...

'Surprise!'

On went the lights, and a sea of smiling faces greeted her through teary eyes. Glewas squeezed her hand.

'Ready?'

She wiped away the tears and nodded.

A glass of champagne was placed in her hand, and the chorus went up:

'For she's a jolly good fellow;

For she's a jolly good fellow;

For she's a jolly good fellow, which nobody can deny...'

*

Glewas moved Darcy around the dance floor with comparative ease.

'Have you been practicing?' she asked.

He smiled and kissed her hand.

'It's not something I ever thought I'd enjoy, but it does have its compensations.'

He squeezed her around the waist, and she giggled. The band's cover of 'If Tomorrow Never Comes' was excellent, even if the lead singer's Ronan Keating impression wasn't. Darcy rested her head on Glewas' shoulder, and they swayed to the music together. She had surprised herself. It truly had been a wonderful night. The fright she'd had completely forgotten now. Nothing could tarnish her happiness.

*

He stepped out into the road, and a car whizzed past, sounding its horn as it went.

What are these metal monsters?

He had never seen anything like them. They were fast and came out of nowhere but seemed to be confined to the hard-surfaced trackway. He cautiously walked to the other side.

Is that music?

He had never heard anything like it before. It had a strange rhythm.

'If tomorrow never comes;

Will she know how much I loved her...'

He did not understand how anyone could enjoy such a noise, but it drew him in.

He opened the door. The noise of the music was so uncomfortably loud that his hands went over his ears instinctively. A few people turned to look as a blast of cold air entered the hall from the doorway. Darcy and Glewas stopped dancing. A spark of recognition and then the inconceivable truth. Darcy breathed in slowly. His name hung between them as her lips parted and she said, 'Gorau!'

EPILOGUE

The darkness fills my eyes.
It grows and creeps, an irresistible menace that
sweeps away all beauty and lays waste to ambition.
I have no choice but to embrace its charms.

The cold stone beneath my feet bites hard.
My comfort is of no consequence in this business
of petition.
The rosary slips through my numb fingers, reflecting
the status of my soul.

Nobody comes here. I am always alone.
The wind whistles through my stone-lined nave
and brushes my lifeless hair.
I stare at the flagged floor below as I wait.
And the waiting is endless.

A GLOSSARY OF WORDS AND TERMS

Ā-cwacian berstan – Saxon. Translated means, to shake and burst.

A'drygan – Saxon. Translated means, to cause to become dry.

Albion – The oldest known name for Great Britain.

Amaethon mab Dôn – The name 'Amaethon' is from the root 'amaeth' meaning 'ploughman'. It was often used in divine names in the pre-Christian Gallo-Brittonic world. Amaethon could, therefore, be translated from Welsh as 'The Great Ploughman' or 'The Plough God'. *Mab* meaning 'son of'.' 'Dôn' refers to a dynasty of crafters that play a central role in the Fourth Branch of the Mabinogi, where they are strongly associated with magic, craft and trickery.

Ā'spryttan snūd – Saxon. Translated means, to grow fast.

Bannog – Keeper of the oxen.

Beorht – Saxon. Translated means, light.

Caliburnus – The oldest reference to Excalibur, the legendary sword of Arthur Pendragon.

Culhwch – Literally translates from the Welsh as, 'hiding place of the pig'. This gives reference to Culhwch's being raised in a pigsty.

Finnabair – Irish. Translated it means, the white Fae or enchantress. It is also a cognate of Guinevere.

Gofannon mab Dôn - Welsh. Literal translation is, 'The Great Smith son of Dôn'. Another member of the dynasty of Dôn and Amaethon's brother. These two men enjoy an almost cult status in early Brittonic traditions.

Huzzah - An exclamation of excitement. Like hooray.

Karregi Gorlewen - a group of uninhabited skerries and rocks in southwestern Scilly Isles.

Materialist - A person who has no knowledge of the existence of magic, magical folk or magical creatures.

Mordred - Morgawse's son. He is also the son of Arthur Pendragon. At the time of Mordred's birth, Arthur had very little knowledge of his own heritage or that Morgawse was his half-sister.

Morgawse - Arthur Pendragon's half-sister. She is the daughter of Igraine (Arthur's mother) and her first husband Gorlois.

Nynhyaw and Pheibiaw - These may have been genuine Welsh historical figures, sons of Erb; but legend has it, they were transformed into oxen for their wickedness.

Rihtan Swipian - Saxon. Translated means, to scourge and put right.

Siluræ Insulæ - Latin. Scilly Isles

Teithiwr - Welsh. Translated it means, traveller.

Ysbaddaden Bencawr - Translated from Welsh, Ysbaddaden means, 'Hawthorn', which often has sinister links in western British mythology. Bencawr literally meaning, 'king of giants'.

DARCY AND SIMON'S GLASTONBURY PLAYLIST

1.	A Design for Life	Manic Street Preachers
2.	Clocks	Coldplay
3.	A Thousand Trees	Stereophonics
4.	Left to My Own Devices	Pet Shop Boys
5.	Dancing in the Moonlight	Toploader
6.	Sail Away	David Gray
7.	The Tide is High	Blondie
8.	Rotterdam (Or Anywhere)	The Beautiful South
9.	You Stole the Sun from My Heart	Manic Street Preachers
10.	Erase/Rewind	The Cardigans
11.	Runaway	The Corrs
12.	Alright	Supergrass

ACKNOWLEDGEMENTS

Special thanks to Jennifer Clement who edited like a star.

For the translation of the Culhwch ac Olwen specifically, I wish to thank Will Parker. His extensive works have been an inspiration.

So many of you have been supportive, and truly care about the struggles of bringing a story to the page. That means the world. I thank you more than words can say.

Shawline Publishing Group Pty Ltd

www.shawlinepublishing.com.au

More great Shawline titles can be found by scanning the QR code below.
New titles also available through Books@Home Pty Ltd.

Subscribe today at www.booksathome.com.au or scan the QR code below.